I0635756

TOXICITY

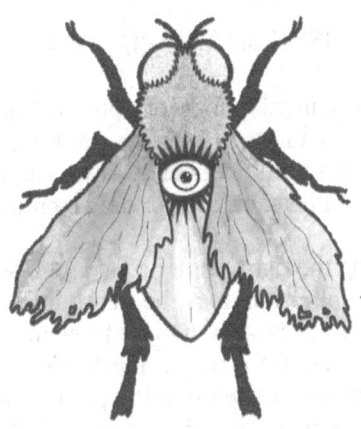

MAX BOOTH III

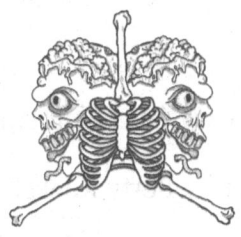

Ghoulish Books
San Antonio, Texas

Toxicity
Copyright © 2024 Max Booth III
First Edition 2014

Second Edition

ISBN: 978-1-943720-30-9

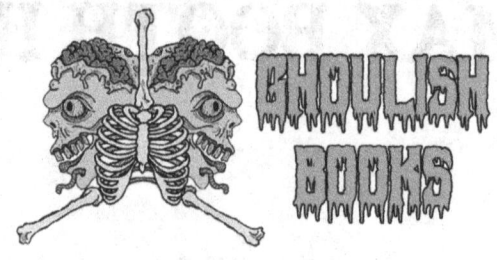

www.Ghoulish.rip

Cover by Betty Rocksteady

ALSO BY MAX BOOTH III

For Lori

CONTENT WARNING

This novel probably deserves every content warning imaginable. It is violent, disgusting, and unhinged. Due to the tonal whiplash nature of *Toxicity* (at times it is simply an absurd slapstick comedy, and other parts of the book play out like a bleak tragedy), I feel it is my responsibility to warn readers that there are multiple instances of graphic sexual abuse throughout the manuscript.

Please read with caution.

—*Max Booth III*

BEFORE

BEFORE

TEN YEARS BEFORE NOW

MADDOX'S FIRST DAY in prison was a memorable one, especially for the other inmates. Sure, random violence was essential in a house of sin, but no one had ever witnessed such anger and hostility over something so stupid.

Not until Maddox.

Everyone told him that seven to ten years was a pretty fair verdict for someone pulled over with a trunk full of cocaine and semi-automatics. He didn't care if it was fair or not—if they had done the deal in *his* car, none of that shit would have ever happened. You could trust a Cadillac. What you couldn't trust was a lousy Honda Civic without a goddamn floor on the passenger's side. He was sure the broken taillights didn't help matters, either.

It was his first day in the joint and, contrary to the theme of every prison musical he'd seen, things weren't looking bright. There was a long road ahead of him. He would have to remain strong if he wanted to survive the years that awaited. This task would be extremely difficult, considering his regular dosage of cocaine had been cut off entirely due to his unfortunate imprisonment.

He got a tray of food and headed for a random table in the cafeteria. His hands shook and he breathed in relief when he finally sat down without dropping anything. His eyes were twitching something awful. He couldn't remember the last time he had slept. All he needed was one goddamn line of coke.

"What do you think you're doing?"

Maddox heard the voice, but ignored him and started eating his breakfast taco. He already figured the food would be horrible and he was not let down. At least there was something reassuring with predictability.

"Hey, shitbird, I'm talkin' to you."

Maddox slowly looked up, yolk dripping down his chin, and spotted a man in a black bandana sitting across from him. Some big motherfucker with the word DEATH tattooed across his throat. He was staring at him with the intensity of pure lava.

"I'm eating breakfast," he said.

"Yeah, at the wrong fuckin' table, man."

Maddox glanced around at the other tables in the large cafeteria. They all appeared the same. "Is there something wrong with this table?" he asked.

"Yeah, there is," said Death. "I'm sitting here."

"Am I wrong in assuming these tables were designed for more than one person at a time?" As he said this, he twitched a little, a tiny clicking escaping his tongue. His eyes felt like sandbags had replaced their lids. And the day had only just begun.

"You a new fish, I'm guessin'."

"You're guessing right."

"'Cause otherwise you'd have to be one crazy white devil to be doin' what you're doin'."

"Maybe I am." *Twitch, twitch.* He slapped at a swarm of flies that weren't really there. *Twitch.* Fuck.

Death raised his eyebrow and studied Maddox closely. "Eh, man, you crashin'? You look like you crashin'."

A trickle of sweat splashed on his food tray. He ran his shaking hands through his long hair. "I do, huh?"

"I was the same when I first got locked up. That llelo will fuck your world up."

"I want to kill someone." Maddox grunted. "When does this stop?"

"It ain't gonna be like no heroin, I tell you that right now," Death said. "Sugar, man, it's gonna be in your system for the long haul. I'm talkin' months here. You're in for one helluva ride."

He twitched.

"My best advice is, you train your mind to think about somethin' and you keep thinking about it, you hear? Distract your mind. It's the only escape."

"Distract my mind."

"Yes."

"How?" Everything was collapsing beneath him. He felt like he was slipping off the edge of chaos, seconds from splashing into its deceiving liquids.

"I don't know." Death shrugged, taking a bite of his own breakfast taco. "What did you do before lockup?"

"I did drugs."

"What else."

"I sold them."

Death sighed. "Besides drugs, pendejo."

Maddox paused, chewed, closed his eyes, took in a deep breath, thought for a second, and exhaled. "Baseball. I played baseball."

"Yeah? Baseball's good, man. I like me some baseball, too. Play nicey-nice to the guards and they'll even let you have a couple mitts during yard time. You play in Little League, or somethin'?" Death laughed. "Some softball tournaments?"

"Try the Majors."

Death held the breakfast taco a few inches from his mouth and looked at him. "I don't think so."

"Well, I was on the roster, at least."

"What stopped you?"

Maddox gestured listlessly at his food tray.

"Well, ain't that a bitch," Death said. Maddox knew he didn't believe him, and that was perfectly fine. "You play any minor ball?"

He nodded. "Down in Iowa, did some triple-A."

Death smiled. "You're distracting yourself like I was telling you. That's good."

"Well, I was until you reminded me." Maddox kept his

idle pupils fixated on the rest of his breakfast. He wondered why it couldn't just transform into a giant mountain of cocaine.

"Guess I did, huh? My bad, holmes, my bad. Breakfast is almost over, anyways. You do know not to sit here after today, comprende?"

"What does it matter where I sit?"

"Don't play stupid." Death gave him a hard stare. "Now go back to baseball. You're starting to shake again. Those gnats aren't really there, man."

"They're flies."

"They're nothing."

Maddox breathed in, breathed out. He rubbed his eyes until they burned. "What do you know about goats?"

"I know they shouldn't cross bridges."

"I'm talking about the Billy Goat Curse. You know about that?"

"The *what?*"

Maddox sighed. He dropped his half-eaten taco on the tray. Hunger had failed him.

"Billy Sianis. You ever hear of him?"

"Nah. He play ball too or somethin'?"

"No, he didn't play ball." Maddox felt his patience dropping. "He was this Greek immigrant who ruined baseball forever."

"Oh yeah?" Death reached across the table and scooped up the rest of Maddox's breakfast. "How so?"

Maddox cracked his neck. Tried to shake his mind off his skull. "He owned this pet goat. A pet goat that he'd bring to league games. Right there in the stadium. I don't know why they allowed that for as long as they did but they did."

"Did he need to buy a ticket for the goat too?"

"I would assume so," Maddox said, although he wasn't exactly sure what the MLB's goat policy was back then. "Anyway, they even went to the 1945 World Series, which was when the shit really hit the fan."

TOXICITY

"Wait, man, that's with the Cubs, right?" Death's face brightened. "This is starting to sound a little familiar."

"Yeah, the Cubs." *Who else would he be talking about?* "Them and Detroit were in that series. It was the sixth game. We had two wins and they had one ahead of us. Sianis and his goat, who he named Billy, they attended that game, the sixth one. They bought box seat tickets, but that wasn't enough. They had to go down and join the crowd so he could brag about owning a goat. No one should ever brag about owning a goat. *Never*." Maddox hesitated a moment before continuing. "Well, it started raining. Now, I don't know if you've ever smelled wet goat before, but trust me when I say you definitely do not want to."

"Goats *do* have a lot of hair, don't they?"

"So you can imagine everyone's discomfort, sitting next to such a foul beast. It was only natural Mr. Wrigley himself would kick the scum right out of the park and onto West Addison. But of course he wasn't fast enough, because Sianis still had time to curse the entire team into never playing in a World Series ever again."

"You really believe in that?"

"How else can you explain a losing streak which started in 1908 and still hasn't ended 'til this day? I mean, it's been over a century."

Death didn't seem to have an answer for that. Instead, he said, "You know what my old man used to call asshole Greeks like the one you're talking about?"

"No, what?"

"Fleases. You know why?"

"Why?" Maddox was always on the lookout for a new way to insult Greece.

"Short for flap grease. You know how these guys work in diners most of their lives, and how greasy their shit usually is? Well, I guess these guys refuse circumcision, so all that grease, it builds up underneath that extra flap. Get it? *Please*."

"That's good." He nodded. "I'll have to use that."

"Yeah, thought you'd like it." Death tossed a tortilla crumb into his mouth. "Don't know why you're sweating over stuff like that, anyway. It's not like it's the Sox or something. Now *there's* a team."

Maddox paused. His hands tightened into fists. "You're a Sox fan."

"Of course I am." Death smiled proudly.

"I didn't know that."

"Well now you do, huh?"

"Yeah. Now I do."

"We're like rivals, huh?" Death laughed. "Guess we *really* shouldn't sit at the same table, anymore. It's against baseball protocol, ese."

"Yes," Maddox said through gritted teeth. He gripped his fingers around the plastic spoon given with his untouched bowl of cornflakes. "Yes, it is."

A piercing horn filled the cafeteria. Breakfast was officially over.

Death never had a chance to stand up. Maddox was on top of him in an instant. The end of the spoon popped his right eyeball like a large grape. An explosion of ocular fluid erupted down Death's face as he screamed for the guards.

When they dragged Maddox away, he was grinning.

For one glorious moment, he'd completely forgotten about the withdrawal.

A FEW MONTHS
BEFORE NOW

THE TITANIUM MERRY-GO-ROUND spun 'round and 'round. Invaded by rust over many years of neglect, it creaked with every little movement, echoing a grungy symphony throughout the park.

Four stoned teens sprawled on it, hands behind their heads as their eyes became lost in the drifting clouds from above. Their feet dragged in the grass.

They all felt completely relaxed and content with the world, which was a rarity for them. Of course, a large part of this had to do with the joint held loosely between Addison Kane's fingers as she passed it to the left. Her boyfriend, Connor Murphy, took it eagerly. And when he finished with his drag, it was then handed over to Candy Blossom—who, in return, gave it to her own boyfriend, Johnny Desperation.

Because of a recent injury inflicted upon his tongue, Johnny was careful to keep the joint clenched in his teeth, rather than touch the sore muscle dwelling within his mouth.

Connor, noticing his friend's struggle, said, "So, how's that tongue treatin' ya?"

"Thut up," Johnny answered, and everyone laughed. Even Johnny. He had to admit, if it had happened to someone else, he would be making fun of them every chance he got, too.

"Man, my mother always told me my body was a

weapon," Candy said, "but I didn't know she meant it like *that*."

Johnny sighed, trying to suppress a grin. It was his own damn fault for talking Candy into getting the piercing in the first place. She had been reluctant at first, which was quite contrary to her character. If there was a place on your body you were able to stick a hoop or a ball of metal in, you best believe it was already inserted in Miss Candy Blossom. Except for that one spot. The ultimate *taboo* spot. But now that position was filled as well. And Johnny had paid the price.

"This is some good shit," Connor said.

"Yeah," Johnny agreed, although he wondered if any of them had ever actually smoked *good* pot in their lives. Maybe they were all just used to ditch weed at this point.

"Trust Dave to supply the absolute best."

"Didn't you hear?" Candy asked. "He isn't just 'Dave' anymore. People, they call him 'One-Arm Dave' now."

"What?" Addison said. "Why?"

"Because he only has one arm."

"Oh," she mumbled, feeling a little stupid. "Well, how the hell did that happen? I just bought from him like not even a month ago, and I'm pretty sure he had two arms then."

When it came to scoring dope, Addison was the one in charge. She once had a brief fling with the local drug dealer at their school, so he gave her outrageous discounts in hopes of getting back together. This made Connor extremely jealous, of course, but he wasn't going to say anything as long as she kept coming back with discounted dope.

"Yeah, it wasn't too long ago," Candy said, clearing her throat for the inevitable lengthy speech. "The way I heard it, anyway, was like this: Dave and that punk dude he hangs out with, Milo or whatever, were out drinking, like, at two in the morning or something, totally fucked up. Milo was driving and Dave sat shotgun, laughing and trying to scare other drivers. I guess Dave has his one arm resting out of the window, holding the vodka, right? So, once it's empty he just drops it out the side of the car, but he doesn't bring his arm back inside, just lets it hang there all limp and shit. No, what I heard was, Dave passed out. And Milo? Well he was just too drunk to notice. Kept on pretending he was gonna run into a car, try to freak 'em out and stuff, ya know, laughin' and havin' just a good ol' time, never realizing Dave was out cold with his arm sticking out the window. When I asked Milo about it later, he told me he had no memory whatsoever about bashing the side of the car into that streetlamp. And people wonder why he's never had his license, huh? Anyway, later on, like a *lot* later on, Dave wakes up in a hospital gurney as a certified stumpy. He says he wants to attach a machine gun or something to it. That'd be cool, huh?"

"Jethuth Chrith." Johnny rolled his eyes. "You're like an Energy Bunny."

They were all used to Candy's extensive tangents. Once she had gone on for two hours about how much she preferred peanut butter and jelly on her waffles to the usual boring maple syrup all those stupid conformists were using nowadays.

Addison sat up. "You're pulling my leg, right?"

"No," Candy said, "but something *did* pull Dave's arm, though."

Connor scratched his chin. "What happened to the arm?"

"I don't think they ever found it."

"Whoa, man, we need to go try and find that shit."

Addison glared at her boyfriend. "What on Earth would you do with a severed arm?"

"Lots of things," Connor replied casually. "Lots."

Johnny sat up, excited. "Maybe there'th a reward!"

"You know, that isn't a bad idea," Candy said. "I know if I lost my arm, I would totally want it back to hang on my wall, or something, like how people nail those giant swordfishes and stuff. It could be like a trophy." She turned to Addison. "Watcha think, Adds? You think your lover boy would pay us if we found his precious jerk-off instrument?"

"I'm pretty sure Dave's a lefty," Addison said. She immediately regretted the words as soon as they left her mouth.

Connor hung his head down and dug his nails into his palm. "Let's just forget it. I gotta jet, anyway. Band practice."

"Would be impossible to find, either way," Candy pointed out. "They had no idea where the accident occurred. Thing could be practically anywhere. Someone probably already found it, too. On its way to Arabia via the black market, is my guess."

Connor inhaled the last of the roach. "Well that's a shame. Could have made us all millionaires. Too bad. Either way, this conversation is pointless, and now I'm gonna be late for practice."

Addison smiled and grabbed his hand. "No one in your band is ever on time."

"Today could be different," Connor said. Then: "Well, maybe I have time for one more."

"Attaboy." Addison reached in her purse for a roller.

"Thounds fun," Johnny said, "but it'th almoth time for dinner. They'll eat mine if I'm not there." Johnny reached over and gave Candy Blossom a quick kiss. "Thee ya later."

"'Bye, baby," she said.

Johnny stood up and jogged away from the park. Connor called out, "Oh c'mon, man, get back here. We won't respect you unless you get high!"

* * *

Johnny Desperation lived in a small bungalow located in the projects of Loathing, Illinois. The house was decorated with a gateless fence, dead grass, and five-year-old Christmas lights no one ever found the energy to take down. A plastic Santa Claus riding a sleigh rested on the edge of the roof, its facial features long melted away by the tyranny of the sun. On the left side of the house, toward the top, resided a large black circle. These were the leftovers marked by the vicious fireballs of a roman candle. One summer a gang of wasps had set up a hive there, and no one could afford any Raid. They did have some spare fireworks hanging around from the previous Fourth of July, though. Worked just about the same.

Johnny stopped in front of his house at the mailbox. The mail had probably arrived a few hours ago, but he seriously doubted anyone had thought of checking. After all, that would require walking at *least* twenty feet. Possibly twenty-five. And he was right: the box was filled with numerous fast food coupons and letters with large red block letters stamped across the front. He shuffled through the envelopes until his vision came across one reading EVICTION NOTICE.

He quickly tore the top open and unfolded the sheet inside. His eyes scanned through the page, widening as they neared the end. He figured they were behind on rent, but seven months late? The landlord was some kind of saint to have tolerated it as long as he had. Johnny studied the dreadful sentence in the middle of the long, dragging paragraph:

The occupants of the aforementioned residence will have no longer than the 15th of September to either pay the sum of $13,000 to amend for outrageous late fees or vacate the premises.

Johnny slammed the lid shut with all his might. It took one bounce off the mailbox and flung right off its hinges. It landed with a clang on the road. He looked up at the sky and sighed.

Shit.

Inside, it was the usual scene. Johnny walked through the door and was instantly bombarded by the eager tongue of their beloved pit bull, Zooey Deschanel.

He found his father sitting on his La-Z-Boy in the

corner, smoking his pipe and playing *Age of Empires* on the cheap desktop they'd scavenged from a garage sale years ago.

"Hey, Dad." Johnny waved his hand out in front of him.

"Fuckin' Brits are going down!" Roland Desperation responded, and relit his pipe. He seemed to light the thing more than he actually smoked it.

Johnny shrugged and headed toward the kitchen, passing his older brother on the couch, who kicked at his legs. "Move!" James shouted. "I'm watching TV."

Johnny paused and glanced at the television set across from them. "It'th a commerthal," he said. "For a Big Mac."

James stared at his younger brother with impatience. "I *love* Big Macs."

Johnny studied the folds of fat peeking from under his shirt. "I can thee that."

"Hey, what's that supposed to mean?"

He found his mother in the small narrow closet calling itself a kitchen. She was hovering over the stove, busting open a packet of macaroni and cheese and breaking into a sweat from the strenuous workout.

"Stop picking on your older brother's weight problem," Ruth Desperation ordered, panting like an Olympic runner. "You know he's just big-boned. Like his momma."

Johnny shoved the envelope in his mother's hands and waited for her to read it. But instead of attempting such a difficult task, she just stared at her son blankly.

"What's this?"

"Eviction notice."

"Weird, we've been getting a lot of those lately." Ruth tossed the mail in the garbage can and returned to the macaroni boiling away on the stove.

"Don't you think thith ith a little therious, Mom?"

"What's that, dear?"

"The eviction notice."

"Oh."

TOXICITY

"Well?"

Ruth waved her hand away. "Nah, it's no biggie."

"No biggie? We only have 'til the thiffteennth, Mom!"

"Until what?"

Johnny slapped his hand against the refrigerator and pushed the eviction notice back into his mother's hands. He pointed at the last three words of the sentence that had stood out the most to him:

. . . vacate the premises.

Ruth scrunched her face up as if utterly lost. "Vacate? Like . . . like a vacation?"

Johnny studies his mother's face to determine whether or not she was being serious. He sighed and wondered how someone could be so blonde without actually being blonde.

He explained the letter again.

"Oh," Ruth whispered. "So that's what they meant."

She shrugged and went back to the noodles. Johnny bit back his lower lip, anything to resist the urge to grab his mother by her throat and shake her uncontrollably. "Mom!" he exclaimed.

"Relax, dear," she said. "All will be well."

"How? We don't have that kind of money."

"Oh, I'm sure a certain large sum is about to hit us soon enough . . . "

"Not the lotto again." Johnny sighed. He dropped his head down a bit and rubbed his temple. She played the same numbers again and again, every week. They weren't even particularly meaningful numbers. In fact, they were the dumbest numbers anybody could possibly conceive.

One. Two. Three. Four. Five. Six.

The magic formula, according to Ruth Desperation.

Here they were, about to lose the house, and she was wasting money on a set of digits that would never be chosen as the winner ever—not in this life, or the next.

He felt his mother's stubby fingers fall on his shoulder. He looked up and caught her eyes. It was obvious she was trying her best to make them reassuring, and it was a little eerie how much they actually were.

"Have faith." She forced a wooden spoonful of the pot's contents into her son's closed mouth, which had since been drained and stirred with cheap Velveeta. "Now taste this and tell me you've tasted pasta more perfect than this."

Johnny gave her the thumbs up. Ruth smiled proudly. He had to admit, he hadn't had macaroni and cheese this good in a while. Sure, they'd had the same thing yesterday, and the day before that, and so on—but all of those times it had been absolutely awful. Tonight, however, something was different. He was pretty sure it was the sudden change from SpongeBob noodles to dinosaur ones. There's just something special about chomping the cheesy head off a miniature Tyrannosaurus Rex.

It was almost time for the drawing, so everyone gathered together in the living room with their individual TV dinner trays. Ruth took the remote from James and turned on the news. Johnny sat in the corner of the room on the floor, picking at his food. Somehow hunger had escaped him.

Zooey Deschanel lay on her stomach beside Johnny, eagerly thumping her tail against the carpet. She anticipated each noodle he flung at her with immense excitement.

"Goddamn turncoat *fucks!*" Roland yelled at his computer. "I'll murder you with a catapult!"

The sudden outburst had sprayed bits of cheddar all over Roland's beard. He didn't pay any attention to this, though. There were still turncoats left to murder with catapults, after all.

"Rollie, now you hush up," Ruth snapped. "I'm 'bout to win us some millions." Her face was serious, even though she held in her lap a porcelain Aunt Jemima doll. It was, in fact, her favorite doll out of her whole collection. She was rotating between giving herself bites of the macaroni and bites to the Aunt. Of course, the doll possessed zero orifices, so the food just smooshed together against the glass into one big mess.

Roland took his eyes away from the computer screen to his wife. He watched the scene with annoyance. "Woman, you are insane."

"The rich are always crazy, dear. Just you wait and see."

They all quieted down as the host began to draw balls from the machine. The first was quite an odd number: **1**.

The one that followed was even odder, despite also being very even: **2**.

The rest . . . well, the rest was lunacy. One by one the numbers popped up, each digit collating within its own numerical order. After it was over everyone just sat there, bodies numb, staring at the screen. The numbers flashed before their eyes over and over again.

There was a **1**. There was a **2**. There was a **3**. There was a **4**. And there was a **5**. And sure enough, next to the mega ball slot, there shone a heavenly **6**.

Even the newscaster was speechless. There simply were no words to fully express the amount of confusion the country was suddenly experiencing.

Johnny let go of his bowl and it tumbled to the floor. Zooey Deschanel was quick to leap on top of it and play vacuum cleaner.

James literally fainted.

Roland dropped his glass of cream soda and it exploded at his feet.

Ruth turned to her husband. "Those things are expensive, for crying out loud." She sighed and told the Aunt to open up wide.

A FEW WEEKS
BEFORE NOW

JOHNNY DESPERATION'S LIFE did a one-eighty.

Growing up, money had always been an evil entity invented to manipulate the good to become bad. Now he realized all that thinking had merely been his natural teenage angst rebelling against society. After experiencing it firsthand, he knew that luxuries weren't in fact such a bad thing, after all.

As soon as they'd cashed that first paycheck they packed their few belongings and went house searching. They moved from Loathing to a nice, gated community off in Libertyville about a half hour away. It was a small suburb devoted entirely to large mansions. The idea that the Desperation family now qualified seemed cathartic to the mind. It was a pleasant change from the direction the family had previously been heading.

He'd never seen a house so big. Hell, Zooey Deschanel's new doghouse out back was larger than his old bedroom altogether. The Desperations went on a spending spree, buying everything deemed valuable by today's standards. Ruth purchased her very own fountain of chocolate syrup that she kept in the center of the kitchen on display for all to see. They never did get an actual dinner table. They all thought it to be foolish thinking. After all, everyone knew the best place to eat was in front of their new seventy-two-inch Sony. Ruth also went to an antique store and bought every single doll they had in stock, and then proceeded to buy everything in Amazon's stock. She was acquiring quite the collection. However, Aunt Jemima would always remain her favorite out of the lot.

Roland hired a team of electricians to transform their new basement into some kind of technological laboratory, which he would go on to dub his "man cave". Each wall consisted of giant computer screens. It was all the makings of expensive equipment that, in truth, he didn't understand in the slightest bit, but, hey, it looked cool. He soon traded in his old history-based war games for something much more entertaining. Instead of murdering Vikings to death with catapults, Roland now slaughtered trolls and warlocks with his large enchanted axe. Now that they had finally come into some dough, he had enough for the monthly subscription of his *World of Warcraft* game he had received as a Christmas gift some years ago. He was hooked.

At first, Johnny was too overwhelmed to comprehend what was going on. He saw his name in the news; people were stopping on the street to talk to him; they were no longer having macaroni and cheese for dinner. His parents offered to buy him the one thing he had always wanted in life, but when he sat and thought about it, he wasn't exactly sure what it was he wanted. After all, they had already gotten him the new iPhone. What more could Johnny possibly need?

Johnny had assumed rich people never went to school. He quickly found this fact to be very false when, a week after moving into Libertyville, his mother signed him up at a nearby private school. As it turned out, rich people just went to schools designed for rich people.

They actually had to wear suits. *Suits*. Johnny cringed at himself every morning while getting dressed. He never thought in a million years he'd be caught dead in a suit. But as it turned out, he actually looked pretty good in them. They were sort of sophisticated feeling.

The teachers didn't give you math lessons. Instead they

taught you how to do your taxes. How to play it smart in politics. The keys to a successfully economy. In a world in where numbers valued over anything else, you either simplified or simply died. Instead of reading Shakespeare, they gave you a biography of Steve Jobs. His first homework assignment had been to write an essay on the Wall Street Crash of '29 and how it could have been prevented if actual enlightened human beings had been in charge instead of the monkeys running the system back in the day.

He saw faces that at first he assumed to be constructed only of greed, promising himself never to socialize with these people. But, by the end of his first week, he had become friends with most of his classmates. He even got a girlfriend. Of course, he was pretty positive she was only interested in him because his name was in the newspaper, but Johnny was willing to ignore that fact as long as she continued taking off her clothes. And he was pretty sure she would.

Memories of his previous life quickly faded away like a bad dream.

A few weeks attending this school—or "academy", as the faculty insisted on calling it—Johnny ran into a group of Goths throwing grapes down an empty hallway. There were three of them, in the same required uniform as he but with stereotypical Goth black makeup, and they all seemed very intent on throwing those grapes. There was a whole stash of the fruit in a backpack they passed between them. He stood there for a while, watching as each one exploded into a tiny grenade of juice.

After around the fiftieth grape, Johnny couldn't take any more. "Watcha doin?" he asked.

"Throwing grapes," said one of the Goths, a spiked dog collar strapped around his thick neck.

"At?"

"Dogs. Don't you see them? They're everywhere!"

Johnny looked around the hallway to make sure he hadn't overlooked anything. "Dogs?" All he saw was a whole lot of squashed grapes.

TOXICITY

"Yeah, man, *dogs,*" said the Goth in the middle. This one sported a spray-painted devilock running between his eyes and down his snout of a nose. "They're, like, everywhere. The stupid fascist janitor gave them the taste of human flesh and now they're all over our shit. These grapes are the only things that'll stop them. Trust us."

"Oh." Johnny thought for a moment. "Why grapes?"

"They're laced with dog poison," said devilock kid.

"Cool. Who spiked them?"

"One of us did. I can't remember which one, though."

"It's doesn't matter!" dog collar kid exclaimed. "We're gonna show these conformist dogs what we're made of!"

Johnny burst out laughing. "You guys are high as hell, aren't you?"

The three Goths stopped throwing the grapes and turned around, completely serious. The one with a collar around his neck replied, "Well, yeah."

Johnny nodded in approval. "Any left?"

The grape-throwers exchanged glances. Johnny noticed their teeth were stained purple. He did not want to know why. Devilock kid shrugged. "Sure, but be aware next time it'll cost you. You're not gonna find this shit on any given street."

He reached in his single-strapped book bag and brought out a small black can. He handed the metallic object over and Johnny took it, puzzled. The thing looked like a can of body spray.

"What the hell is this?" he asked. "Tag?"

Devilock kid grinned. "In a way," he said. "Only think of it as instead of making your body smell good, it makes your *soul* smell good. Ya know?"

"No, not really. How do I take it?"

"Just spray it in your mouth. The rest takes care of itself."

Johnny raised the can and hesitated. "If this turns out to be Windex or something, I'm going to kick your ass."

"Dude, it is a hundred times better than Windex," said the one with the dog collar. "For real life."

The tardy bell filled the remote hallway. It was like the gun of a race shooting off to signify it had officially begun. *Well, here goes nothing*, Johnny thought, opening his mouth and squeezing down on the can's trigger.

A bitter substance shot down his throat. It was the sourest thing he had ever ingested. He felt it sticking to the inside of his throat, melting into his innards like some kind of misty acid. His vision turned inward and traveled inside his own body. He watched as a purplish rain incinerated his organs. His heart bubbled and withered to nothing. The charge running through his body was blissfully painful. It was the most euphoric feeling he had ever experienced.

And it was just a little too much.

Johnny let loose a cough, and then another, and another, and so on. Each cough struck a match against his lungs; so intense yet so pleasurable at the same time.

He heard the Goths laughing from every direction. "What . . . what *is* this?" he managed to spit out.

A chubby hand clasped his shoulder. "The Brit calls it Jericho. We just call it *purple*. We don't know much else, besides it's fuckin' killer."

If Johnny had been capable of saying anything else, he would have absolutely agreed on the Goth's last statement, but everything was spinning so fast he could barely keep his own balance, let alone speak. He saw the line of lockers, then the Goths, then a door, then the Goths, then the dogs, then the lockers again all in a matter of nanoseconds.

Hold up. Dogs?

All around, surrounding him and the three Goths. Closing in, drooling, stomachs growling. Hellhounds of the universe.

Suddenly it was all so clear to him. The hungry canines had been there this entire time. Whatever he had just sprayed down his throat, it had opened up a brand-new way of seeing the world. A world in which flesh-craving dogs now roamed.

He wondered if perhaps it would be better to live in a world where such monstrosities were not visible to the human eye. He suddenly yearned to return. But then he thought, if he couldn't see them, would they still be able to attack? He gulped. Dying by the fangs of hounds you couldn't even see would be the worst death ever. It was a miracle he had stumbled upon these Goths before it was too late.

Johnny looked at the kid on the left, who thus far had been deafeningly silent. "Why haven't you said anything? People aren't that quiet. Who are you? Imposter!" The imposter clamped his hand over his mouth and looked away, embarrassed. What was he hiding?

Dog collar kid laughed. "Nah, his voice is just unusually feminine."

"Oh," Johnny said. "My bad."

"It's okay," the quiet Goth squeaked. Dog collar kid was right. His voice was indeed incredibly girly.

"So, how do you feel?" asked devilock kid. He was smiling.

Johnny reached into the fruit backpack and grabbed a handful of its contents. "I feel like graping some dogs," he said.

And that's just what they did.

NOW

DAY ONE:

EGG

1

MONTHS HAD PASSED. The merry-go-round remained still. The group of teenagers had returned, minus one, making it only three now. This time instead of pot they passed around a bottle of tequila. None of them were exactly in the right spirit to be spinning so they just sat there and drank. None of them realistically liked the taste of tequila, but they were teenagers and thus couldn't be choosy over what types of liquor they were able to scavenge.

Candy Blossom took three turns for every single turn. The other two didn't mind.

"I just can't believe it," Connor said after a while.

Addison shook her head. "Out of everyone I ever knew, Johnny was one person I never thought would do something like this."

Connor gave her a hurtful look. "What about me?"

Addison shrugged. "It's the way it is, baby."

"Bitch."

"Either way, I still can't believe it," Addison said.

"Well, believe it," Candy said coldly. She stared into the pearly night sky with damp eyes and wondered why people were the way they were. Despite how hard she tried, she couldn't seem to come up with an answer.

Connor ran his fingers through his overgrown red hair, trying his best to comprehend the situation. "I mean, his ma wins the lotto and bam, he transforms into a totally new person. It all seems like a strange dream, ya know?"

"Yeah." Addison nodded.

"Candy," Connor said, "what exactly happened when you went over there? What did he do to you?"

"Gimmie." Candy snatched the tequila from Addison. She took a long swig, paused, and took another. "I went up there to his new place to, like, surprise him, you know? Have you guys been there? It's fuckin' huge, I kid you not."

"Yeah," Connor said. "I've been there a few times. I don't think Addy has, though."

"No, I haven't gotten around to it, yet."

"Don't bother." Candy splashed more liquor down her throat. Her piercings glistened in the shadows of the forgotten park. "I get up there, right? He ain't alone. And I'm not talking about his family, either. Bastard goes to a new school not even two months and he's already screwing some slut. He answered the door in his underwear and she was standing behind him wrapped in a blanket. I guess everyone else was out on errands or something."

Connor turned to her, staring incredulously. "Are you serious?"

Candy returned the look. "Why would I make something like that up?"

Addison kicked his foot. "You're right," he said. "I'm sorry."

"He told me he was now among a more superior, civilized class of human beings and I would no longer be required of any further services," Candy continued. "Those are his exact words. Can you believe that shit? I told him all that money changed him and he said he didn't change, he just grew up. I told him no, you just grew down. Then I spat in his face and left. I'm never talking to that piece of shit again, I swear to God."

"I'm sorry, Candy." Addison put her arm around her. "That's horrible. Know that we're here for you, okay?"

"Thanks. That helps."

Connor stood up and walked out a few feet away. He finished the last of the tequila and whipped it off into a nearby field of weeds. The sound of the glass shattering interrupted the night's eerie silence.

Connor turned back to the girls. "And don't worry," he said to Candy. "He won't get away with this. He *will* suffer the consequences of his actions."

"What did you have in mind?" Candy sniffled.

"Uh, I don't know, I guess we could, like, set a bag of dog poo on fire and leave it on his porch . . . or something."

The two girls stared at him. Candy sighed and lay down on the merry-go-round.

Addison shook her head at him. "God, you're such a nerd."

2

"STAY BEHIND THE yellow line, please."

The prisoner in the neon blue jumpsuit ground his teeth together. It took every ounce of him to resist jumping over the line, reaching under the bulletproof glass, and choking the guard until he coughed up the goods. "My candy is missing," he calmly explained. "I would like it returned."

"Look, dipshit," said the guard. "I already done tol' ya, ain't no candy here, ain't no candy to give ya."

The prisoner cracked his neck. He had gone ten years without any candy, he could surely hold off his craving another couple of hours. It probably wasn't even that long of a walk to the nearest gas station, anyway. There was around fifty bucks in his wallet—assuming the Ratman hadn't snatched that, as well.

The guard pushed the prisoner's personal belongings through the slot in the window. He spoke into the intercom: "Now, if you're done throwin' a fit, please change out of your uniform and back into your personal attire. Where I can see you, if ya don't mind. You're still a con 'til you leave these doors, as far as I'm concerned."

The prisoner unzipped his jumpsuit, stepped forward, traded the uniform for the garbage bag discarded at his feet, and returned behind the yellow line. He changed into the street clothes he had been wearing when he'd arrived here all those years ago. They were a little tight.

Boxers, socks, jeans, combat boots, white T-shirt, a faded light blue jean jacket. He snuggled the Cubs cap around his bald scalp and risked a weak smile. After ten whole years, he was no longer Prisoner #070411. No longer was he a serial number. Once again, he was a man with a name.

Maddox Kane.

"I don't give a shit who you are," said the Ratman. "Now get out of my prison before I decide to throw your ass back in. You'll be hearing from your PO by tomorrow, so make sure that address is still valid. Otherwise I'll be seeing you soon, cupcake."

Maddox walked out the door, trying to act tough, although secretly he would've done just about anything for an actual cupcake right about now.

He made it two feet outside the prison before stopping. This was different from being out on the yard. There was no longer barbed wire around him. Sure, there were still towers everywhere, but the guards had ceased pointing their rifles at him. They didn't even give him a second look as he walked away. It was so goddamn beautiful.

The air, it smelled different. It'd been a while since he had breathed air this clean. He was a free man now. Everything was going to be better. Even the snowflakes floating down on his cheeks felt wonderful, and he had never really been much for the cold, either.

Maddox walked away from Megaton Corrections a free man.

He wondered how many others were allowed such a privilege. Most of the cons he had encountered inside were either in for life, held an appointment with Old Sparky, or succumbed to the piercing bite of a burnt toothbrush. Sure, there had been a few instances when Maddox was the one wielding the toothbrush, but then again, when it's shank or be shanked, there's only so much you can do.

He turned onto the long narrow road leading from Megaton to the parking lot some miles away—or "drop-off", as they called it. Cherry-top escorted the convict to drop-off and a bus transported them to their new hellhole, for however many times the judge pounded his mallet. It was a cycle repeated each week. Of course, friends and family were allowed to travel this road as well, whether it was visits or release pick-ups.

No one would be coming to pick up Maddox, though. He thought the art of surprise would be in his favor. Otherwise a certain someone might just decide to up and run—such as his ex-wife. And that would be a very bad thing indeed. They still had some things to talk about.

So he walked, figuring he'd hitch a ride once he reached the drop-off. He buttoned his jacket and stuffed his hands in his pockets. The snow fell in light clouds.

Maddox had never really been one for winter. He'd rather live somewhere that was warm all year—a place where you could play a game of catch without having to suffocate yourself with an Eskimo coat. Someplace like . . . Florida? Nah, Florida was for retirees and Marlins fans. And he wasn't that old yet; only turned thirty-three two months ago, for Christ's sake. Maybe in twenty, twenty-five more years, then *maybe* he'd begin to consider the idea. Florida, a place for golfers and alligator poachers. No thanks, man, that's quite all right.

California, he thought, and smiled; *that's where.* L.A., Lake Tahoe, maybe San Francisco—who knew. California, now *there* was baseball weather if he had ever seen it. He'd been down there a couple times working a few jobs for a man named Vincent King. A couple drug deals with some big-time Hollywood execs looking to get their noses white, and knowing King was the man you went to when you needed such a thing. It was pretty nice, he thought— possibly even perfect. He imagined buying himself a little boat, settling down somewhere in the Pacific with his family, fishing and relaxing, playing baseball wherever they docked. He liked this idea, despite how impossible it probably was in reality. He was, after all, on parole. California, if it could happen, was still a long way.

A white bus became visible in the distance. As it

neared, black painted letters on the side came into focus, reading MEGATON CORRECTIONAL FACILITY. He remembered how he had leaned his head against the window, watching the vanilla fields as they went by, wondering what starting for the Cubs would have been like.

The bus honked as it drove by, the driver tipping his Stetson at him—*Jesus,* he thought, realizing it was the same cowboy who'd been driving a decade previously. He remembered the hat clear as day, the hick spitting out globs of snuff wherever he pleased—especially at the feet of his passengers. He could still smell the driver's hideous breath and nearly gagged.

Maddox shot him the bird and continued onward.

* * *

Two hours later he finally reached drop-off, which was about as busy as the pisshole road he'd just traveled. He hopped over the little guardrail, boots slapping against the icy black pavement. The parking lot was too big for a small dingy office like that.

Maddox debated whether or not to go inside and search for something to drink or eat, but decided the clerk, used to dealing with ex-cons just released, would probably treat him like some kind of lowlife thug. And he wasn't a lowlife, no sir. He wasn't some tweaker or rockhead. He'd actually earned his high school diploma; even went through two semesters of college before being drafted down to Mesa for the Rookie leagues, working his way up the A-ladder. Of course, he was never exactly Mr. Do-Right either. Grand theft auto? Nothing difficult about that. Drug trafficking? Easy peasy. Murder? Well, never anyone that didn't already deserve it in the first place. No, he was no lowlife, that was for sure, but it still made him angry just thinking someone would accuse him of such.

*Low*life.

He was no thug, either. Maddox had decided a long

time ago that he was putting all that shit behind him. There was no more jeopardizing his future. He was free now—and intended on keeping it that way. There weren't many second chances in this world, but if there ever was, this was one of them. He needed to stick around and provide for his little girl—make up for all the lost time he caused.

He tried to think of different *legal* jobs he could acquire now that he was a free man, but always seemed to end up in the middle of a bank robbing daydream. He was sure there were other ways to make money besides living a life of crime. Maybe he could become a car salesman.

Supposedly his parole officer was going to set him up with a job at some factory come Monday, so at least there was that.

Maddox approached one of the few vehicles left in the parking lot, a minivan that had just pulled up. A woman stepped out of the driver's seat and slid the backdoor open, grabbing a crying baby from the backseat as he neared closer. No doubt going to check-in at the office up ahead. Probably to visit the infant's homicidal father.

"Why, hello there," Maddox said. He hoped his tone sounded friendly enough. It'd been a long time since he'd held a conversation with someone out of a uniform.

The woman turned around quickly, surprised. She gave Maddox one look and backed against the van, protectively squeezing her child against her chest. "What do you want?" she asked, quick and to the point.

He cracked a smile to lighten the mood. "Relax, ma'am, no need to be scared. I'm not gonna hurt you."

"You're going to rape and kill me, aren't you?" the woman asked, becoming teary-eyed. "Oh God, not in front of my baby girl!"

"What? No, why would you think such a thing?"

The woman shrugged. "I don't know. I thought maybe you had escaped from the prison."

"I was just released."

"How was it?" She shuffled the wailing baby in her arms.

"It was okay."

"That's nice. What do you want?"

"Was wondering if you could give me a ride into town."

"Not a chance." The woman turned around and walked toward the office.

"Well, um, thanks," he mumbled, and ventured forth to try his luck with the next car. After five more turndowns, he finally said screw it and hotwired the minivan, taking off with that familiar rush running through his body. He skidded away from the parking lot, speeding down a street he hoped led into town, wondering how long it would take for the police to pick him up again. The woman would undoubtedly be able to identify him in a lineup. They sure talked long enough.

The drop-off probably had cameras, too, Maddox was thinking, and sighed.

So much for staying clean.

* * *

Maddox strolled up and dropped the items in his arms on the counter. The cashier gave him a funny look and he exchanged it with a wink.

"That sure is a lot of candy and cupcakes," she said.

"And the Pepsi." Maddox held up his fountain drink.

"Of course." The girl rang up the contents.

He hesitated, offering a guilty smile. That grand theft auto couldn't just go unaccounted for. Such deeds had to be reciprocated. "You might as well charge me for two pops. I downed one back there and refilled it."

"I saw." The girl gave Maddox a look like he was a cute little puppy. "It's no biggie. Everyone does it."

"Thanks."

"Sure."

Maddox watched her package the sweets into a plastic

bag, facial piercings swinging with her every movement. She couldn't have been any older than what, seventeen, eighteen? About the same age as his own daughter. Except this girl possessed spiky pink cotton candy hair while Addy's was long and black.

He paid and made toward the door, but something drew him back. He'd never had a single spot on his body pierced before. He had never really understood the point of a chunk of metal hanging from your flesh twenty-four seven.

"Don't they hurt?" Maddox asked, standing at the entrance. The automatic door slid open and the status remained the same; no one left, no one entered.

"At first," the girl replied, as if expecting the question, "but you get used to them pretty quickly."

"You get asked that a lot, don't you?"

"Not as much as you'd think. Most seem too afraid to ask."

"Why's that?"

"I'm not sure. Maybe they think they'll hurt my feelings or something. Or maybe they're just shy. I saw your face, though, and knew you wanted to ask. Didn't think you would, to tell you the truth. You just got out, didn't you?"

Maddox cocked his head, grocery bag swinging in his hand. "Yeah, how'd you know?"

"Ain't a sweeter tooth around than a man freshly outta the joint."

He smiled. "Well, you got me there."

"I also bet candy and cupcakes ain't the only things you got a sweet tooth for, huh?"

His smile faded away. "I think I better go."

"You know which one hurt the most, out of all of them?" the girl asked.

Maddox stayed put, curious. "What?"

"My clit."

He winced, regretting his failure to depart the gas station when he still had a chance.

TOXICITY

"Know why I had it removed?"

"The pain, I'd imagine."

"Nah, like the others, you get used to it."

"Then why?" Maddox asked, although he really wasn't sure he wanted to know. All he had wanted was a simple Twinkie.

"Made oral a bitch. My ex? It sliced his tongue to shit, bled all up in me. I don't care too much about him anymore, though. Come to think about it, it wouldn't have been such a bad thing if it had cut his tongue off all the way—the asshole that he is."

Maddox paused for a moment, trying to think of what to say to something like that. After a while he concluded the best course of action would be to flee. He turned around and jogged out to the minivan and stuffed a chocolate Hostess cupcake down his throat, hoping his own daughter wasn't the same as whatever that thing back at the gas station was.

A cotton candy-haired demon from Hell, he thought, and shuddered.

HE WASN'T SURPRISED to find their old place empty. She had warned him in advance that they were moving far away from the Midwest.

However, Maddox sincerely doubted their new home would be located even two towns' distance, and his suspicions were proven correct when he looked up his ex-wife's maiden name in the phonebook. Shit, she hadn't even moved out of town.

Sheryl Landers, it read, his finger halting on the listing. He tore the page out and folded it into his pocket. There was no use in trying to call. It would only end with her hanging up the phone. No, this sort of interaction needed to be face-to-face.

Driving over to the address listed in the book, Maddox popped in a butter rum Lifesaver and wondered how he had managed to go without candy for so many years. The craving had even been worse than the cocaine, ridiculous as it sounded. He was a patient man, he liked to tell himself, and looked down at the steering wheel of the car he'd just stolen.

Well, sometimes he was, at least.

He swung into the apartment complex his ex-wife now lived. Nearly passed it—a jungle of snow-covered bushes and trees hid the parking lot entrance from normal street view. The place was in need of a serious trimming. And shoveling. Jesus, he hoped he didn't get stuck trying to pull out. In some places the snow was past his ankles.

He passed the residential mailbox, noticing an

infestation of graffiti along its dented steel, and read their inscriptions. On the side, in large block letters, graffiti read: *JEREMY WAS HERE! LONG LIVE THE WHITE MAN!*

Below that, another rogue suitor—this one wielding red ink—raised the question of said Jeremy's arguable sexuality.

Maddox scanned past this to the tenant labels. He spotted the name in the middle, at 3C.

S. Landers.

There was no working buzzer within sight, so he allowed himself in the building and made his way up the stairs. He stopped at 3C and raised his fist to knock on the door, but slowly lowered it back down.

He was about to see his family for the first time in a decade. They had no idea of his release. Somehow he didn't see this ending well. Would Addy remember him? Surely she would. She was only seven when he was put away; not like she had been three or four, or something. There had to be some kind of memory the girl still kept of him.

He did, however, fear what Sheryl might have told Addy about her father. Was she aware of the type of man he used to be? Did she think he was dead? The only way to go about this would be to peel off the Band-Aid and just knock.

So that's what he did.

Maddox could hear the distant babbles of a television as the door swung open. It was loud, any hint of dialogue drowned out by an obnoxious laugh track. His muscles tensed as a woman appeared before him, one with long black hair covering her left eye. She wore baggy pants and a tight black T-shirt with the words SICK PUPPIES printed across it, white sleeves from an undershirt covering her arms. She stood there barefoot in the doorway, granting visibility to the black nail polish that matched her facial cosmetics.

He knew who she was right away.

"Yeah?" The girl raised her eyebrow. "Can I help you?"

He realized he was just standing there with a goofy smile like some sort of creep. A great first impression with his daughter after so long. He cleared his throat. "Hello, sweetheart."

She sighed. "You a friend of Del's?"

"Who?" Maddox wasn't sure he wanted to know who that was. "No. I'm here to see you."

"*Me?*" She pointed to herself for clarification.

"You don't remember me, do you?" What else had he expected?

"No . . . sorry?"

Maddox thought for a moment, trying to figure out a way to sharpen his daughter's memory. Finally he said, "Here, try to picture me with a lot of hair, 'bout this long? Ring any bells?"

The girl shook her head. "No, sorry, who are you?"

Maddox held his arms out, welcoming her fleeing embrace. "I'm Daddy, baby."

"*What?*" Addison Kane took a step back.

"I'm home." He smiled, following her inside.

The living room made him grimace. Nicotine stained the ceiling, holes in the wall, dirty carpet. A small TV rested in the corner of the room on a brown cardboard box. The place reeked of expired milk.

He looked back at his daughter. This was definitely no place to raise a little girl in. Not that she was very "little" anymore.

Addison kept backing up, face fixed in a confused stare. Maddox attempted to say something else, but was interrupted by a woman's voice coming from the kitchen. "Who's at the door? Jeremy?"

Addison shook her head slowly. "Some guy." She never took her eyes off Maddox. "Says he's my dad."

There was a brief silence, then a sharp "*What?*" from the kitchen. Heavy footsteps headed toward the living room. They were confronted by a woman in a flannel, revealing her bare legs. Same remarkable hair as their daughter. It didn't take Maddox long to notice the large stomach on his ex-wife. The stomach of a pregnant woman. They stood there staring at each other; Sheryl's expression that of puzzlement and Maddox's of pity. She was so unhealthy-looking, skin incredibly jaundiced, dark bags hanging from droopy eyes. It appeared that while Maddox had given up his drug addiction, his formal spouse had acquired her own. The tracks imprinted within her inner thighs didn't lie.

Poor Addy, he thought.

The room remained quiet for a moment longer, like the short span that occurred before a gunslinger duel commenced in a cheap spaghetti western. Just staring each other down. Then Maddox winked and showed off that grin of his.

"Don't tell me you forgot about me, too," he said.

"Addison, go to your room," Sheryl said.

"But Mom—"

"Now!"

Addison sighed, gave one last good inspection of Maddox, and walked to the hallway and entered the second door on the right. Maddox repeated it over in his head; made sure he wouldn't forget which one was his daughter's room.

He redirected his vision back at his ex-wife. "Now, that isn't any way to speak to our daughter."

"She's not your daughter," Sheryl said coldly, lips snarling. "Not anymore."

"Now, that simply isn't true."

"Oh, it is. Now I'm going to call the police. I would advise you to get the hell out of here before they arrive." She stormed back into the kitchen, torso and above visible by the opening in the wall.

"Why would you call them?" Maddox asked.

"Sure, you bust out and you think you can hide out here? You fuckin' loser, you best think again. I'm not putting up with your crap, anymore."

"Honey," he said, "do the math. I didn't escape from anywhere. I got paroled. I'm free, baby. Free."

Sheryl rolled her eyes up as if in deep thought. After a while she placed the phone back in its cradle, pulled out a knife from the drawer, and headed back in the living room, blade pointing out. She halted a few feet short of Maddox, who hadn't budged an inch.

"I don't care if you did or didn't bust out," she said. "I still want you out of here right this instant. I never want to see your pathetic face ever again, you got it? And you can forget about Addison. You lost her, understand? This isn't your family, anymore."

"Well, you don't have to be so mean about it." Maddox held out his arms. "I come in peace."

His ex responded by waving the knife in front of his face, inches away from carving a new set of eyes in his flesh. "Maddox, dammit, I told you to go so you best go!"

As if signaling the welcome bells, an annoyed voice from down the hall suddenly shouted, "What the *fuck* is all this goddamn noise?"

"Uh-oh," Sheryl whispered, amused, "you gone and done it now."

He heard footsteps stomping toward them, and there appeared a man in just his boxers, sporting a mullet while scratching his balls. "The fuck are you?" he asked, looking at Maddox suspiciously.

At first, Maddox remained silent. Then he said, "I'm Dad, that's who the fuck I am."

"What you say, boy?"

Sheryl leaped in front of the two men, putting her hand on the guy's bare hairy chest. "Del, remember I told you about Addy's dad? The guy locked up? This is him. I guess he got paroled. Now he's here and keeps threatening me and he just won't go away!"

"Oh yeah?" said Del, his ex's new lowlife boyfriend. Although judging from the wedding rings on both their fingers, he was a lot more than just a boyfriend.

TOXICITY

The guy looked Maddox up and down, smirking. "You're the junkie, huh? That right?"

Maddox stayed quiet. If there was one thing he had learned locked up it was that it was usually better to let the other person speak. The more you spoke, the fuller of shit you usually were. The advantage of silence, you had all the time in the world to plan out your next move. All of this while the opponent flapped his gums off about things that would never matter once the actual action started.

"Don't know what you're doing around here, boy," Del went on. "Ain't got no smack for ya."

"You sure about that?" he asked.

"Yeah, I'm fuckin' sure, man. What, you wanna start something? Huh?"

"I was just thinking those needle marks on your arm tell a different story."

Del glanced down at his arm and back up. "You mind your own fuckin' business, ya hear? Now get the hell outta here 'fore I knock your fucking skull in."

"After I speak to my daughter."

"She ain't your daughter anymore, bitch," Del sniggered. "She's my kid now, but don't you worry—I takes real good care of her."

Then he winked.

Maddox didn't think—it only took one right hook to the guy's jaw to knock him out cold. He went up in the air and landed squarely on his back, sending a vibrating thud throughout the living room. Sheryl screamed, dropping the knife, and put her hands to her mouth.

Maddox cracked his knuckles and turned his head to his ex-wife with utter disgust. "What do you see in this guy?"

Sheryl backed away, shivering. "I'm calling the police."

"I figured."

* * *

Maddox wiped down the minivan clean of all prints before abandoning it on the side of the road. All his sweets were gone, wrappers crammed into a plastic bag that he buried in the snow ten feet from the scene. He crafted a little cardboard sign and left it sticking in the driver-side window:

GONE TO GET GAS

Sucking on his last Lifesaver, Maddox started down the snowy road leading toward the trailer park. The trailer park where his brother lived. Well, at least used to.

He didn't bother sticking his thumb out. Hitchhiking seemed like a bad idea. It'd just lead to having to deal with some nosy asshole begging for one across the face. He was pissed and he knew a nice long walk would help cool him down a little. It always did.

It had felt pretty good sticking one to that dipshit back at Sheryl's apartment. He'd met hundreds of his type before, in and out of the joint. All they ever did was make him mad, and he ended up hitting them. It was the cycle of life.

As he walked, Maddox wondered once again what Sheryl was doing with somebody like that. Did she have a thing for drug addicts? True, Maddox used to dip into the cocaine once in a while. Nothing too serious, just a little taste of King's own product, free of charge. Of course, his old boss had never been aware of this, and that was probably for the best. Also, okay, maybe his habit had been more than just a habit, and in fact had been a full-blown addiction. But once he got sent up to Megaton, his regular dosage had been cut off entirely. Sure, there were ways to smuggle certain substances in, but then you would owe someone a favor. And in prison, once you owed one person a favor, you were never out of debt until you were witnessing a body bag zip closed from an interior point-of-view.

But, what had seemed the impossible turned out to be the reality as Maddox no longer found himself relying on his next hit. He knew then this was the beginning of a transformation into a better human being, a more suitable father figure for his little Addy.

Climbing the slick porch, Maddox gave three rapid pounds to the screen door, waited a second, and then added three more for good measure. He doubted his younger brother had actually moved residences in the last decade.

He waited for someone to answer, glancing idly around the trailer park. He appeared to be the only one moving about. It was around mid-afternoon, meaning everyone was either at school or work. Or sleeping, of course. The snow had long stopped falling, thank God, and now the air was still, the world taking a moment of silence.

The walk, like he knew it would, had helped calm him down some. He was less stressed out now, telling himself he was a free man and could do whatever he pleased. There were no more bars to keep him confined from all the endless possibilities awaiting his future.

The front door swung open and a shirtless man in jeans peered through the doorway with greasy hair. "Yeah, help you with somethin'?"

"I was thinking maybe you could," Maddox said.

"And what would that . . . " He paused, adjusting his vision, and dropped his jaw. "Holy shit! Is that you, Mads?"

"The one and only." Maddox nodded.

"Hell, man, I haven't seen you in like . . . what, five years?"

"Ten."

"Yeah. Shit, too long. You just get out?"

"Today."

"And you come straight here, huh?" Benny Kane asked, grinning. "You miss your brother, that it?"

"Yeah, something like that," Maddox said. "Hey, it's freezing out here."

"Yeah, of course. My place is your place, you know that."

Maddox did indeed know this. This was why he had

given his parole officer the trailer's address as his new home on the outside. His brother had a way of never being able to say no to him.

Benny stepped aside to allow Maddox to enter. As he closed the door behind them, he gave Maddox an odd look and said, "Dude, what'd you do to your hair?"

4

JOHNNY SAT AT the lunch table, staring down at his tray of food in disgust.

The cafeteria was animated by the shrill laughter of his so-called peers, chattering away like jackrabbits on crack.

Of course he didn't want to eavesdrop, but he was left with little choice. They all talked so loud, they were practically begging him to. Why else does someone even talk if not for others to hear them? Everyone sounded like the same dying starstruck hyena.

He looked down at the piece of toast in his hand, shaking just inches from his open mouth. The little round purplish balls spread across it sickened him. He took a bite. He'd eaten this shit before but still he grimaced as each egg popped, releasing its horrid salty flavors into his taste buds. It was hard to believe that this was the most expensive food in the world, costing up to five grand a kilogram. Sure, they served other types of caviar at lunch, but since he was considered one of the "richer" students, he was rewarded the ever-luxurious Beluga.

Johnny found it laughable that this was a reward even in the slightest. He would have laughed, too, if it wasn't for his sudden urge to vomit. He dropped the barely touched slice of toast back on the tray with the rest of his food. It made him wonder how much his parents were paying the school to cook this type of shit. How else could they afford it?

Doing his best to reject his need to puke, Johnny studied the rest of the food laid out before him. In the center of the tray was the main attraction: a big juicy piece of Kobe beef lathered in A1 sauce. It was the most expensive meat there was and, to Johnny, it tasted like any other meat.

There was a cup of Bird's Nest soup, a calm liquid poured in a Styrofoam bowl that looked like a big old puddle of snot. In the corner of the tray was his dessert: a buttery looking slab of disaster called *foie gras*—or, duck liver. According to the chef who served their food, the school was very lucky to be located out of Chicago. Apparently the dish was banned there. Johnny wondered if perhaps it was for good reason.

Not for the first time he wondered if things were only popular because poor people couldn't afford them. If he took a dump and registered it on eBay for ten thousand dollars, would everyone want to bid?

"What's wrong with you, dude?"

Johnny turned to the side where a peer of his sat. He was pretty sure they were friends, but Johnny had no idea what his name was. That wasn't the problem with the kid, however.

There was something wrong with his face: he didn't *have* one.

It was as if someone had wrapped a skin-colored blanket over his head, erasing all identifiable features. What was left was just a head; minus eyes, minus a mouth, minus a soul.

Johnny blinked a couple times, adjusting his vision—*this is what you do when staring straight into the dark*—and the kid's face cleared back up. Normal again. Or at least doing a good job at pretending.

"What?"

The kid pointed at Johnny's tray. "You're not even touching your food. What's going on with you, man?"

"Nothing," Johnny said, shaking his head. He managed to catch a handful of students out of the corner of his eye. At first, he wondered why their faces were missing, too, but then they reappeared after a short session of rapid blinks. "Just a headache. Really, it's no biggie."

"Well, if you're not gonna eat that, do you mind if I take it off your hands? I just adore this foie gras."

"Sure, whatever. Take it."

Johnny pushed the tray to the side and sprang to his feet. It felt like someone had strapped him to a merry-go-round and applied tape to keep his eyes wide open. It reminded him of the one he and his old friends in Loathsome used to hang out on. A mixture of nausea and intoxication overwhelmed him. He was spinning all right; it was just that his body couldn't catch up with his mind, and his mind couldn't catch up with his thoughts, and yet his thoughts couldn't catch up with his mind. None of it made sense, but when did anything really make sense when your eyeballs suddenly turned into tiny rolling globes? Who was spinning these plastic planets? It certainly wasn't him.

The faces of everyone in the cafeteria were blurry. Like someone had painted all these facial features on them, but had accidently smudged it before the ink could dry. He felt sick to his stomach. He was going to puke. All that Beluga caviar and Kobe beef would go spewing all over these inanimate stand-ins and that would be that. Jesus Christ, this school taught him more about expensive foods than anything else. Fuck algebra. All you needed to know in life was how to properly eat an oyster.

Johnny ran. He didn't care if he fell, he still ran. He pushed past the plaid mannequins and hurried for the boys' bathroom. Any second, he knew his balance would go tumbling out from under him but he didn't care. He just needed a couple minutes to himself, to take a few deep breaths like a human being without everybody in the whole goddamn universe taking his picture. Plus . . . he needed to check something out. He had to confirm his face was still intact. He had to make sure his fears were silly and that the eraser hadn't struck him, too.

Johnny kicked the bathroom door opened and before

he could do anything else, a wicked explosion of purplish goo discharged from his mouth and splattered against the sink. The smell was horrendous but it felt marvelous finally leaving his system.

Puking wasn't so bad, he thought. Definitely a hobby he needed to take up more often.

He looked up at the mirror in front of him and for one frightening moment all he saw was a miserable black hole swallowing the space where his body should have been; a vortex, and what it led to was nothing at all. The worst possible destination imaginable.

Then he blinked and reality snapped back into focus.

He could see the gallon of sweat pouring over his skin; damn near on the verge of a heart attack. Kids weren't supposed to be this stressed out—this paranoid. He needed help. He needed a fix. What he needed was some more purple. It'd been at least five hours since his last hit. Too long. Way too long.

"*Now* who's tripping balls?" said a voice from behind him.

Johnny squealed and leaped around, nearly falling into his own puddle of puke. Standing next to the urinal was a real-life bloodsucking vampire.

No, not a vampire. Just a Goth.

Johnny relaxed. The kid had spooked the hell out of him.

"Jesus Christ, where did you come from?"

The Goth laughed. He was wearing a dog collar. "I was taking a piss."

"That makes sense."

"So, have you started seeing the demons yet?"

Johnny coughed, trying to get a hold of himself. "I don't know what you're talking about."

"Just wait," the Goth winked. "They'll start showing up before long—and once they do, believe me, there's no escaping them."

"You're crazy."

TOXICITY

"You're in denial," he said. He started to walk off but turned back at the last second. "And remember, don't ignore the buzz. It'll end up eating you alive."

And with that, he was gone.

Looking back down at the sink, Johnny discovered his puke had also mysteriously vanished. It was almost as if he hallucinated more when he wasn't high.

He turned the faucet on and splashed water in his face. He needed to go home, relax, breathe in some purple. Then he would be able to think clearer. He'd be able to finally focus.

Stepping out of the bathroom, Johnny realized that while inspecting his own features—or *lack* of—in the mirror, the Goth's reflection had failed to show up along with him.

He shivered and returned to the cafeteria for a nice hot cup of *kopi luwak*, the rich man's coffee. It was made from beans ingested and then excreted from a weasel-looking animal called the Asian Palm Civet.

5

"**Y**OU WANT A beer, man?"

"I don't drink anymore," Maddox said, examining the trailer's shady interior.

"What? You don't *drink* no more?"

"That's what I said."

"Well, why the hell not?" Benny came back from the kitchen with a beer in his hand. He lay down on the sofa, planting his feet on the armrest, and pointed to the recliner next to him. "Cop a squat."

Maddox hesitated for a moment, looking around some more, wondering why the room was so clean. It wasn't like his brother to pick up after himself. Finally he gave in and sat down, settling back in the chair's cushion.

"Comfortable, ain't it?" Benny asked.

"I guess."

"Found that beaut 'bout three trailers down next to some garbage cans. Man, the stuff people throw away, it's amazing."

Maddox didn't say anything; just rested his head on the chair. He wouldn't have cared if a dog had pissed on it—anything was better than one of those god-awful bunks back at Megaton.

"So, man, you're finally out!" Benny said, breaking Maddox's tranquility. "Five years, ain't it feel good?"

"*Ten,* and yeah, it feels good."

"Well, what do you wanna do?"

"I want to sit here for a bit, be quiet, and relax." Maddox closed his eyes.

"All righty then," Benny said. "Get your relax on, no one's gonna stop ya. I'll just watch some TV and relax, too."

"There isn't a game on, is there?"

"It's the middle of November, man. What do you think?"

"Yeah, that's right." It'd been a long day. "Would have been nice, though."

Once in a while on the inside, the wardens would broadcast a game on the intercom, usually only postseason. By the 7th inning stretch, he'd have already won two cartons of cigarettes, betting on the outcome of each play like they were at the races. As kids, he would make his brother crouch down in the dirt with his glove and he'd fire them in at him. He was only twelve and already reaching 85mph. A future playing ball seemed inevitable—assuming he didn't fuck it up. Which was, of course, exactly what he had done.

Thinking about his mistakes got him thinking about his Cadillac, making him wonder just how badly his brother had damaged it while he had been locked up.

"Hey, Benny, you still have my car, right?" Maddox refused to open his eyes in fear of what his brother's facial expression might have held.

"Yeah, of course I still got it. It's parked out back."

"You didn't wreck it or anything, did you?"

"No, man, the same condition you left it in. Shit, what do you take me for?" He tried to sound offended, but was doing a poor job at it.

"Just making sure," Maddox said. "Calm down."

"I'm calm."

"You have any clothes?"

"What?"

"Clothes. I want to take a shower."

Benny directed him to his bedroom and downed the rest of his beer, skimming through channels. Maddox stumbled through the darkness of the trailer and located his brother's room. He snatched the first set of clothes he came across and left.

As he strode toward the bathroom his brother called out for him.

"What?" he asked, standing in the doorway, a towel hanging over his shoulder and a ball of denim and Fruit of the Loom bunched up in his hands.

"Just thought I should warn you," Benny said, sipping a new beer, "that the soap in there is extra-slippery."

* * *

Maddox flicked the light switch on in the bathroom and froze.

Something was seriously wrong.

The tiled floor had not one discarded piece of clothing on it. There weren't even misguided urine puddles surrounding the toilet. The water was actually clean. Where were the brown, crusted stains in the bowl? The pubic hairs curling on the seat? The sink was even scrubbed.

He decided he would have to bring this up later, ask Benny what new drug he was on that possessed him to be so neat. Maybe suggest to increase the dosage, see what happened.

Maddox watched himself in the mirror as he undressed, revealing his naked form. He looked over his oblong scars. He inspected his tattoos, all three representing his love for the game. There was the giant red C on his chest, where his heart would be. There was the rabid bear gashing into his right shoulder, tearing out of his flesh like some kind of demon fleeing from Hell. And, of course, there was the last tat he had done, a little over a month before getting busted. Two digits located in the center of his back in bold ink:

23

The number they had assigned him after being drafted into the Big Leagues. Wrigley Field, baby. His dream, supported by a tough ivy shield. He didn't like thinking about his dream, anymore. Instead he turned away from the mirror and stepped into the shower. Regret was an emotion he had never particularly cared for.

After he was done he got dressed in a black T-shirt and dark blue jeans. He felt good—no, more than good. He felt *fantastic*.

Maddox came out of the bathroom and found Benny exactly where he'd left him. "What's this?" he asked, gesturing to the TV.

"*Wife Swap*," Benny said. "I swear, man, I'm addicted to this show."

"What's it about?" Maddox slipped his boots on.

Benny sat up on the sofa, suddenly bursting of excitement. "Well, they take these two different families, right? And then they switch the broads up and live like that for a couple weeks. It's like a reality show for swingers—only there's no fucking. Well if there is, they don't show it, at least."

"That doesn't sound very entertaining." Maddox sat down in the recliner. The shower had energized him quite a bit. He hadn't realized how much he actually missed that kind of privilege, to bathe under hot water—*alone*.

"It's not," Benny agreed. "But for some reason I can't stop watching it."

Maddox cracked his neck. He didn't want to just sit here, watching reality television and doing nothing. No, he wanted to go out, have a burger, catch a movie, do *something*. "You got any money, Benny?"

"A little . . . Why?"

"Get it and come on. I'm starving."

"What, you broke?"

"It's kinda difficult to earn a paycheck behind bars, Benny."

"Now, that sounds like losers' talk, but okay."

Benny threw on some clothes and they made their way around the back of the trailer, approaching a black automobile parked beside a couple of steel trashcans.

Benny fished the keys out of his coat pocket and tossed them to Maddox, who barely caught them as he stared at his car in a near-hypnotic state.

"We gonna go or are we just gonna stand here all day?" Benny asked.

"Let's go." Maddox slid in the driver's seat of his precious '74 Cadillac Eldorado. He settled down in the leather, finding his comfort zone before inserting the key in the ignition and starting it up. He loved the feel of his hands around the steering wheel as the engine roared to life. It was enough to make a man cry.

Benny got in the passenger side. "See? No dents."

Maddox glanced down at the floorboard and spotted a pile of fast food wrappers and empty beer cans. The seats were stained with God knew what. The interior smelled like pot. He tried to shrug it off.

"So, where're we going?" Benny asked.

"I don't know. Where's the best place to get a burger around here?"

"With the money I have? Probably McDonald's. Dollar menu, man, can't beat it."

"No, McDonald's was always smashed and oily. I hate that place."

"Actually, they've changed a lot since you've been away," Benny said.

"Oh yeah?"

"Yeah, they recently decided to add more grease."

"Funny. Where else? I want an actual good burger. Something big and juicy."

"Oh, well why didn't you just say so? I got somethin' big and juicy for ya right here," Benny said, and winked. Then he paused, less confident, and added, "I'm talking about my dick."

"Would you like to be bitch-slapped, Benny?"

"No, that's quite all right, thank you."

"Thought so. Now, where else can we go?"

"You know what? There's a truck stop up there in town.

Easy to find. I'll give you directions. There's this restaurant inside, ya know, has the best fuckin' food you'll ever have. Cheap, too."

"Yeah?" Maddox pulled out of the trailer park and turned onto the main road. "They have burgers?"

"Of course, they got burgers." Benny lit a cigarette. "They got anything you want, man. Burgers, steaks, spaghetti, fuckin' chow-mein. Hell, I could probably even get you some ass if you wanted some."

"That's okay, Benny."

"No, it's not okay. It's been like, what, five years, right?"

"Ten."

"Yeah, shit, that's even worse. Go ten years without, man, you gotta be on the verge of exploding at every pair of tits you pass, huh? Unless you're batting for the other team now. Is that it? You drop the soap too many times?"

"That bitch-slap offer is still on the table, if you want it. And I'm thinking you do."

"Okay, okay, sorry." Benny smirked. "Hey, ain't you got a wife? Why the hell are you here and not over there stickin' it in her?"

"We're divorced now, Benny."

"Oh, shit, well. I always thought she was a bitch, anyway, if it's any constellation."

"Do you mean consolation?" Maddox asked, flicking on the radio.

Benny thought for a moment, then shook his head. "Nah, man, I don't think so."

6

ADDISON KANE ENTERED her bedroom and sat at the edge of her bed. A peculiar wave of familiarity washed over her. The man in the living room, when he opened his arms out to her, there had been some sort of subconscious current trying to drag Addy to the man's embrace. Somehow she had managed to resist, and now she wondered if perhaps that action had been a mistake on her part.

Her mother had always told her her father was long dead. But then again, her mother wasn't exactly known for her honesty. Could this guy really be her father?

Then, from the living room: "You blew your chances of being a father!"

Oh, well that settles that, she thought.

Addison sat there for a little longer, thinking how her mother had just saved her from a lot of aggravating questions. Some she most likely would have been slapped for asking in the first place.

Then she heard a loud thud. Her mother screamed bloody murder. She said she was going to call the police. The door slammed. Silence.

It was going to get ugly here. It would probably be in her best interest to leave the apartment for a few hours. She threw on a hoodie, some socks and her shoes, and slipped out of the place as quietly as possible. Her stepfather was unconscious on the floor. She made sure her mother wasn't looking when she pressed the heel of her shoe down on Del's stomach. It was enough to make her smile as she jogged down the stairs and out into the cold.

TOXICITY

* * *

Loud, obnoxious music could be heard reverberating down the street. This was how the neighborhood usually sounded at this time of day. The neighbors had given up complaining long ago. It was never any use.

The sun was just going down when Addison approached her boyfriend's house. She didn't bother knocking on the door, but instead walked around to the side of the garage and pounded her fist against its dusty window. She continued this act until the music abruptly ceased and an intoxicated head poked outside. At one glance of Addison, the head went back into the garage. She heard it saying, "Dude, it's your chick."

Another voice: "Hey, man, I thought we agreed no girls at practice. It throws off my mojo, you know that."

Then Connor: "Oh shut up, we're done here, anyway."

One by one, the band marched out of the garage door, hopped on their bikes, and rode home. They were dressed as wizards. Addison waited until they had all left before she entered the garage. Her boyfriend sat behind the drum set, wearing a blue silk robe with golden stars stitched into the fabric. A pointy hat matching the robe laid at a tilt on top of his head. He was lightly tapping a pair of drumsticks against his thighs. "Hey," he said, looking up. "What's going on?"

Addison raised her eyebrow. "I could be asking you the same thing."

Connor smiled. "Like the costumes? Got a deal at the Salvation Army. Pretty sweet, huh?"

"You're actually going to wear that while performing at shows?"

"Yeah, why not? Assuming we ever get one booked, of course."

"Very . . . cool." Addison had always found her boyfriend's heavy metal band, Asswarts, a bit strange. Every song shared the same central theme: Harry Potter. She hoped he would have grown out of his J.K. Rowling phase a long time ago, but apparently it was not meant to be.

"Oh, yeah, check it," Connor said. "Thought of a new song today. You know Severus Snape, right?"

"Yeah."

"Well, what about 'Severus *Rape*'?" He smiled at her as if he had just revealed the greatest work of art ever conceived.

"Dear God."

"I know, right?" Connor grinned. "It's brilliant."

Addison shook her head. "Yes, it sure is," she said. The boy was truly lucky she loved him. "Can we go outside and talk for a minute?"

"Yeah, of course." He stood up and Addison placed her hand on his shoulder.

"Um, do you mind unwizarding yourself first?"

"Oh, sure, sorry." Connor blushed.

They left the garage and found a seat on the porch swing out front. It was a little chilly, but after covering up with Connor's large magic robe, it wasn't too bad.

"So, what's up?" he asked.

"I think I met my real dad today."

"*What?*"

She told him everything that had happened before leaving the apartment. When she was finished, Connor sat a moment in silence, staring into the sky.

"So, you gonna talk to him again?"

She shrugged her shoulders. "I don't know. I mean, what if he left again for good? Maybe freaked out because of the cops or something. I don't even know how to get a hold of him."

"Maybe he'll contact you."

"Maybe."

"Do you want him to?"

"I think I do, yeah," Addison said. "Anybody has to be better than *Del*."

Connor nodded. "You really stepped on him when you left?"

"Yeah." Addison smiled. "It felt good."

"I'm glad. That guy's an asshole."

"Yeah," she agreed, thinking her boyfriend really had no idea what kind of despicable monster the guy actually was. Her hands self-consciously buried themselves in her hoodie pocket, although the scars were already protected by wristbands.

"Hey," Connor said, "what do you think of 'Her Heinie' as a song name? Like, instead of Hermione? It could be an ode to butts or something."

Addison giggled. "I love you."

"Love you, too," Connor said, and kissed the top of her head. They snuggled together on the swing and stayed there, enjoying the moment. Addison was already feeling better. She always did when he was holding her like that. It made her feel like everything would be all right in the world, even though it probably wasn't true.

She fell asleep in his arms.

7

DONALD WAS SICK.

He didn't think he was going to live much longer. His condition had been on the decline for a while now, and as the hours ticked by, it only worsened. There wasn't a lot of time left. Maybe a day or two at the most, then his brain would just give up and his body would fall down wherever it was standing. And that would be the end of good ol' Donald. The world would be minus one junkie.

There was nothing that could save him either. Except for one thing.

Jericho.

But that was too expensive. Donald slept in a cardboard box. He used newspapers as blankets. Who in his situation could possibly afford what he so desperately craved?

It was starting to rain. Lying face up in an alley, arms crossed, teeth chattering, body shaking, he wondered how his life had gone so downhill. And how quickly it had progressed. Hell, he had once worked at Wal-Mart. It was a good job; he had worked himself up to assistant manager.

Then that goddamn door greeter got him hooked on the purple and everything started to go wrong. Donald liked to believe his first act of insanity was when he stapled his nametag to his boss's forehead, but he could have been crazy long before then, too. He couldn't really remember too much of his past now. Jericho had helped in that department, as in many others.

Around the same time he was fired was when Donald

64

started noticing people. *Really* noticing them. Not just some sit-in-a-park and observe the joggers type of noticing. No, this was more of a cryptic image noticing, and it was his job to decipher the hidden messages.

He discovered a different layer of humanity. There wasn't just skin and bones. There was *so much more*. He couldn't explain it at first, not until he encountered the UPS driver.

See, the man's employment with the United Postal Services had all been just a clever ruse. His real work was with the Devil.

Donald saw through the man's disguise right away. He buried the demon's head in his back yard, ditched the rest of the body down Lake Michigan. This was before the bank repossessed his home, obviously. Now the severed head was some other joe's problem.

Besides opening up his eyes, Jericho had also amplified his other senses. He could smell the scum of the world as they traveled from point A to point B, pretending like everything was normal. Pretending like they were human. Sure, they might have been able to fool the average pedestrian, but in reality they were horrible actors. Donald could smell their real intentions. Their real evil.

He found his hearing was stronger than ever, too. Traffic became one of his most loathed enemies. Always honking, always yelling—it was too much. Colors became too bright, gave him agonizing migraines that resulted more often than not with him passing out cold from the pain.

His sex drive was at its limits as well. It was a lucky day if he could last longer than an hour without acquiring an erection. Between Jericho and hookers, Donald had run out of cash rather quickly.

Now he spent his days sleeping in a cardboard box, caught in a binge of masturbation. When he was finished he used the rest of his spare time shaking and crying, wondering how he could score some money for his drug fund. He also feared the demons that inhabited every third human being that passed his alley. But before he could come up with an actual solution, he was rock hard again. It was a never-ending cycle of humility.

None of it mattered really. If he didn't get a fix soon he would die. It was as simple as that. Once the purple entered your system, it didn't leave until it sucked you dry. The only way to prevent death was to constantly refill. And he hadn't refilled in almost two weeks. It was either shit or get off the pot now.

Donald slowly climbed to his feet, letting the rain wash away his sweat. The rain was more solid than normal rain, like tiny droplets of piercing ice, but it didn't seem to faze him. He was burning up—yet freezing at the same time. He shook the snow from his hair and stumbled out of the alley.

The night was calm. He kept his head down, letting the demons go on about their false business without bothering them. He had other agendas to attend to tonight. If Donald planned on living, he would need to come up with some cash. He wasn't sure what he was going to do yet, but he knew he had to do something. And fast.

8

THE CADILLAC SWERVED into the gas station's wide icy parking lot. Metallica blared from the car's speakers. Just like old times.

Maddox and Benny got out and entered, passing through the convenience store area and finding the restaurant built further inside. They sat down in an orange leather booth, a brother on each side, picking up the menus from the matching Formica table.

As they scanned the various meals available, Benny muttered, "Anyone ever tell you, you drive like a goddamn lunatic?"

Maddox smiled. "I missed speeding."

"Yeah, I think every car within a three-mile radius could back that up."

His smile widened, trying to focus on the menu in his hands. He had felt terrific after taking that shower, and his good mood only seemed to be increasing. Driving the Cadillac again had been therapeutic.

Maddox had tried the radio shortly after departing from the trailer park, but was disappointed when all he came across was pop and rap shit. Fortunately, he was able to locate one of his old Metallica cassettes in the glove compartment. He sighed, thankful that his brother, who favored Tupac and Ice Cube, hadn't thrown it away. He cranked up the volume and followed Benny's directions to the gas station, every couple minutes pushing his foot harder on the pedal, grinning like a fool, until he was going seventy-five and banging his head back and forth to "Battery."

The waitress, a cute little number wearing a green uniform and a ponytail, approached the booth notepad in hand. "Hi, my name's Amanda," she said, displaying a shiny beam, "and I'll be serving you fine gentlemen tonight. Can I start y'all off with somethin' to drink?"

Maddox gave up with the menu. His brother hadn't been lying when he said they had everything. "I want a Pepsi, and the biggest, juiciest burger your cook can make. And fries, too. Big fat ones."

"And as for me," Benny said, "I'd like some coffee and the bottomless spaghetti and meatballs. That come with garlic bread?"

"Just the first helping," Amanda said.

"Well, that hardly seems fair." Benny frowned, and paused, as if to debate over the menu one last time. "I guess I'll take it."

"'Kay," the waitress said, jotting their orders down. "I'll have it up for you in no time."

"I bet," Benny mumbled, as she backed away and headed into the kitchen. He lit a cigarette and leaned back in the booth with his arms resting on top. "She's pretty fine, huh?"

"Go get 'em, tiger," Maddox said.

"Shut up."

"Relax."

"I'm relaxed."

"Good."

Shortly thereafter their food arrived.

"You had the spaghetti and meatballs, bottomless," said the waitress, setting down the pasta. "And you had the big juicy burger, extra big and juicy." Followed by a wink. "Enjoy your meal."

"I wonder if she's on the menu . . . " Benny trailed off, watching her walk away. "Will you check out the—"

"Eat, Benny," Maddox said. He already had a quarter of his burger gone. He created a puddle of ketchup on his plate and drowned a couple French fries in it.

TOXICITY

It was his first real meal he'd had since released, and it tasted like heaven. Sure, you got used to prison food after a while, but it's nothing compared to actual human food. There was nothing like praising in glory as he re-experienced the bliss of a double bacon cheeseburger.

"Jesus, man, you're eating like you just got out of the pen or something," Benny said.

Maddox only looked up.

Benny giggled and said, "So, what are your plans?"

"Plans for what?"

"I dunno." Benny shrugged. "About anything, I guess. I mean, you just got out. You must have some kinda plans, right? You gonna go working for King again?"

"No," Maddox said, and he meant it. He never wanted to see Vincent King's face again. It was because of him that Maddox went to prison in the first place. He was through with the crime shit—this he was absolutely positive of.

"You gonna stay with me, then, are ya?"

"Just 'til I get back on my feet, if that's all right with you," Maddox said. He stuffed the rest of his burger down his throat and washed the meaty entrails away with a swig of pop. "Still jobless?"

Benny looked up from his plate of pasta, a saucy noodle dangling down his chin. "Nope, got me a job at Starbucks now."

"The coffee place?"

Benny nodded, and Maddox had to laugh. Surrounded by an endless supply of caffeine was not such a good idea for his brother. "So, you went from dealing crank to dealing frappaccinos?"

"Yeah, but I think the crank paid better, though." He grinned. "As a matter of fact, right now I'm on temporary suspension."

"What'd you do?"

"Oh, just my stupid boss. He got tired of the customers complaining every time I took a sip from their drinks.

Hello, it's called 'sample tasting'. I'm just looking out for the safety of my fellow Americans."

"Should have known." Maddox tossed a fry in his mouth and leaned back in the booth, sighing in content. The plate had been scrapped clean, really hitting the spot. He felt alive, rejuvenated. Like a free man should feel. Sitting in this truck stop, Maddox was satisfied for the first time in what he reckoned to be a long time. Now if only he could speak to his daughter . . .

"Hey, waitress!" Benny called out, signaling Amanda over, who'd just finished taking the order of a large graying male with a beer belly.

She came over to them and nonchalantly muttered, "Server."

"What?"

"We're not supposed to answer to waitress anymore. It's *server* now."

Benny cocked his brow. "What? Why?"

"I dunno." She shrugged. "Guess it's sexist or something. What did you want?"

"Oh, yeah. You think you can get me a box?"

"Full already?"

"Yeah . . . good stuff."

"Shame, you didn't even ask for seconds. That bottomless order must feel like a waste now, huh?"

"Yeah, well . . . "

"Tell ya what," Amanda said. "I haven't even had a chance to ring you guys up yet, the place's been so gosh darn busy. How 'bout we just say you wanted the single plate instead?"

Benny smiled. "Now that's a fine idea."

"Thought so," said the waitress.

Benny watched her as she walked away, turning back to his brother. "She is one piece of work, huh?"

"She's all right," Maddox said, finishing his Pepsi.

"All *right*? Man, you've been away way too long. Speaking of which . . . " His eyes traveled toward the convenience store area. "I'll be right back. Sit tight."

TOXICITY

And just like that, Benny was up and out of his seat and leaving the restaurant. It crossed Maddox's mind that he might've been ditching him with the bill, but then he remembered he was the one with the car keys, and relaxed. A few minutes later Benny returned, shivering.

"Shit," he said, "since when did it start to rain?"

"Where'd you go?" Maddox didn't like the look in his brother's eyes.

"Never you mind. You ready to jet?"

"Sure."

"Good," Benny said, laying down some money on the table, "'cause I gotta surprise for you."

"I don't even want to know," Maddox said, as he was led out of the truck stop, thoughts drifting to his daughter again.

It wasn't like Sheryl was just going to hand Addy over to him. Therefore, he'd have to hire a lawyer—a helluva good one, too, considering his ex-con status and all. The dreadful reoccurring question bounced back and forth in his head: would it even be possible to obtain custody? Maddox didn't like the probable answer, so he created his own.

He wouldn't rest until it was a reality.

* * *

She had the scariest face Maddox had ever seen.

At first glance he mistook her for a man. It just wasn't every day you came across a woman with a shaved head. The next thing he noticed was the dragging fishhook scar lined from one ear to the other, hopping over the mouth like some sort of sinister clown's grin. Her jagged lips held a white discolor to them that made Maddox cringe, bubbling sores ringing her mouth. But perhaps the most horrifying feature of this wretched woman was the milky glass ball inserted in her left eye socket. He had never seen a cursed object before, but after one glance at this glass eyeball, he was relatively certain this thing was cursed as fuck.

He gulped in horror, sincerely fearing for his life.

Using the rearview mirror as a translator, Maddox's eyes and the girl's *eye* connected, locked together. She winked her good eye, the one dressed up with long black lashes, while the opposite held not even a brow.

"Benny, what is this thing behind me?" His arms tensed, hands tightening around the wheel.

Benny patted Maddox on the shoulder, smiling. "This is the surprise I was telling you about. Mads, meet Jazzy." He turned around and said, "Jazzy, meet Mads."

9

BY THE TIME Addison awoke, it was already raining.

The time of night was undeterminable. The air was cold and wet. She snuggled closer into her sleeping boyfriend's arms, seeking stronger warmth. The sound of rain pounding against the tough steel of car roofs hammered into her ears like nails.

Ever since she was little, bad weather had always given her a sinus headache. Her temples felt like they were inflamed with the hottest fire known to man. Usually if she went back to sleep she'd feel a hundred times better in the morning, but it appeared the icy temperatures of the night weren't going to let her do such a thing.

She pulled the wizard cape against her, wrapping her body in it, when Connor asked about the time.

"I don't know," Addison whispered. "It's late."

"Is it raining? Jesus, it's coming down hard."

Addison nodded, adjusting herself on the swing. "I should probably be heading home, anyway."

"Why don't you stay here? We can sleep in my room."

She debated the idea for a second, and thought it would probably be in her best interest to stay as far away from her stepfather tonight as possible. That punch must have been one hell of a throw to knock him out like that. He'd be hurting still, and undoubtedly in a rage. She knew he'd be drinking and shooting up, and Addison tried to stay away from him when he was high. Bad things happened.

"Okay, I'd like that," Addison agreed. "But I need some aspirin. Bad."

"The rain again, huh?"

"Yeah."

"Lemme go see what we have." Connor kissed her, kicked the robe off him, and jogged into the house. A short time later he came back outside with an apology. "I guess there isn't any. Sorry."

"It's okay," Addison said. She gave long drawn-out blinks, trying to force the pain from her brain, but to no success. She rubbed the spot between her eyebrows, wincing. "Let's just go to sleep," she said, although she knew full well it was going to be hell trying to fall back asleep now. She would be up most of the night tossing and turning, blowing her nose and pushing a pillow in her face to cry. It was how it always was.

And Connor knew this. "C'mon," he said, "I'll take you to Walgreens. Get you some good medicine. It should still be open."

"Connor, no," Addison said, shaking her head. "That's really nice of you and all, but really, I'm fine. It's raining way too hard to be driving around in."

"What are you talking about?" Connor said. "I'm the best driver there ever was."

Despite the headache, she still managed to snort.

"Are you saying I'm not?"

"No," Addison said, "I'm just saying good drivers usually don't play bumper cars at red lights."

"I told you, that light was *green!*"

"I was there with you. That light was red and you know it."

"Whatever," Connor said. "The guy had a Colts bumper sticker, anyway. He deserved it."

"And that's exactly the type of talk that makes me hesitate when getting in the same car as you when it's storming out."

Connor sighed and gave her a look that told her to quit

being so stubborn. "Babe, need I remind you who beat *Grant Theft Auto IV* in *one day's* time? Me, that's who. And you think I'm a bad driver? You should be ashamed of yourself."

She risked a soft laugh, which she immediately regretted. She really hated the rain. "Fine, but just as long as you remember red means stop."

"Yeah, it also means kiss my ass," he said, and stuck his tongue out.

She chased him off the porch and ran through the rain and snow, piling into his 1987 Ford Fiesta parked in the driveway. It was a cheap little bucket of bolts, but, unlike most kids' cars at their high school, it actually drove. And drive they did. Miraculously without failing to stop at a single red light, too.

Her head was hurting more than when they left, so she said she'd just wait in the car while he went in and got the meds. They kissed and she leaned her head against the cold window, resting her eyes as Connor closed the car door and jogged into the drugstore.

Her lips curved faintly into a crescent as she thought about what a great guy her boyfriend really was. Not any man would drive out in the middle of the night in the pouring rain to buy a bottle of aspirin for his girlfriend. They just weren't like that. Unless, of course, there was the possibility of sex; then they'd be rushing out any time of night to buy her whatever she desired. But Connor already knew how she felt about that, and seemed perfectly understandable, even if he didn't know the reasoning behind it. Addison felt lucky. She really had someone special. She knew he would always do his best to protect her from harm, and she loved him dearly for it. She knew he loved her, too, if not more.

One day they'd even get married, she was thinking, and dozed off into a light sleep.

* * *

Connor strolled into Walgreen's feeling pretty good about himself. Hair dripping from the rain, he made his way across the store to the pill aisle. He grabbed a bottle of ibuprofen and headed toward the refrigerated section for a couple Cokes, going past a bin of pink ski masks that were on sale. Walking to the front to pay, he found himself wishing pop still came in glass bottles. Glass always made liquid so much better. He didn't know why, but it was true. Not that he'd been alive when pop was sold exclusively in glass bottles. But he'd seen enough movies to speculate.

"That all?" the cashier asked, a kid only a few years older than Connor.

"Yup," Connor said.

"It letting up any out there?"

"Getting worse," he said, shaking his head and paying for his items.

"Well, be careful." He handed over the plastic bag.

"Thanks," Connor said, and exited the drugstore.

He stopped a few feet short of his car. Addy's door was wide open, and she was nowhere to be seen. He looked around.

"Addy!" he called out. "Addy, where are you?"

He got in the car and set the bag down in the backseat. Maybe she went into Walgreens to use the bathroom and forgot to close the door. Didn't seem particularly unrealistic. Then he noticed a spatter of something brownish red on the passenger seat, where Addison had been sitting before he left her, and all logical thought escaped him.

Blood. Fucking blood.

Connor dove out of the car and yelled his girlfriend's name. He searched the parking lot anxiously but came up with no results. She was gone. Just like that, missing from the face of the Earth.

TOXICITY

What the fuck?

He thought he heard something, but wasn't too sure. The rain was too loud, made it near impossible to hear anything unless it was right in your ear.

Connor paused. That time there *was* something, he was positive of it. A scream? A girl's scream. Connor gulped. He didn't like the sound of it, but it'd have to do. Somewhere off to the left. He didn't hear it anymore, but it had come from that direction. He was sure of it. He ran off and shortly found himself entering a small-wooded area. Addison screamed again. Much louder now. He was getting closer.

Jesus, please be okay, he thought, mind growing into a state of complete panic. *I'm coming, baby, I'm coming.*

10

DONALD WAS USED to the rain.

The snow stabbing his bare feet as he trudged through town no longer affected him. While Jericho had heightened some of his senses, it had also diminished others. The ones he really didn't need. The ones that without, he became stronger. A more powerful entity. A superior being.

Donald was on the prowl tonight.

There was only so much longer he could withstand the withdrawal before death's wicked breath inhaled his soul. And then even Jericho wouldn't be able to help him.

If he wanted to continue living, he'd need a fix. A fix cost money, money of which Donald did not have. Money was everywhere but in his pocket. It was all around him, up for grabs. He just had to reach out and grab it.

The rain was a criminal's advantage. Camouflage. Especially in the middle of the night, like now. He stumbled through the Walgreens parking lot, scoping out cars with the keys still in the ignition. There weren't many choices, as it turned out. A pick-up truck here, a Toyota there. All of which were securely locked.

He supposed he could just smash a window and hotwire one. The rain would cover up any noise of breaking glass, but it still didn't help the fact that he had no idea how to hotwire a car. He'd probably just end up electrocuting himself. Still, there were probably valuables in them that he could snatch. Stuff he could pawn. Maybe even some cash, perhaps a wallet or purse. And if anyone gave him any trouble, well, that was what the knife was for, wasn't it? He wouldn't mind taking out a few demons. Hell, he'd even enjoy it.

He always did.

Donald found the knife in a dumpster a few weeks back. It was a big 'un, a weapon akin to something Arnold Schwarzenegger would've been packing in *Predator*. The blade was a little rusty, and the handle was a bit rough, but it'd still do the job. He decided to keep it around in case any more of those pseudo-mailmen tried to convert his pure Christian soul into something of a darker kind.

Just when he was about to smash his fist through the pick-up truck's window, another car pulled up. This one pretty dingy, but he thought he'd give it a look before committing to anything permanent. He waited 'til the driver got out and entered the store before progressing. Donald crept forward and peered inside. The keys were still in the ignition, just dangling there. Which meant the driver didn't plan on being in the drugstore long. There was no time to waste.

He opened the door and slid behind the wheel. Getting ready to pull the gear from park to reverse, he paused as he spotted something out of his peripheral vision. He slowly turned his head to the figure in the passenger seat. A girl. Sleeping, by the looks of it. If she was awake she didn't seem very fazed by the sudden intruder.

His eyes focused on the hump in her hoodie where it curved outward. Toward him. Almost as if they were begging for his touch. There was a familiar tightness in his pants as he licked his lips. All thoughts of stealing the car temporarily subsided, as did the inevitable return of the driver. He suddenly found himself faced with more pressing issues. The last time he was this close to a girl was over a month ago when he still had a few bucks left. It was the cheapest prostitute he could afford, yet she had still been afraid to touch him. He took care of her, though. Now she wouldn't be touching anyone.

Donald reached his hand out and rubbed it against the

girl's breast. The contact alone was enough to make him gasp. The caress only continued for a second further, however, for the car was suddenly filled with a piercing shriek.

He directed his vision from her chest to her face. Eyes wide, mouth in an oval, screaming. He felt nails digging into his cheek and he recoiled. The girl, frantic, opened the passenger door and jumped out. A warm trickle of blood dripped down his face. Donald climbed out after her. He gripped the knife tightly in his right hand as he scanned the parking lot. He was sure she would've fled straight into the drugstore, but he didn't see the automatic doors sliding open. So where?

There, to the left, running wildly through the rain, toward an outskirt of trees. He booked after her. Fast, fast—soles of his bare feet slapping against the snow. He followed her into the woods. Ahead, gaining speed. Then an abrupt stop as she tripped over something on the ground. Within seconds he was leaping on top of her. She screamed for help and Donald backhanded her across the face to shut her up. People never knew when to shut up. That was their problem. Just shut up, he told her. Or maybe he only thought it in his head.

She just would not keep still no matter how hard he smacked her. He kept trying to knock her out, but the bitch was tough. And aggressive, too. He sorta liked that. It turned him on.

They fought on the ground, rolling around in the snow. It was almost fun. But he was growing impatient. He wanted to get down to business before he exploded.

All he had to do was show her the knife and she stopped resisting. Her eyes widened in terror, choking on her own air.

He asked her if she was going to scratch him again. No response. He reached under her shirt and grabbed her nipple and twisted until she cried. He repeated himself. Still nothing. He was about to twist her tit again when he realized he hadn't actually been talking out loud. He shook his head in frustration. It'd been a long time since he conversed with someone who wasn't a demon.

"You done scratching?" he asked, voice hoarser than he remembered. He coughed a few times, globs of blood spraying from his mouth. The girl was terrified, seeing the color of his blood was purple and feeling the cold steel of the knife pressing against her throat. He asked again. "Well?"

"Yes," she replied, nothing more than a whimper.

"Good. Next time you scratch I cut off a finger. Understand?"

"Yes."

"And if you scream again you lose your tongue. Got it?"

"Yes," she said. She was shaking uncontrollably now, tears blinding her vision.

"Do you believe me?"

"Yes."

"Good. I'm not fucking around. Now let me ask you something. You one of them?"

She frowned, confused. "What?"

"*I SAID, ARE YOU FUCKING ONE OF THEM?*" he yelled, twisting her tit all the way around. She started to scream again but bit back her tongue just in time. "*ARE YOU?*"

"No!" the girl answered, biting down on her lip. Lines of crimson drool seeped from the corners of her mouth.

Donald smiled. "Good, I didn't think you were. You look nothing like a demon, do you? Nah, you look good. You look real good. I like it. I like it a lot. I want to see more of you. Turn around."

"What?"

She was getting on his last nerve. He would kill her after he was finished just for this alone. This time he grasped her entire breast within his palm and squeezed hard enough to make her cry out again.

"I said, turn the fuck around." This time she didn't ask

him to repeat himself. Fumbling in the snow, she managed to turn around on her stomach. His greedy hands grabbed the end of her jeans and pulled them down to her ankles, revealing only a pair of black underwear, which he cut open with the tip of his knife. He ran the blade along the smoothness of her buttocks, reveling in the whimpers it invoked. He leaned his head down and allowed his tongue the same path the knife had taken.

It was all too much for him to handle. It was either now or never. He flipped her over on her back again and pushed himself on top of her. "Spread your legs," he ordered gruffly, unbuttoning his own pants and releasing his throbbing cock. The girl clamped her thighs together and he pulled them apart, not bothering to argue with her any longer. Donald reached over and held the knife against her throat. She stopped fidgeting.

He really fucking needed this. He thanked God for having the patience to wait in the parking lot. Look at what he had found! Maybe today was Donald's lucky day after all. The girl might even have some money on her as well, maybe enough to score a small dosage of purple, but he wouldn't be upset if she didn't. This would be good enough for tonight. Nevertheless, he'd still go through her pockets after he was sated and she was dead. Which would be soon. He was almost there. Oh God. Oh sweet fucking almighty Christ.

Then something hard bashed into the side of his face, sending him flying off the girl.

A deafening ring devoured every ounce of his consciousness. He could feel part of his cheek hanging there, torn off from his face. He turned around just in time for another blow, this one connecting below his jaw. Some kind of log. Hard as a brick wall. Raining down upon him. He never had a chance to see his attacker, blood and rain clogging his eye sockets.

Everything went black.

11

ONNOR DROPPED THE log and rushed toward Addison. She was still lying there in the snow, partially naked, curling into a ball and shaking. He kneeled down and put his hand on her. Her body seemed to be drenched in blood. Whether it was from her or the rapist or both was too hard to tell.

"Jesus Christ." He didn't know what else to say. What words of comfort could he possibly offer her? He grabbed her hand and squeezed it lightly. She responded by squeezing back, clamping tightly down like a set of canines. She was in shock. It was freezing out, the rain coming down hard as ever. She'd catch pneumonia out here long enough, exposed like this. He gently pulled her pants back on and lifted her up.

He took slow steps, careful not to trip. It seemed to take an eternity to find the parking lot again, but he did. He opened the backseat and guided her down on the cushion. There was a throw blanket back there that he kept in case they went to the park or the beach. He wrapped Addison with it and kissed her on the forehead. "You're okay, now," he said. "No one else is going to hurt you."

She whispered something but it was too distant to make out.

He leaned closer.

She whispered it again, this time just loud enough to hear. "Help," she said. "Help me. Please."

"I know," he said, wiping back his own tears. "I know."

He stood there for a while looking at her. At all the blood. It set off something in his head, made him snap.

"I'll be right back, okay? I promise. Just sit tight and when I get back we'll go to the hospital, okay? I love you, Addy. God, I'm so sorry."

Before leaving, Connor turned the car on, exposing Addison to the heater. He turned around and headed back into the woods.

He found the cocksucker right where he left him. He had regained consciousness, but was just lying there, wheezing and looking up at the sky. There was a knife nearby in the snow. He picked it up and walked over to the monster. There were no words to say. There was nothing. He grabbed the guy's hair and yanked his head up, then slit his throat and watched as all of the life drained from his body.

Connor tossed the knife in a bush and returned to the car. He drove away without saying a word, Addison in the back, equally quiet.

DAY TWO:

MAGGOT

12

JOHNNY WAS IN the kitchen the first time he saw the Fly.

He was standing at the counter, drinking a glass of water. It was three in the morning. He hadn't been sleeping well lately. Mostly just bouncing back and forth against the walls in his room, singing old TV theme songs, and smacking himself across the face. It was his little way of clawing the bad thoughts from his mind. So far no success, but there was still time.

He took a sip and it caught in his throat. He gagged, wrenching, and coughed out a glob of purple phlegm.

And the Fly.

Came buzzing right out of his throat.

It landed on the brim of his glass and stared at him.

When It spoke, it was hell trying not to drop it.

"Hello, Johnny."

He wasn't sure how to respond, or if he should at all for that matter. Conversing with insects was a whole new territory for him.

"It's okay," said the Fly. **"I'm not used to conversing with humans, either."**

It seemed almost as if the Fly's words were forming in his head. But he wasn't the one thinking them up. Or was he?

"If I were to speak aloud you would never possess the precise hearing functions required to understand me. Instead, I am sending my thoughts directly to your brain, and vice-versa. I think it is much easier this way, do you not?"

This was just a figment of his imagination. Ever since those grape-throwing Goths had introduced him to the purple, he'd been seeing a lot of weird shit. Just hallucinations. Johnny scratched an infected sore on his neck and wondered why it had to be a fly of all things.

"Why, of all things, do you have to be a boy?"

"Touché," Johnny whispered. He waited for It to say something else. When It didn't, he asked, "Well, what do you want?"

"Ultimate destruction."

"Yeah, who doesn't?" Johnny sniggered. Then he thought if anyone were to walk in right now, they'd catch him standing in the middle of the kitchen, holding a glass of water and laughing at nothing. He did his best to form a straight face.

"I also want to save the world, though I can understand how those two goals could contradict themselves. But what do they say about sacrifices? Yes. Sometimes tragedies are necessary to prevent complete horror."

Johnny wasn't sure what to say about that. He just wanted to go back up to his room and sleep. Maybe do some more purple first. Jerk off a little.

"Imagine your life existing within the confines of a sandcastle."

"A sandcastle?"

"Yes. And one day the tide washes it all away. All that hard work is now nothing, thanks to one little wave."

"'Kay."

"But let me ask you, what if that wave hadn't been so innocent? What if, instead of merely wiping out your puny sandcastle, it had grown to the colossal proportions of a tsunami, and it destroyed an entire city? A state? A country? A *world?*"

"Tsunamis aren't that powerful," Johnny pointed out. "You are one ill-informed bug."

TOXICITY

"You're missing the point, Johnny. What would you rather have happen? The destruction of the sandcastle or the extermination of the city?"

"Uh, I don't know, probably the sandcastle."

"Right. So, let me ask you this question again, a little differently."

"'Kay."

"Would you be willing to sacrifice your life, along with others, for the greater good?"

"The greater good?"

"Yes, Johnny. The greater good."

"What's the greater good?"

"It means you'd be saving the world, dummy. Don't you want that?"

"I don't know." Johnny thought about it for a moment. "Saving it from what?"

"Demonic possessions, among other things. Mainly you would be dealing with the highest ranks leading Lucifer's army of evil."

"Whoa, man, hold up, that sounds kind of dangerous."

"It's *highly* dangerous! You would have to *sacrifice* yourself! You do know the definition of the word 'sacrifice', right?"

"Wait, you mean I'd have to die?" All of a sudden Johnny did not like where this was heading. This insect was nothing but bad news.

"Yes, you'd have to die. You'd have to kill. You'd have to serve your planet for the greater good."

"Or what?"

"Or else all is lost."

"Which means?" It was amazing to him how bugs always beat around the bush like that. Why couldn't they just come out and say what they were getting at for once? Jesus Christ.

"Which means the world ceases to exist! The

Army of the Dead prevails and everything succumbs to darkness!"

"And that will happen unless I kill myself?"

"In so many words," the Fly said, **"yes."**

"Oh." Johnny looked away from the glass of water and examined the empty kitchen. He wondered once again if he was still dreaming. He returned his stare back to the Fly in the water. "Well, I think I'm gonna have to pass."

"What? You can't *pass*."

"Sorry, dude." Johnny raised the glass to his mouth and finished off the rest of the water, swallowing the Fly along with it. It screeched in agony as It was dragged down his throat into the acidic purgatory of his stomach.

"I gotta stop taking drugs," he whispered to the refrigerator, and went back up to his room to sleep. In the morning he had forgotten all about his late-night encounter with the Fly. It was a Saturday, so he spent most of the day taking hits of Jericho and playing the piano in the living room. It didn't occur to him until later that his family didn't own a single musical instrument. What the hell had he been playing?

13

ADDISON WOKE EARLY the next morning, curled in Connor's arms. She tried to convince herself last night was just the scene of a very nasty nightmare, but it didn't do any good. She lay in bed and didn't move. Her stone-cold eyes stared ahead into the darkness. The warmth of her boyfriend's arms gave little comfort.

She hadn't even moved yet and was already feeling the pain. She wondered how badly she was torn, how much damage there was. She had bled between her legs for a while. Everything had gone so bad so fast. It was all fucked.

Last night after leaving Walgreens, Connor had driven straight to the hospital. He parked in the lot and just sat there, staring at the steering wheel for a while. Addison was still in the backseat, whimpering. She sat up, gasping at the pain and the shock of the situation.

"Did you kill him?" she had asked. He didn't answer. She leaned forward and saw his hands still gripped around the steering wheel. They were covered in blood. "You killed him." This time it wasn't a question.

"I couldn't let him be," he whispered. "I just couldn't."

She squeezed his shoulder. Tears blinded her. "Thank you."

Connor cleared his throat. "Can you walk, or do you want me to go get a wheelchair?"

The idea of going into the hospital made her shake. She thought about all the nurses and doctors putting their hands on her. Like the guy in the woods. He'd had his hands all over her. Grabbing her. Rubbing her. Squeezing her. Now she was expected to go inside this building and let others grab her. No. Fuck that. She couldn't do it. No way.

"I don't wanna go."

Connor looked over his shoulder at her. "You have to go. You're hurt. You've been attacked."

She trembled harder, lips quivering. "Please. Don't make me go. I don't want them to see me."

Connor rubbed his eyes, then winced. He held his hands out and stared at the blood. He looked back at Addison. "I don't know what to do, Addy. I just don't know."

"Neither do I."

"I think we need to go inside the hospital. This isn't right."

Addison stared at the building outside the car window. The rain had let up some, albeit a little too late. She tried visualizing walking into the hospital lobby and approaching the front desk and telling the clerk that someone had just raped her. That someone had chased her through the woods and violated her. Then, afterward, her boyfriend had killed him. She tried to imagine what kind of reaction the front desk clerk would make and every possibility made her want to vomit.

She turned back to Connor, crying harder now. "Please . . . can we please just . . . just go to your place? I . . . I can't . . . I can't fucking do this . . . I just can't . . . "

"Yeah." Connor stared at his hands again. "Okay. We'll go. I'm sorry. I'm so sorry, Addy."

He drove back to his house. Connor had helped her into the shower and, following her wishes, left her alone while she tended to her injuries. Every muscle she moved sent a volt of pain through her body. It was like walking on knives in a room swallowed by fire.

It took her forever, washing all that blood off. Some of it crusted onto her skin, not wanting to come off for the life of her. Afterwards she inspected herself in the mirror, wiping away the fog and wincing at the beaten girl it revealed. Her eye was severely swollen, black and blue—nose just as bad. At least it wasn't bleeding anymore, wasn't broken or anything. She was lucky her nipple hadn't been ripped completely off.

The tainted touch of the monster glowed over her skin. A radioactive infection of disgust. She saw the trails his hands had made, where they had squeezed. She saw where he had entered her, where he had licked her. Addison turned around and hurried back into the shower, twisting the knob frantically until the water was practically steaming. Her flesh became red as she washed all the filth away. But no matter how hard and fast she scrubbed, the shame wouldn't leave. It remained there, eating at her soul—a stigma of the worst sort.

There was an embarrassing limp to her walk as she left the bathroom and headed to the bedroom. Connor was in there waiting. He helped her into bed and crawled next to her, holding her. An hour or so later she managed to find sleep. It was a sleep fueled by the same scene stuck on repeat. Over and over, she felt the pain, the fright—the horror.

Now it was morning and Addison was still just as traumatized from the night before. She hadn't so much as changed her pattern of breathing yet when Connor asked, softly, "You're awake, aren't you?"

"You sure he's dead?" Addison said.

Connor's arms tense around her. "We gotta talk."

"Not yet."

"Okay."

"Wanna be quiet for a little longer."

He kissed the back of her head. Her body shivered at the brief contact. The gesture was faint, but still present: she had pulled away from him. She hoped he hadn't noticed.

They lay in silence for about an hour longer. There was

the sound of the front door opening in the living room, and Connor said, "I think my dad's home."

"Yeah," Addison said.

Ten more minutes passed.

Then he said, voice kind of cracking, clearly fed up with the silence, "What can I do for you, Addy? I just don't know what to say. I think you should go to the hospital, something. Let me drive you."

She stayed quiet. She didn't want to talk. Why couldn't she just lie here in silence? How fucking difficult was that to understand?

"Will you at least let me look?" Connor asked. "I don't even know what all he did to you."

"What do you think?"

"I know, but it was dark. Did he cut you, too?" He paused. "I . . . I found a knife."

"No, no cuts. Can we please not talk about this?"

"Okay," Connor said. "But we're gonna have to, you know? Something has to be done."

"What's done is done," she said, trying not to cry again.

"I'm not so sure about that."

"You killed him."

"I had to."

"I know."

"Okay."

"Are you sure he's dead for good?"

"Yes. I think so."

"How did you do it?"

Connor paused. "Let's just lie here for a while."

* * *

Later in the afternoon, Addison woke up to an empty bed. It felt colder in the room without him there. Made her feel silly for pulling away from his kiss earlier. It wasn't that he repulsed her or anything, it was just the gesture in general. Too soon, she thought, way too soon. All it did was bring back the crazed man from last night, how he had kissed her too, but instead of affection it had been out of evil.

So much evil.

She shivered.

Addison slowly worked her way out of the bed and walked with a slight limp to the bedroom, wincing with each step.

Connor was in the kitchen, hands folded out on the table, staring at the wall in concentration.

She sat down across from him and gave a weak smile. "Hi."

"How're you feeling?"

She didn't see a reason to hide the truth. "It hurts," she said. "Bad."

"I'm sorry. Let me take you to the ER, okay?"

Addison sighed. "Connor, I don't want to do that."

"Why not?"

She looked at him.

"I'm just worried something bad will happen if you don't get some treatment, you know?"

"Something bad already happened."

He made a grimace like he was choking back a tear. "The bleeding stop?"

"Yeah."

"Addy, tell me the truth. How bad are you hurt?"

She thought about it for a minute, remembering her inspection in front of the mirror from last night. "It's pretty ugly, but I think it'll heal by itself. Maybe some ointment, I don't know. Hurts worse than it looks."

She lowered her head. It hadn't even been twenty-four hours, for Christ's sake. Didn't he understand that she just did not want to talk about this, ever?

"You're positive you don't want to go?"

"Connor, please."

"Okay, I'm sorry." He shook his head. "You want some coffee?"

"That'd be nice. Your dad sleeping?"

Connor's dad worked a night job. He was a good man, but mostly kept to himself. Hardly said anything to Addison; same went toward Connor. He was a man in perpetual mourning; the death of his marriage still hit him as if it had happened only yesterday.

"Yeah," Connor said, pouring two cups of coffee and stirring the necessary cream and sugar in it. He set one down in front of Addison and placed three pills beside it. "The ibuprofen . . . from last night. And a Vicodin that I stole from my dad."

"Thanks." She swallowed the tablets. She noticed he was just standing there, looking at her. "Connor, please, I'll be fine. It's just going to take a little bit for me to recover from this, okay? I'm alive, the guy's dead. There's nothing else anyone can do about it."

"Well . . . " He trailed off and pointed at her chest.

She looked down, saw the circle of red forming at the tip of her nipple, and frowned. "Oh." She sighed. "Can you please get me a couple Band-Aids and some peroxide? Maybe a bag of ice for my eye, too?"

He didn't say anything, just remained where he was, face slack, his eyes red and sore. This was one of the main reasons she didn't want to go to the hospital. She hated that look. She'd experienced it enough last time she was stuck in the emergency room. It suddenly struck her, with complete mortification, that all the shit with her stepdad could've been perceived as practice runs for what went down last night.

"Connor? Hello?"

He snapped out of it and wiped his eyes. "Yeah, sure," he said. "Anything you want. I'm here for you. Always."

* * *

After tending to her wounds, Connor drove her home. Neither said anything. He pulled to the curb and parked. They sat in silence.

Then Connor said, "I think I'm gonna have to hide out for a while. Maybe leave the state."

Addison turned her head. "What? Why?"

"I killed someone, Addy. Sooner or later they'll find the body."

"Yeah, but I was being attacked. You saved me . . . "

"An attack we still haven't even reported? Kinda suspicious, don't you think?"

She closed her eyes. She hadn't even begun to consider what would happen to him as a result of all this. "Well, if it comes to that, then I'll show them what he did to me."

He put his hand on her shoulder. "I know," he said, "but there's something else."

"What?"

"There has to be a camera outside of Walgreens, right?"

"Yeah, so it has the recording of that creep chasing me," Addison said, a little hopeful.

"But it also shows us coming to the car and me leaving you in the backseat. It'll show that I went back to finish the job. They'll know we could have gotten away without killing him, but I still went back, anyway. I could get convicted of murder. I can't go to prison, Addy. I just can't. You know?"

She didn't say anything at first. If it wasn't one thing it was something else. The passenger window was frosted over, shining her distorted reflection back at her. This was the same place she'd been sitting when that monster had grabbed her. There was still blood on the seat. She wondered how much of his cheek was scraped into her fingernails. She lifted her fingers to her nose and tried to smell him.

"What if you said you went back because you dropped something? Like your wallet?"

Connor seemed to consider this. "I guess that might work. I don't know if I want to risk them believing me, though."

"Who's going to stick up for *him*?"

"Good point. Let me think about it. In the meantime,

is there anything else I can do for you? You got the ibuprofen?"

"I got it, thanks. I'll be fine. Call me later, okay?"

"I will," Connor said. "Gonna think about a few things. I don't know if I'm going to turn myself in."

"Well, if you do," Addison paused, making sure what she was about to say was the absolute truth, "I'm coming with you."

He looked surprised. "Really?"

Addison reached over and gave him a kiss. She expected to draw back as soon as their lips connected, but the reaction was absent this time. She smiled. "Thank you for everything you've done. I love you, Connor."

"I love you too, Addy."

"Call me." She got out of the car. The weather had cleared up some since the night before. She tried not to limp too much as she made her way along the sidewalk, and to her amazement, she found it barely showed. It wasn't even hurting as bad.

Connor waited until she entered the building before driving away. She really would run away with him. For one thing, he had saved her life. For another, she loved the boy. She honestly didn't think she'd ever be able to find someone who was better than him, who'd take care of her as good as he did.

Besides, this fucking town would kill her if she didn't get out sooner or later.

Climbing up the stairs proved to be more difficult than the sidewalk, but she still managed. Addison wasn't new to pain. She knew how to make do. It was almost one o'clock when she came through the door. It had already occurred to her that Del wouldn't be too happy with her disappearing like that. Plus, given the terrific K.O. her real father had delivered, anything was possible.

Del was sitting on the recliner watching some action movie. It was a little hard not to notice the large cage installed in his face, steel wires running in and out of his mouth. She bit her hand to subdue any sniggers. She started heading to her room when he raised his arm in front of her, blocking the path.

"Hell you been?" he asked. You could see how much of a struggle it was for each syllable. Addison loved it.

"Out."

"What you wearin'?"

"Clothes," she said. He was talking about the clothes Connor had let her borrow, since her own outfit was no longer of any use. Some baggy jeans and a homemade band T-shirt.

"That say? *Asswarts*?" He seemed confused.

"You can read? Whoa."

"Shut your trap."

"Where's my mom?"

"Scoring. Want some?"

Addison looked at him, a sneer stretching across her face. "You do realize she's pregnant with your child, right?"

"Yeah, so?"

She shook her head—guy was a lost cause. The phone rang. She turned around but was stopped by Del's hand, which had jerked forward and grabbed a hold of her bottom.

"She won't be home for a while." He winked.

Addison smacked his hand away and broke for the kitchen, picking up the phone. "Hello?"

"Hello, sweetheart," said the voice on the telephone.

She froze, her breath disappearing. "Hi . . . "

Addison listened for a few seconds, then said, "Yeah, meet me outside, fast as you can. I'll be waiting. Bye."

She hung up and headed toward the front door.

"Who that?" Del asked.

Addison ignored him, wincing as she hobbled down the steps. She sat out front in the cold, thinking about her situation, until a black Cadillac pulled up with loud rock music blaring from the speakers. One of those terrible bands everybody's dad loved for some reason.

14

IT WAS ALMOST 1:00 P.M. by the time Maddox woke up, sprawled on the sofa and feeling a nasty sugar hangover. A line of watermelon-flavored drool dripped from his chin. Someone was shouting. Maddox spotted a twenty-something-year-old kid standing in front of him with his arms held out, shaking.

"Who . . . who . . . what?" trembled the intruder. He was dressed in a business suit.

"Um . . . hello." Maddox sat up, allowing the sticky cupcake wrappers to avalanche off of his now alert body.

"What *happened* here?" The kid gestured to the general living room area, where empty pop cans, beer bottles, pizza boxes and sweets now reigned supreme.

Instead of answering, Maddox stood up, brushing the plastic guitar controller out of his way. He stretched his limbs to their limits and yawned.

The kid crossed his arms and tapped his foot impatiently. "You mind telling me who you are?"

"Me? I'm Maddox—Maddox Kane. And you?"

His brow slanted. "You're related to Benjamin?"

"Yeah, I'm his brother."

"His . . . " The kid stopped. He gave Maddox a once-over and slightly gasped. "Oh, my God. You're the convict, aren't you?"

"I'm the one." Maddox snagged a half-empty can of Pepsi from the night before and downed its contents. It was flat and warm as piss but he didn't care.

TOXICITY

He noticed the kid had raised his fists and spread his legs apart in some sort of poor attempt of a martial arts stance. "You're an escapee?" the kid said. "Back off, scumbag! I know karate and I am *not* afraid to use it."

"Are you going to hit me?" Maddox didn't want the poor kid hurting himself.

The door to the bedroom creaked open and out came Benny, wearing nothing but his underwear, hair wild from a night of booze and sex. He was coughing in his elbow when he spotted the scene in the living room.

"Floyd, what the hell are you doing?"

"I think he's going to hit me," Maddox explained, and shrugged. He sat back down on the couch and dug for a Twinkie hidden under the cushion.

Benny smirked. "That right?"

The kid, Floyd, backed away as if suddenly placed on trial. "I will not tolerate living in the presence of wanted criminals. I have to draw the line at this."

"He didn't escape, Floyd."

The kid paused, slowly turning his head to Benny. A wind of puzzlement fluttered about him. "He didn't?"

Benny shook his head.

"I was released." Maddox licked his fingers clean of cream filling.

"Oh." There was a faint hint of disappointment in Floyd's tone. "Sorry 'bout that."

Benny sighed and turned toward the kitchen, most likely to retrieve his morning beer. Maddox just woke so he hadn't had the chance to peek in the refrigerator yet, but he was willing to bet there were at least half a dozen of those babies still slumbering away in that good ol' icy coffin of mold and forgotten condiments.

Sometime last night when they returned to the trailer, Maddox had opened the fridge so he'd have somewhere to store the twelve-pack of Pepsi his younger brother had bought for him at the truck stop. Unfortunately, when he swung the door open a golden glow had blinded his eyes, and he was momentarily reminded of that emblematic briefcase they carried around in *Pulp Fiction*.

The kid stuck out his well-groomed hand. "I'm Floyd."

"So I've gathered." Maddox said, taking his hand warily.

"Are you staying here, or something?" Floyd sat down on the chair next to him, scratching his smooth scalp of a head as if in deep thought. The sharp, dark unibrow resting above his eyes gave Maddox the sensation of uneasiness.

"For the time being," he said. "What business of it is yours?"

"Well, I happen to live here. Therefore, I believe such information may be quite essential."

"What do you mean, you live here?"

Benny returned from the kitchen with his fingers wrapped firmly around the golden neck of a beer bottle. He plopped down on the couch next to his brother and reached for the remote.

"Floyd's my roommate," he said. His eyes stayed focused on the TV as he talked, half of his attention in their discussion, the other lost to the aimless flicking pastime universally labeled as 'looking for something good to watch'. "Had to get one when I got busted for possession. I got lucky, though, they didn't stick me with intent as well, and just let me off with some community service . . . and a ton of fines. Plus the rent for this place was getting outrageous, so I did what I had to do."

Maddox let that all sink in and realized straightaway something didn't fit quite right; a slice of illogic that only his little brother could be a part of. "Benny, why are you still paying rent on a trailer you've been living in over a decade? Don't you own it by now?"

"You'd think so." Benny shook his head. "But that stupid goddamn law Obama passed way back when screwed us trailer residents over. My landlord really felt bad about it, too. Odd, since he gets paid longer, but he's a pretty nice guy. I swear, one of these days I'm gonna get a duplex or something."

"What law?" Maddox asked, but Floyd cut him off before he got an answer.

"None of this explains what happened here." He nodded toward the mess on the coffee table, on the carpet, on the furniture. "Do you realize how much time I spend cleaning this place up? All I ask in return is for a little common courtesy and to *keep it neat*. Why can't you do this one little thing for me, Benjamin? What could it possibly hurt to be less of a slob?"

"Floyd, if you don't shut that trap I'm kicking your ass out on the curb," Benny said, finally coming to a halt on the Bravo channel. "Now, if you'll excuse me, I got me some *Housewives* to watch."

Floyd sighed in defeat and stood up from the recliner. He picked up a dirty dish and began stacking others in his arms, cursing under his breath as he trudged off toward the kitchen. He twitched as he struggled to balance the miscellaneous paraphernalia of last night's *Guitar Hero* sessions. Pausing every few steps to assure himself each object was stacked evenly with the next, he slowly arrived at at the sink. The water came on and they didn't hear a peep from him for a long time.

Watching Floyd furiously scrubbing the dishes for phantom crusting, Maddox couldn't help but recall a guy he met back in Megaton. He wasn't sure what his name was anymore, but the guy had worked service duty in the cafeteria, standing behind the sneeze-guard at lunch with his little scooper and latex gloves. He always made sure each tray held exactly the same amount of food as the others. One solid scoop of beans, identical helpings of glop, even placed the milk cartons facing in the same direction. Maddox had heard that the guy was in for life, due to an argument he had had with his neighbor. Apparently, the neighbor allowed his poodle to do her business on the soon-to-be convict's lawn, and after numerous requests for this disturbing activity to cease with no improvement, the guy had picked up the poodle, stormed next door, and proceeded to beat the neighbor to death with his very own dog—presumably, with an even number of thwacks to each side of the face.

Benny was asking him if he had ever seen some show that was on TV.

Maddox started to turn his head to the television when he was distracted by the sight of his brother's back. Deep red lines rode diagonally from the left side of his hip, ending at the top of his right shoulder. It appeared to be the gruesome leavings of a thin, fierce strand of leather.

The thing from last night shot back to memory.

"Benny." He tapped him.

Irritated, Benny said, "What? Hurry before they start talking again."

"Where's the girl from last night?"

Benny thought for a moment, as if struggling with what to say, and finally winked. "Oh, she's in a safe place."

"Close by?"

"Yeah, you can say so."

"Is she dead?" Maddox said, hopeful.

"What? Who the hell do you think I am? *Dead?* Nah, man, she's sleeping on my bed for Christ's sake."

At least it was worth a shot.

"Isn't she, you know, still mad from last night?" Maddox asked. They kept their voices low.

"Of course she is. Wouldn't you be mad if you did a job and didn't get paid for it? She's *pissed*, man. Says she's gonna stay here and not leave our sides 'til we cough up the dough. And that could be like weeks—hell, maybe months."

It was suddenly very difficult to remain quiet. "Jesus *Christ!* What the hell did you have her do, Benny?"

He winked again. "Oh, a little of this, a little of that. Don't you worry, bro, we'll get the money somehow."

"What do you mean, *we?* I told you last night I didn't want anything to do with this."

Maddox chugged another warm Pepsi and for the first time in years he thought about how satisfying and welcoming an actual drink would be—a *man's* drink, not any of this kiddy sodapop shit. He could easily see how this would end up, and it had bad news written all over it. Barely a day out and he was already caught up in the middle of a prostitution feud. He desperately wished his release had waited until April; a game would do his nerves some good, cool him down. Where was his loyal 7th inning stretch when he needed it the most?

"Well," Benny said, taking a sip of a beer that looked way too desirable in Maddox's eyes, "judging from your attitude, you don't want her around either, right? She scares you, doesn't she? Yeah, she scares me too. But man, she is a *freak* in bed. Still, though, she has to go. I'm sure you'd agree with me on that. And since you want her gone just as much as I do, it turns into a *we* situation, get it? Because I certainly don't have that kind of cash floating around here. Shit, I'm on suspension as it is."

Maddox had stopped paying attention to his brother about halfway though his speech. A deep, gargling snore had risen from Benny's open bedroom door, and the horrific noise was seeping under Maddox's fingernails, like a demented glass eyeballed chalkboard.

With the empty Pepsi can held glumly in his hand (a peace offering, he briefly thought, a white flag) he asked, "How much?"

Hesitant, Benny turned back to the TV, feigning deafness.

Floyd was finished with the dishes and now had a broomstick in both hands. He swept lividly—yet neatly—across the hard wood of the small living room floor, all the while muttering curse after curse under his Listerine-fuming breath.

Feeling at a loss, Maddox repeated himself. "How much do you owe, Benny?"

He coughed. "Three."

"Hundred?"

The silence from his brother sent shivers down Maddox's spine.

"*Thousand?*"

Benny turned back around, an innocent smile forced through his teeth. "Sorry, Mads. I guess I lost control of myself."

Maddox clenched his fist around the can of Pepsi, smashing the aluminum into a sharp metallic ball. He whipped it across the room—missing Floyd's head by mere inches—and watched it bounce off the wall.

Floyd stopped and glanced down at the small indention the can had created upon the wall's surface. His one eerie eyebrow irately crunched down. He let go of the broom and threw his hands up. "That's it! I'm done! I've tried, I've really tried, but if you disgusting creatures insist on living like pigs, then a pen is where you'll live! You've won! Congratulations!"

Benny giggled uncontrollably. "Floyd, you're too much, man, really."

Floyd pointed at them and yelled, "No! Don't you laugh at me! I am *SERIOUS!*"

This only demolished the final barrier between Benny's presence on the couch and the floor, for he rolled off nearly in tears, banging his head on the coffee table along the way.

"You know what?" Floyd's face transformed into an infuriated one-browed tomato. "*Fuck you! Fuck you, Benjamin! I hate you!*"

He spun around in an attempt to storm off to his rented room, but his path was blocked by the colossal chest of the rancid lot lizard. Floyd shrieked and staggered backwards, tripping over the rug and falling on his bottom. He slowly lifted his head, petrified.

The beast glanced down at the new guy, who looked a little creepy even to *her,* and smiled. "Hey dere, sugar."

Floyd tried to talk but the only thing he could muster out was a series of feeble mumbles. She raised her index finger and slowly shook it—like a mother would, Maddox thought, but immediately brushed the idea away, afraid of what type of hellish spawns this unholy monstrosity could produce.

"Now, now, dere," she said, "no reason be scared. I ain'ts gonna hurt ya. Well, unless you wants me to."

"Wh . . . wha . . . what?" Floyd stammered.

Benny continued to laugh while Maddox remained silent. Godzilla wore a large black thong mostly swallowed by an untamed bush and nothing else, her eyesore breasts meeting her wide, quarter-sized bellybutton.

She leaned down closer to Floyd. "You next in line to ride the Jazz train, baby?"

"Huh?" he mumbled. It was perhaps the only material left that hadn't fled and went turncoat on his vocal system yet.

"Yeah," she smirked, "youse ready all right." Jazzy grabbed Floyd by his collar and tossed him up on her broad linebacker shoulders. He started pounding on her back, pleading for freedom. Maddox and Benny could only watch as she carried him back into the bedroom and slammed the door shut.

The screams, moans, and other demonic noises that followed would haunt Maddox's sleep for the rest of his life.

15

THE WAY HE remembered meeting his new girlfriend was like this:

Johnny had been hanging out at this pool hall all the local rich kids attended. Of course, no one there actually played pool. He had learned this the hard way. His first time there he picked up a stick, inserted some change in the table, and challenged some random patron to a game. The kid took one look at the skuzzy table and laughed.

The kid had said, "Please, do I look like I eat Ramen Noodles to you?"

And Johnny had lowered his head in shame. "But Ramen's so delicious . . . "

Then the kid had placed his well-manicured hand on Johnny's shoulder, saying, "You still have a lot to learn about being rich."

"Apparently." Johnny sighed.

"First thing's first," Johnny's new mentor said, "you don't *play pool*. Pool is for fools, you understand? Look, it even rhymes, so I doubt you'll have an easy time forgetting it."

"Rhymes are cool."

"When you visit a place like this it is not to play silly little games. It is to *socialize*. To socialize with other wealthy kids like yourself. Only they will actually know how to act rich, which you obviously do not know how to do. Because we have lots of money, the bartender will serve us whatever the hell we want. It does not matter that we are only teenagers. We are better than everyone else. I am not trying to be cocky, I am just stating the facts. Remember that. We are better than everyone else. Now say it."

"We are better than everyone else," Johnny said, liking the sound of it.

Sure, rewind a couple months ago and he would have probably beaten the shit out of someone talking like this. But that was the past and this was the present. People change; futures are altered. If God wanted to throw him a fortune, why shouldn't he play ball? It wasn't like he was hurting anyone or anything. He was just some kid trying out a new lifestyle, warranty included. He promised himself the second things started going sour he'd rewrap and return it to the store, receipt in hand.

So why not have a little fun?

He remembered thinking at the time that his girlfriend, Candy Blossom, would get a kick out of the stories he would be able to tell her now that he was undercover in the deepest depths of Snob Town.

Oh, how'd they laugh!

"Another thing," said his mentor. "Do not tell anyone else that you think Ramen Noodles are . . . delicious." He grimaced. "That kind of shit will get you blacklisted. Seriously. You are lucky I am such a good friend."

"I don't even know you."

"We sit together in Apple 101. You are the kid whose mother won the lottery, correct?"

He nodded. "That's me."

"Yes, we know more about you than you do. It is all good. This kind of lifestyle takes some getting used to. Just remember . . . no more cheap noodles, okay?"

"Okay."

The mentor grinned and slapped a boastful hand on Johnny's back. "Attaboy! Now, let us go *socialize*."

Johnny paused, a little embarrassed. "Uh, how do we do that?"

The kid gave him a look, seeing if his leg was being

pulled or not. "What do you mean, *how?* We are going to go have a lot of strawberry daiquiris and ponder Elon Musk."

"*Who?*"

He laughed. "Now I know you are messing with me. Come on, let us do this thing!"

So he led Johnny away from the wretched pool tables and into the bar area. Some very fruity tasting drinks were served with fancy umbrellas. Johnny didn't particularly care for these, but after a few quick hits of Jericho in the bathroom everything tasted like the best thing in the world. Even the air was top-notch that night.

Despite the pool hall lacking a dance area, he clearly remembered dancing with a whole lot of people. It was very magical. He also remembered licking the counter, so there was that.

Then later on, around twenty minutes until closing, Johnny was sitting at the end of the bar with some kind of pink drink in his hands when this girl he had never seen before sat down next to him. He noticed her out of his peripheral vision but chose not to acknowledge her presence. Given the strange hallucinations he had already experienced (a cocktail infested by a million flies, for example), he wasn't so sure she was real.

Then he heard her voice, and knew she was no more a hallucination than he was.

"So, you gonna buy me a drink or what?"

He nodded and bought her a drink. He didn't know what she ordered, or if she ordered anything at all. It didn't really matter, he supposed.

"So, you're the lottery boy," the girl said. It was then that he looked up, although the next morning he could not exactly recall what she looked like. He wanted to say her hair was red, but it could just as well have been blonde.

"Who told you that?" he asked.

"No one told me, silly," the girl giggled. "Practically everyone knows. It's common knowledge."

"That's what my mentor was telling me earlier."

"Your mentor?"

"Yeah, he told me to stop eating Ramen Noodles," Johnny said, adding a little slur in his words. By then he was eighty percent booze and fifty percent Jericho. At that point, numbers no longer made sense and he was perfectly fine with that. Who needed accurate statistics when the ceiling was swimming?

He pointed behind them at a juke box/iPod machine where his new mentor was chilling. "That's him. He is very wise."

His mentor waved at them.

The girl looked over and started giggling. "Where? There's no one there."

"Right . . . there." He realized he had been gesturing to a trash can. "Oh. Never mind."

"All night you've just been sitting here talking to your drink. You told it to quit buzzing?"

"Who the hell are you to judge me, huh?" Johnny snapped, and threw his glass against the wall. He watched as, instead of shattering, the glass absorbed itself into the wall as if it was a bubble and disappeared completely. He dropped his head and discovered the glass to have already returned in his hands, still full of whatever the hell kind of alcoholic fruit he was drinking. "Whoa."

"What?" the girl asked.

"What do you want with me, woman?"

He felt her long fingernails scratching against the back of his neck. "Your family really win that much in the lotto?"

"I guess."

She smiled and leaned forward, whispering in his ear, "Come with me."

She took him by the hand and led him into a limo waiting out front. It took off and seemed to drive forever, all the while leaving Johnny and this new mysterious girl in the back by themselves. A long tinted window separated them from the driver.

"Tell me, lottery boy. You gotta girlfriend?"

Johnny nodded regretfully. "Sorry."

"How much is she worth?"

"Uh, well," Johnny began, and cracked up. "She lives in Loathing, you see . . . "

The girl smiled. "Ah, a rag gal."

"I suppose."

"Pretty far away, don't you think?"

Johnny shrugged. "Not that far, maybe twenty minutes."

"I don't know." The girl scooted closer against him. Her legs were folded under her ass, sitting sideways with one arm slung around his neck. "If I lived twenty minutes from *my* boyfriend—that is, *if* I had one, which I certainly do not, but that can easily be changed, if I met the right man, of course—and if I suddenly found myself in an, uh, how do I say this? a . . . feverish mood, and my guy lived so far away, and, say, I was a little tipsy, I dunno . . . seems to me I might end up doing something stupid. God knows I have before. Who doesn't, right? Hey, does your girl drink?"

Johnny gulped. "Um, a little, yeah. Why?"

The girl threw her hand in the air, as if reaching for an answer that wasn't there and never would be. "I dunno, was just wondering. To be honest with you, I don't rightly believe a girl like that deserves such a masculine man of luxury like yourself. I mean, just look at those abs!" She gently rubbed her hand against his abdomen and cooed in awe. Johnny tried not to let on how ticklish it felt. "Oh God, a man like yourself, you deserve to be on a magazine. Have you ever been on a magazine? Who am I kidding, of course you have, being all rich and famous like you are. That must be pretty cool, having all that money. I bet you like to buy stuff, huh? You buy your girlfriend lots of jewelry, don't you? I don't know why when she's probably off twenty miles away doing God knows what. You don't deserve that kind of treatment. Not at all. I mean, God, just look at that bulge. I bet you're humongous."

Johnny jumped back when she grabbed his cock, his

voice cracking as he shouted, "Hey! What do you think you're doing?"

Her cheeks flushed red. "I'm sorry. It's just . . . I dunno, looks so . . . you know? I wanted to feel it, all right? I felt it get hard, too. You're really gonna be faithful to some rag gal who's off doing whoever she wants? Some poor white trash? Really? You're Johnny Desperation! You are a king. You could do so much better. You could do *me*. I would take care of you, ya know. I would take care of *that*." She reached over and gave his cock another tug. This time Johnny stayed put, watching her with wonder as she unzipped his tightening jeans.

"I don't know about this," he said, and gasped as she wrapped her fingers around his shaft. He dug his nails in the limo's leather, telling himself this was wrong, this wasn't who he was. He liked Candy Blossom.

But did he really?

He wondered if maybe this strange girl had a point. What had she actually ever done for him? He couldn't think of a single thing.

"Stop . . . " He tried his best to keep a coherent train of thought, but failed miserably. "I am with . . . No, Candy . . . Oh, God . . . "

"Oh, don't kid yourself," the girl said. "You're one of us now, lottery boy. And I am your girl . . . "

Then she leaned down with an open mouth and Johnny forgot everything else.

16

"I THINK THEY'RE asleep," Benny whispered.

"What?" Maddox said. He sat on the sofa, knees shaking.

His brother leaned forward in the recliner. "I haven't heard anything in a while. I think maybe they finally fell asleep."

"Probably." Maddox didn't show the slightest hint of relaxing. A breath exhaled too loudly could wake the beast, he reckoned, and this was definitely something he did not want to ever do. Especially not after hearing all those screams from the bedroom.

As if reading his thoughts, Benny asked, "You think he's still alive?"

"Of course he is. Don't be stupid," he said, although he wasn't too sure of himself.

"What if she killed him, Mads? What if she kills all of us? She scares me, really scares me. She seemed okay at first, I'll admit that. Even a little sexy. But . . . you don't know the things she did to me last night. I'm still in pain, man, I'm still hurting."

"Well," Maddox began, but was cut off when the phone started ringing. His eyes widened at the possibility of the lot lizard awakening, but Benny was leaping toward the coffee table and answering it before any real damage could be done.

He handed it to Maddox and said, softly, "It's for you."

"Me?" Maddox took the phone. "Hello?"

"Yes, is this Maddox Kane?"

TOXICITY

"Who is this?" He didn't recognize the voice. It was male, and a little too business sounding for his taste.

"This is your parole officer, Mr. Kane. My name is Lionel Turner. Pleased to meet you."

Shit. He had completely forgotten the prison assigned him a PO. With all this hooker business, it had been a little hard to remember.

"What do you want? Now is not a good time."

"What seems to be the problem, Mr. Kane?"

"You don't want to know."

"Actually, I do. It's kind of my job to want to know, as you can understand."

"Why are you calling?"

"First, I will warn you not to use such a tone with me again. I will remind you that, if provoked, I can make your life hell. So next time you speak, keep that in mind." The parole officer cleared his throat. "Now, I called to make sure the residence and phone number you listed were correct. I also wanted to remind you that you will begin working at your new job come first thing Monday morning, eight o'clock sharp. You do remember where you are to go, yes?"

"Not at all." The beat of his heart pounded harder and harder against the interior of his chest, making it feel like any second the organ would burst through his breastbone and go tumbling out on the carpet next to his feet. *Bump, bump*, it would go, *bump, bump*. And then finally die.

"You'll be reporting at the Booth Bacon packing factory north of Megaton. You know where it is? It's really hard to miss."

"Okay," Maddox said, and hung up.

"Who was that?" Benny asked, cautious but intrigued.

"Bacon Nazis." Maddox found his boots and pulled them on.

"What? Where are you going?"

He leaned down. "I need to make a phone call."

"But you just got off the phone!"

"Yeah, and I need to get back on."

He left his brother in the recliner and slowly creaked the front door open, slipping through the crack. Standing out on the porch, chilly winds slapping against his cheeks, he dug into his jean pocket for the page he had torn from the phone book the day before. He unfolded it and dialed the circled number. It rung three times before a girl's weak voice said, "Hello?"

Maddox smiled. He couldn't help it. "Hello, sweetheart."

* * *

Maddox wasn't sure why, of all places, he brought Addison to this truck stop, maybe because it was really about the only place he knew, anymore. Either way, it appeared less dangerous during the day than it had at night.

At first, neither of them said a word. Addison sat with her head slumped, black hair dangling in front of her face, trying to hide the injuries Maddox noticed right away. He didn't know how to ask his daughter about the black eye, the swollen nose, without risking upsetting her. He didn't want to do that, so he decided to let this one play out on its own. Who knew, maybe the girl would bring the subject up herself.

The awkward silence they were enduring was interrupted when a waitress approached them asking what they wanted to drink. Maddox opened his mouth to order his usual, but was cut off by the melodious whisper of an angel:

"Coffee."

"All righty." The waitress turned his way. "And you?"

"The same."

"Very well." The waitress left for a short period to fetch a pot. She returned moments later and filled their mugs. "And will either of you be ordering food today?"

"No, thank you," Addison said, and Maddox let out a

breath, relieved. He barely had enough money for coffee—anything else and they would have been slipping out the back door.

Maddox watched as his daughter added sugar and cream to her cup. He furiously tried to come up with something to say.

"So, how's school?"

"School's okay."

"Good grades, I trust?"

"Of course."

"Good," he nodded, "that's good." He watched her drink coffee, thinking how much he wanted to ask if it was that asshole of a stepfather that had bruised her face up like that. Of course it was him. Who else could it have been? Maddox made a mental note to kill this guy before everything was set and done.

"I'm sorry I didn't remember you at first," she suddenly choked out. It was so unexpected that it took Maddox a second to realize what was happening. He saw tears rolling down her cheeks, listening to her apologize for his own stupid mistakes.

He reached over and gently laid his hand on top of hers on the cold Formica. "Hey, don't be crying for my wrongdoing. There's no reason to feel bad, Addy. It's my own fault you didn't remember me—*mine*. So don't you shed a single tear, okay?"

"Okay," she whimpered back, wiping her eyes with the back of her free hand.

"I want you to know another thing, too." Maddox squeezed her hand. "I'm a changed man. Yeah, I've made some mistakes, I admit that. But inside, sitting on my bunk all day and night, it gave me a long, *long* time to think. Mostly about you, Addy, and how badly I screwed things up. I want to make things better for us, sweetheart. I want to be the father you never had a chance to have. Can I do that for you?"

Addison wiped her face dry with her bare arm, nearing

pulling off the wristbands she wore in the process, and smiled. "I would like that very much, Daddy."

His heart leaped a mile as the word left her lips.

He squeezed her hand a little more and said, "I'm glad, sweetheart. I'm very glad."

"I don't wanna live with him no more, Daddy," she sobbed quietly. "Neither of them."

"He did that to you, didn't he? To your face?" He couldn't help it. He needed to know.

Addison turned away, looking at anything but the man sitting across from her. "Yes."

Yeah, Maddox was thinking, *next time we meet, you're a dead man.*

"I don't want to talk about that," Addison said. "I just want out of that house. I want to live with you. Can I?"

"Yes. Of course you can live with me. It might take a little bit of time, since I don't have full custody, but . . . "

"How long will it take?"

"Well, I doubt your mother is just going to hand you over, so I'll have to get a lawyer."

"When?" Her tears were now replaced by a gleam of excitement.

"I don't know," Maddox said, "but even then, I'm not so sure it would work. I was in prison, Addy. Courts tend to look down on that."

Addison squeezed his hand in return. "What are we going to do? What are we going to do?"

"I don't know," he said at last, lowering his eyes in shame. "I've been thinking about it, but I just need more time."

"What if you gave them money?"

"Gave *who* money?"

"Mom and Del," she said. "Maybe they would let me go if you paid them enough. I bet they would. I *know* they would."

"Yeah?" He felt a sadness overwhelming him as he sat before his daughter; a daughter who thought her own mother would sell her away for dope money. This wasn't how things were supposed to work. Not with *any* family.

"Yeah, of course they would," Addison went on, giving his hand another squeeze. "So, what do you say?"

"I don't know, sweetheart. Maybe there's a more reasonable way to approach this."

"No," she said, panicking, "no, there's no time. I have a year until I'm on my own, and . . . and I'm not sure I'll survive until then. I can't take it anymore. It's unlivable. The drugs, the booze, the—"

"Okay!" He didn't want to hear any more of this. It was becoming too much. "We'll try it your way. How much are you thinking here?" Maddox raised the coffee to his mouth and gulped it all down in one swallow.

Addison settled back in the booth, taking a drink herself. "A lot," she said. "They're not gonna just let me go for a few hundred. It's gonna take a couple thousand I'm guessing. Maybe more than just a couple. Like, I don't know, ten?"

If he hadn't just finished his coffee it'd have been spat all over the table. "Ten *thousand*? Do you think I'm made of money, honey? I was only released yesterday. I don't even know if I have enough to pay our bill here."

"Don't worry about the bill." Addison pulled out a pocketbook from God knows where. "I can cover this."

"No, that's okay . . . "

"Don't you have connections? Can't you get them to help you?"

Maddox sighed. He was at a loss. "Yeah, but Addy, I told you I'm not doing that stuff anymore. I've changed."

"But can't you go back, just this once? For me?" Her lips quivered and Maddox could already spot another treacherous army of tears breaking through the barricades. "I want to be a family again. A family with *you*. Please?"

"I'll . . . I'll think about it. Okay?"

"Okay." She held a firm grasp on his hand now. Hadn't he been the one to grab hers in the first place? What happened?

* * *

Once again the Cadillac was occupied by another lingering silence. If he had spotted a hitchhiker, Maddox would have probably picked him up just to break the tension. This awkward, avoiding eye-contact business was an absolute nightmare. He gave his daughter a hug and risked a kiss on the forehead before pulling away from the apartment building, fighting away tears of his own.

Maddox cranked up the radio and banged his head back and forth like some kind of rabid animal being put down. It was a desperate distraction, but it did the trick and stifled any cowardly crying that may have taken place. There was only one thing he could do and he despised the mere thought of it—yet, it had to be done. Yeah, he had been a cruel bastard at times, but there was no way he was going to reject the pleas of his own daughter. He couldn't just turn his shoulder on the way she had begged him to save her.

Maddox pounded his fist against the steering wheel as he headed toward the Dan Ryan.

Daddy . . .

Who could say no to that? It didn't matter what he had promised himself while rotting away in his cell; the only thing that he truly cared for was to live a life with his daughter and, if it was still possible, patch up a broken relationship. The way Addy had talked to him at the truck stop gave him hope for a future that wasn't as lost as once feared. And if breaking a vow he had quietly swore so many times to himself while sulking in his cot was necessary to accomplish such an objective, well, then so be it. He didn't care. He only cared for Addison.

Back before 2001, Maddox would have turned on Randolph rather than Ohio, but according to prison gossip, King had picked up shop and moved elsewhere: a boxing arena located across the street from a methadone clinic. There was no trouble at all finding the place.

Maddox pulled the Cadillac alongside the curb and stepped out, regretting this already as the cold wind slapped his jean jacket roughly from side to side like a weak, surrendered flag. He cracked his neck, took one last deep breath, and approached the building.

There was a small dark green sign nailed above the door with a detailed drawing of a beaten butterfly. One of its wings was torn completely off and blood oozed down its fragile little body. Over the butterfly's black and blue head, in bright yellow font, there rested the boxing arena's title:

THE STING

Float like a butterfly, sting like a bee, Maddox thought, and sighed. He walked through the door wishing he was back in prison where life was less complicated.

17

IT DIDN'T MATTER where Johnny went, there was always that goddamn buzzing following him around.

In the shower, it was there. He could crank up his speakers to its maximum capacity and the buzz would still manage to outweigh the music. It could be loud when it wanted to and it could be quiet when it wanted to—but no matter how loud or quiet, it was always there.

Buzz buzz buzz.

Even when his thoughts decided to take a break for a change and he found time to sleep, every dream was occupied by a deep blackness, and the only sound he heard was a buzz that seemed to increase in volume as the blackness darkened.

It never ended, whatever it was that was happening. He didn't even know. One night he goes downstairs for a drink of water, meets a talking fly who tries to convince him to kill himself, is refused by a good, old-fashioned chug, and now he's being punished with the Fly's—what, dying screams? Would this be a scar branded into his psyche for the rest of his life? Would he be eighty and still be going on about a phantom buzzing that only he could hear?

Maybe he ought to have killed himself, after all.

But that was exactly what this insect wanted! He didn't know what to do. It was growing impossible to ignore. Pretty soon he'd crack; it was only a matter of time. He'd be strolling casually down the hallway, gritting his teeth and trying his best to look normal, and then he would break down and scream. He'd pound his palms into the side of his head over and over until either the Fly died or he died.

He had a sickening feeling it would end up being the latter.

For a long time there was this knot at the bottom of his stomach that kept tightening no matter what he did. It felt like a wave swaying back and forth, trapping all sensation in the center of some ghetto raft, slapping him into the greatest seasickness anyone had ever experienced in the history of water.

The decision to get help was not made by him, but rather by his new girlfriend. The one who'd been awfully kind to him back at the pool hall, whenever that had been. Time easily escaped him lately. He'd be sitting there and nod off and a whole week would have passed.

"You're not well," she commented one afternoon in the school cafeteria. The table was mostly empty, save for a few hipsters fiddling with their latest handheld gadgets. He and his girlfriend had some books laid out around them, attempting to study for their Mac vs. PC exam with little progress. She was too busy twirling her fingers in her hair and he was too concerned about eternal damnation to really care.

"What makes you say that?" Johnny asked. He had just sunk his teeth into a $150 slice of pizza (toppings including caviar, lobster, crème fraiche and chives) and wondered why anyone would pay so much money for such garbage. It was the most expensive pizza in the world and it took all he had not to spit it back out on the table. He instead forced himself to swallow what he bit into and discarded the rest on the tray. Well over a hundred bucks wasted.

When did the money end? Did it ever?

And to think, he would have just been happy buying a five-dollar buffet at CiCi's.

"Well, for one thing," his girlfriend said, "you only take

like a thousand years replying anytime someone says something to you."

Johnny waited another nine hundred ninety-nine more years before saying, with a smirk, "I do not."

She playfully slapped him on the shoulder and he could have sworn—just for a second—that her hand went straight through him, like he was a hologram. "Okay, smartass, it isn't just your response timing."

"What else?" Johnny took a good long drink of his chocolate frappacino and belched loud enough to startle the insects strangling his sanity.

"You keep scratching your head."

"It itches."

"Do you have lice or something?"

Johnny shook his head. "Just flies."

"Yeah, see, that's another thing. You keep going on about these flies but no one else ever sees them. They're not really there. Also, I didn't want to bring it up, but it's been almost two weeks since you bought me a present."

Johnny sighed. He didn't remember Candy Blossom being such a greedy pain in the ass. "Didn't I give you earrings Wednesday?"

"Um, first off, those weren't real rubies. Secondly, I saw the sticker. They were marked 75% off. And thirdly, I may have lost one of them."

Johnny took another bite of his $150 pizza and regretted it immediately. "I would think you'd want me for me and not my money."

"Yeah," his girlfriend snorted, "and I would think you'd want me for me and not my pussy. This isn't some lovey-dovey public high school relationship, understand? You've moved on, Johnny. Welcome to the world of adulthood. You like what you see here? Of course you do. I'm fucking hot—even I know that. Well if you want to continue having me then you better step up on your game and quit screwing around. It's that purple shit, right? You're taking too much of it. I would advise dropping that vice before it consumes you whole. I've seen it happen to too many people, and normally I wouldn't care, but this time it's getting in the way of my presents and I will not stand for that, dammit!"

Johnny smirked. "I'm fine, really. If anything, I should be taking more of the stuff."

"Is that so?"

He nodded.

"Then would you mind telling me why the hell you're sticking a butter knife in your ear?"

Johnny hesitated. He felt the cold steel of the silverware in his clenched fist, in his ear, and wondered how long he'd been going at it.

"How else do you expect me to get any peace and quiet?" he asked. "You try living with these things and see what you do."

"For God's sake, Johnny, you're bleeding!"

He laughed. "Nah, I don't think that's my blood. Enjoy your time in fly hell, you little bastards."

Slowly scooting off the edge of her stool, his girlfriend said, "Okay, that's it. You are getting some help and that's that."

Johnny rested the crusty knife back on the tray and finished off his chocolate frappacino. Afterward he said, "Hey, I can't hear the buzzing anymore. I think it's actually gone. Isn't that wonderful?"

But of course it wasn't wonderful, for not even five minutes later Johnny found himself once again tormented by the droning of a thousand winged devils.

18

ADDISON STOOD OUTSIDE the apartment building and watched her father drive away. She had managed to stop crying shortly before exiting the Cadillac. Her father had helped comfort her some, but for the wrong reasons. There was no way he would ever know the true influence of her embarrassing burst of sobs back at the truck stop. How could someone reveal such a terrible secret to another human being? And Connor expected her to go the hospital.

Exhaling a frosted cloud of air, Addison turned around and entered the apartment building. Her face was still a little numb, and certain places hadn't eased on the soreness, but all in all she felt loads better than the night before. Though that wasn't to say everything was all right, either. She took small, slow steps up to the third floor, and the door was locked. She hesitated. The door usually wasn't locked unless her parents were shooting up and paranoid about a SWAT team barging in. Understandably, they didn't want Addison's presence during these memorable family moments.

But where else was she supposed to go? She wasn't dressed for the weather outside. It was either wait out in the hallway or risk it.

Addison inserted her key into the knob and turned it. The door creaked open and she stepped inside, doing the best she could not to make any noise. She closed the door behind her and tiptoed into the living room. She froze in place, gasping, then choking on her own breath.

TOXICITY

There, on the carpet floor, beside the cardboard TV stand, were two figures. The one on top, with the wired cage mask, was thrusting rapidly into the woman underneath. Pants down to his knees, hairy bare ass sticking up in the air. It wasn't the first time Addison had walked in on her mother and stepfather having sex. She thought about turning around and leaving the apartment, but the fear of having nowhere else to go overwhelmed her. There was simply no energy left in her body to walk over to Connor's.

So, she lowered her head and strode past them toward her own bedroom. Only she never made it. Her pace stopped as she stole a glimpse of her mother. Something wasn't right. Her eyes were wide open, but her pupils were barely visible, rolled up against her skull. Her tongue lay limp out the corner of her mouth. There was something that appeared to be foam dripping down her chin, down her cheeks, down her neck.

She was dead.

No. Oh God no.

Her heart skipped a beat as she looked at her mother, white foam staining the carpet beneath her head, her stepfather violating the corpse. He hadn't even noticed Addison had walked through the door.

Oh God, she thought, *the baby . . .*

"*Del!*" Addison screamed. "*Get off of her!*"

She leaped on top of her stepfather, smacking him in the back and trying to pull him off her mother. He was too strong. With a simple shove he pushed her away, knocking her against the TV set. It tumbled off the cardboard box and crashed onto the floor.

"Fuck off," Del muttered, focusing on his wife. He continued to thrust into her, grunting. Addison held back a mouthful of vomit and jumped back on him. She clawed at his shirt, tugging it with all her might.

"She's dead!" Addison screamed. It was as if someone had turned a faucet in her tear duct, tears running down her face. "Get off of her! *Get off of her!* Oh my God, don't you see what you've done? She's dead! *Get the hell off of her!*"

She pulled his shirt one last time before he shot out his elbow and bashed it against her nose. She fell back in a sitting position, hands cupping her face, a fountain of blood streaming from between her fingers.

Del looked over his shoulder at her, squinting his brow with annoyance. "The hell's the matter with you?"

Beginning to shake, Addison sobbed. "She's dead, she's dead, oh my God, she's dead."

"What? Shut the fuck up. No one's dead." He turned back to the woman lying limply beneath him and grabbed her jaw. He moved her head to the left, then to the right. "Right, honey?" He released his grip and sighed. "See what you went and done? What I say about interrupting us, huh? She fell asleep, that's all! I hope you're fuckin' happy, you stupid bitch. Now what am I supposed to do?"

Addison stared at him in disbelief. The man was insane. Insane and extremely high. For some reason, his mouth was stained purple. She spotted the used syringe abandoned on the carpet next to them, next to a couple of strange black canisters. That must have been the fix her mother had gone out earlier to get.

"She's dead," Addison repeated.

Del let loose an incomprehensible howl and spun off Sheryl, tackling Addison with the force of a fierce lion. Pants still around his ankles, she felt his pathetic erection poking her stomach as he wrestled her on her back. He cocked his arm around and brought his fist down upon her mouth.

"*What the fuck did I just tell you?*" Del screamed. "She is *not* dead!"

"*YES SHE IS!*"

He punched her a couple more times until she stayed quiet, spitting up a glob of blood. She saw that he was crying just as much as she was. Then he hit her again.

TOXICITY

"All you fucking people are so fucking stupid sometimes, I swear," Del said. "Why is it up to me to teach everyone a lesson? I don't know. But I have to, and you know that."

"*What?*" Addison cried out, trembling in terror as she felt her stepfather's hands ripping at her jeans. "*No!* Get off!"

She heard him snigger. "That's the plan, ain't it?" he said. His incompetent fingers grew impatient and finally decided to tear her pants off. She slapped him away and was rewarded with another punch to the face. The back of her head bounced against the floor and she closed her eyes, waiting for it to be over.

It was just like last night all over again. She felt utterly helpless, and it sickened her. Connor wouldn't be here to the rescue this time. Addison clenched her teeth as tears fell down her cheeks. Her hands searched blindly for some kind of weapon, anything of use within reach. She came across something long and thin; some kind of plastic tube with a sharp point. The syringe.

She swung it wildly in the air. It struck its target on the first shot, the syringe plunging straight into her stepfather's eyeball. She let go and it stayed there, sticking in his socket as he squealed.

Addison lay there beneath him, breathing heavy, blood squirting across her face. Acting on pure instinct now, she reached back up and wrapped both hands around the wire cage installed in his broken jaw. She yanked the steel as hard as she could, the metal tearing from Del's mouth, ripping several holes in his cheeks like a fish caught on a hook.

He flung himself off her and fell into a fit of convulsions, grabbing at the ugly mess that was now his face. Addison bolted to her feet and fled from the living room, smeared blood blurring her vision. Her original intended direction was the front door, but she soon found herself bumping into the door of Del and her mother's bedroom. The gargling cries of her stepfather were nearer, chilling her spine. There was no time to return back to the living room. Addison opened the door and closed it behind her, locking it with an unsteady grasp.

Del was yelling now, although what he was yelling was incomprehensible. In a normal neighborhood the police would have already arrived, but the tenants in this building were used to such commotions. They kept to their own business and no one bothered them. It was fucking pathetic.

Addison could hear him stomping back and forth, colliding with the walls and falling down, getting back up again only to repeat the same actions. It wouldn't take too much longer for him to find his way to his bedroom, and then who knew what would happen.

Whatever the case, she had to prepare for a fight.

Addison ran to the closet and slid it open, searching for a weapon. Shoes, coats, more shoes, a bowling ball. Her eyes glued themselves to this with pure hatred. So many nights he had come home drunk from tournament night; more often than not they had ended with black eyes and broken glass.

She heard him kicking at the door now. A few bangs and the wood splintered away, swinging open by a strong breeze of monstrosity. Everything was happening so fast. It wasn't like how it was in the movies. There was no time to think—just react. And react she did.

"*Addison!*" Del gargled, an endless crimson waterfall streaming down his neck, soaking his T-shirt. His pants were now pulled back up, but not without a dark circle near the crotch area. He managed to stumble five feet inside the bedroom before Addison swung the bowling ball at his gut, knocking the wind out of him and sending him down to his knees. Desperate hands broke the fall. It left him crouched, head slowly lifting up to spot his prey.

Addison looked away and brought the bowling ball down on her stepfather. Even with her eyes squeezed shut, it made her cringe. The cracking of his skull pierced her eardrums. Del collapsed on his stomach. She no longer heard his raspy breathing. His body remained still.

Addison turned around and went into the living room. She sat down on the couch and watched the stillness of her mother. The sight was too much to take in, covering her face, she sobbed into her shaking hands. After some time she walked into the kitchen and picked up the telephone and dialed a number. She settled back down on the couch and closed her eyes for a while, and waited.

19

"**W**ELL, AIN'T YOU a sight for sore eyes!"

Vincent King's large arms folded around Maddox's spine and squeezed, lifting him off the floor. He had been compared to a bear before, and it wasn't much of an exaggeration. Medium height, maybe a little shorter, but wider than a bison. Arms, legs, torso, all engulfed in bulging muscle. Maddox had never seen his old boss with a head of hair, and today was no exception. He wore a black and gray pinstriped suit, shoes waxed to a shiny gloss. The man was practically born to be a gangster.

"Yeah," Maddox gasped, "good to see you too, Mr. King."

Realizing he was on the verge of crushing his lungs, King loosened his grip. "My apologies, mate. Just a wee bit surprised, seeing you is all."

"It's okay," he assured, slowly regaining normality in his color.

"When'd you get your release papers? You paroled, are ye?"

"I was let go yesterday morning."

"Wow, seems like just yesterday you were arrested and lost all my drugs, huh?"

"Uh, yeah."

King's office was underground, below the boxing arena. It was a large empty room. An echo could go a long way in a place like this. Two rows of stone ivory pillars were scattered from one end of the room to the other like a set of Greek dominos, forming a narrow walkway from the entry door to a wooden door attached to the opposite wall. The mystery of the contents beyond it gave him the chills. He gulped and tried to direct his attention elsewhere.

The floor, the ceiling, and the walls were crafted out of black marble. Located on the right side of the office, away from the pillars, was a fountain running the entire vertical length of the room. Clear, clean water streamed down into the small stone pool; countless pennies residing at the bottom. The peaceful sound made him have to pee. Maybe that wooden door was something simple, like a bathroom. Except, why had Vincent King emerged from it earlier with his hands raw and bloody, like he'd just finished beating somebody half to death?

"So, how was prison and all that?" the Brit asked.

Maddox cracked his neck. "Over with, as far as I'm concerned."

"Ten years is a long time, me boy. A long time indeed."

"Yes. Yes it is."

"How did you get through it?"

"I don't know." He shrugged. "I guess I read a lot."

King laughed. "I can't believe you're already out. I had marked my calendar and everything. Of course I never check the fookin' thing. We should celebrate! Except, well, now's not exactly a good time." He caught Maddox staring at his hands and blushed. "As you can probably tell, I'm in the middle of some business."

"Yeah," Maddox said, forcing the syllables from his lungs, "well, that's kinda what I came to see you about."

There was no going back now, watching the man's smile widen. "Ah, so this isn't just your simple welcome back visit, eh?"

"Not exactly."

"Excellent!" King clapped his hands together diabolically. It was a gesture that reminded Maddox of a small child finally getting hold of the cookie jar that'd always been out of reach. "Always ready for work, that's me boy!"

King leaned forward, clamping a large bloody paw on

Maddox's shoulder. "Listen here, lad," he said. "I know you just got here and probably want to catch up on old times and all that jazz—" Maddox cringed at the word *jazz*, "—so my apologies for rushing like this, but Mads, there is some *major* top-secret shit going on back here. Now, it just so happens that I *do* need a guy for a very important job—one that'll pay quite handsomely, I might add. So, why don't you come along and follow me into the back and get a clearer picture of what exactly we're dealing with here, eh?"

Maddox nodded solemnly and allowed King to lead him toward the wooden door.

King wrapped his sausage fingers around the knob and twisted it open. A draft of cool air exploded against their bodies. They stepped into a room fueled by numbing darkness. A dimly lit light bulb attached to a thin chain hung in the center of the room. It swung back and forth over a man's head. The man in question sat in a shabby kitchen chair. His hands were tied behind his back with a length of rope; crusted blood covered more of his face than an actual expression. His drenched tank top and camouflage jeans were also stained and torn. He would be dead within the hour without serious medical attention.

Despite the gruesome injuries, Maddox was still able to detect the ruined eye patch hanging idly from his face. He looked incredibly familiar.

A malice grin spread across King's face. The man was so giddy it made Maddox want to turn around and go running for the hills. *Think of Addy*, he told himself. *She called you Daddy.*

"This, Maddox, is Felipe," King said. "Or, as we like to call him, test subject number eighteen."

"Fuck you, King!" the man spat out.

Before the words had barely left his mouth, a figure sprung out from the dark and struck him across the face. Felipe yelped like a punished dog and fell silent. The attacker slunk back into the shadows before Maddox could get a good look at him.

"And that was my good ol' chum, Winston." King chuckled. "Now, Maddox, since there is not a moment to waste, allow me to begin our demonstration. You see, Felipe here has been a naughty little cunt—haven't you, Felipe?"

"It wasn't me!" he cried. The man in the shadows backhanded him across the mouth.

King went on. "We received word that he was pocketing *my* product from one of *my* clockers. So now the wanker's test subject number eighteen. And the next name he'll have will be attached to his toe. Just ask the previous seventeen subjects." He snickered.

Maddox focused on the dying man sitting before him. He felt sickened that there was nothing he could do to help the poor guy. Where had he seen him before? He was sure he had. There was something about that eye patch.

"A while back," King continued, "an associate and I underwent a series of experiments, conducting a very scientific trial of chemistry. Well, at least he did, and I supported him financially. Fuck me if I understand any of that bollocks. It doesn't matter, though, because the experiments were a success."

"What experiments?" Maddox asked.

"Oh, no worries, they only affected filth like Felipe here. You see, my partner and I have effectively developed a brand-new drug; one that hasn't seen the light of day until this past year. Something unlike anything anybody's ever experienced before."

Maddox tensed as King reached in his suit pocket and brought out a miniature spray bottle. There was nothing threatening about this, for Maddox had laid eyes upon dozens of similar bottles containing men's body spray in the past. The only feature he thought shady was the lack of a logo. The bottle was completely black.

"A revolution in narcotics," King said, presenting the

bottle up in the spotlight with pride. "This is a significant psychedelic piece of history, my blue-blooded friend. Nothing like this has ever been completed with such outstanding results. This is a hallucinogenic chapter in future schoolbooks; each word transfused into particulates that spray out of this little bottle right here. One whiff of this shit and your ol' noggin' grows a damn near supernatural dependency for it. It is the most addicting and ingenious creation ever to be conceived, and it is mine. This is the beginning of the new drug era."

Maddox remembered where he'd seen the hostage before. Standing there trembling in Vincent King's Room 101, he gaped at the man tied up in the chair with absolute horror. Ten years or so ago, during his first day served in Megaton, he'd had a very powerful conversation with this man. Then he had stabbed him in the eye with a plastic spoon. It was because of him that Maddox had served the whole ten years instead of the minimum seven.

"Jesus," Maddox said. He didn't realize Sox fans could have so much life in them. "What are you going to do to him?"

"Watch and learn, Mads," King said softly. "You're about to witness something magical."

He stepped forward and told the hostage to open wide. Felipe just sat there with a cold stare, refusing to budge. King gently chopped him one in the throat, laughing as he began choking and searching for breathable air. It was the chance King needed to squirt the bottle's substance in his mouth. It was sort of a drizzly, bright purple mist.

Felipe continued gagging as King sprayed another dose of the product down his throat, as if he was being force fed too much garlic, or perhaps had swallowed too much phlegm and it was now blocking his airways. It was a sickening retch, droplets of purple spraying from his lips. He didn't nudge his finger from the trigger until the bottle started shooting blanks.

Empty.

TOXICITY

King moved away and watched the man shaking in his chair, that evil grin never leaving his face. King was proud of his work, the evil fucker.

It took a few minutes before Felipe managed to settle down enough to speak. "What the fuck . . . did you . . . give me?"

"Jericho, baby," King said, "just Jericho."

Maddox cleared his throat. His brain told him to flee while he still had the chance, but his feet kept him glued to the floor.

The hostage yelped.

"Now watch very closely, Maddox," King said. "This is important."

Maddox bit his lower lip and watched. What else could he possibly do? It wasn't like he could make the hostage undo the purple mist ingestion. What's done was done. Now all he could do was watch and learn. And hope for the best.

Felipe fell into a disturbing series of twitches, teeth clacking together rapidly. He swung his head around wildly, all the while a low steady hum escaped his throat, volume rising higher and higher, bouncing off the cement walls. His head was still shaking, resisting an offer visible to only him, when he suddenly froze in mid-swing. He focused on the two gangsters standing in front of him. Maddox saw his pupils transforming into a mystical purple and he found himself wondering just what the hell he was getting himself into.

"Why is he looking at us like that?" he asked.

"Shh," King said.

"Faces," Felipe muttered hoarsely. "Where are your faces? *Where are your faces?*"

The hostage resumed rocking, this time with much more force. Violet tears drained down his cheeks as he shrieked. "*Faces!* You have no *faces!* Dios mio, what is *happening to me?* Get off! Caras! Caras! Sin caras sin caras sin caras! Quítate de encima, Dios mio, por favor, para, por favor, para, por favor, por favor, por favor, para. No puedo, no puedo . . . "

His frantic shaking led to the chair legs' ultimate destruction. He slammed to the floor and rolled against the wall, screaming and defending himself from faceless intruders.

The man King had dubbed Winston came out of the shadows again and cautiously approached the hysterical hostage. Maddox didn't have a chance to view any more of this frightening scene, however, for King grabbed a hold of his shoulder and led him back out into the office. King shut the door behind them, miraculously drowning out the ear-bleeding madness they had just witnessed.

"Well, that's enough of that," King said.

Maddox couldn't have agreed more.

"So, what do you think?" he asked, after settling down behind his desk.

I think you're insane, Maddox thought, and said, "It certainly is . . . interesting."

"Indeed." King sighed contently. "This bad boy's been on the market for a little under a year now, and the number of buyers increases by the second. This is a fortune in the making, Mads. I can't even begin to imagine where this will be next year . . . or where I'll be, for that matter. Hell, I could probably retire—maybe move on to a new location. Chicago's growing old."

Despite the horror Maddox had just observed, he still couldn't help but find some humor in what King was saying. "And you couldn't retire before?"

King smiled. "Oh, of course I could retire. I could've hung up my guns half a bloody century ago. But I haven't, and I doubt I ever will. You know why?"

"Why?"

"I love this shit too much! I was born to be a gangster, Mads, and I'll always be one. Just like you."

"Me?" Maddox said, ignoring the Brit's own contradiction about expressing an interest in retiring only a few moments ago.

TOXICITY

"Well, you're here, aren't ya?"

Maddox vomited in his mouth, then swallowed it back down his throat.

"Speaking of which," said King, "you came here for a job. I assume you're still interested."

20

ADDISON WAS STILL sitting on the couch when Connor arrived. The door was unlocked so he barged inside, breathing heavy from the winding run up the three flights of stairs. Given her call earlier, which had been a short, "Help, please, dead, all dead," one could understand his frantic haste. He saw Sheryl in the living room and nearly passed out.

"Oh, fuck," he said, leaning against the wall.

Addison was off in her own little universe, oblivious to her surroundings. Her mouth was hanging open and she didn't appear to be blinking. He walked over and sat down next to her. It felt good not to stand. He wrapped his arm around her. "Jesus Christ, Addy, what the hell happened?"

But she didn't say anything. After a while Connor ventured into the kitchen for a glass of water. He also planned on calling the cops. Halfway in, however, he spotted something from down the hallway. The door was kicked open; shards of wood splintered all over the place. He didn't want to know what was waiting for him in the room but he knew he had to look, anyway.

He found Del with part of his brains crushed in from the bowling ball beside him. It made his stomach turn. He bent down and sprayed a mouthful of vomit over the front of his Chuck Taylor's. Connor turned around and returned to the couch with Addison. He decided to take a short little vacation to her getaway world. It was nice. Even with the reek of corpses and puke on his shoes, it was nice.

But then Addy told him what had happened and he

threw up again. The odor was getting to the both of them so he got up and opened the set of windows in the living room. He looked outside into the falling snow and watched people getting in and out of their vehicles. He wondered where they were going, where they were coming from. How many of them had just returned from a murder scene? How many were about to walk right into one?

Connor sat back down on the couch and held Addison against his chest. They stayed like that for quite some time until Connor asked her if he should call the police.

"No," she said.

"Why not? You didn't do anything wrong, baby. Just reacted in self-defense. There's evidence of this. A lot."

Shit, he thought, *didn't we just go through this same situation last night?*

"I just turned seventeen," she said. "I thought about this before you got here. I don't know of any other relatives. They'd make me a ward of the state and I'd go off to live God knows where. I can't do that, Connor. You know that."

"What about your father?"

She shook her head. "You really think they'd give him custody?"

"Sure they would. Why wouldn't they?"

"He just finished serving, like, a decade of prison time. I doubt they will see him as very fit to take care of me."

"Addy, they don't have any other options."

"I don't care." She started to cry again. "I don't want to do that!"

"Okay, okay . . . "

"I want to be with you and get the hell of this place already. I hate this town! I hate the people here. They disgust me so much. They're all pigs. I hate it. I hate it!"

"So, let me get this right," Connor said. "You're saying you hate it?"

She slugged him on the arm. "I'm glad you can find humor in this."

"You'd rather I cry with you?"

"No. Yes. I don't know. I'm confused and scared and tired and I just want to get away from everything. This town is killing me. And now *this*. I want to leave it. Leave it all. Go to the city, maybe. Do you want to go to the city?"

Connor squeezed his arm around her. "You said you'd run away with me. Of course I will with you, too. Is that what you want?"

She was shaking, like she was about to burst of emotion. "There's something I need to tell you."

"What's that?"

"I lied to you before, about being a virgin."

Connor went to say something but then stopped. "Oh-kay," he said.

"I'm not talking about last night, either."

"It's all right, Addy," he said. "I don't care."

"No, it's *not* all right!"

"What happened?"

"Del," she said. "He's done things to me. Some really bad things."

"Oh."

Addison took off her wristbands, something she had never done as long as he knew her, and showed him her veins. Horizontal scars ran across both wrists.

"It got so bad that I wanted to die," she explained. "I tried to, but I was young and stupid and didn't know how to die properly, I guess. I'm glad he's dead, Connor. My mother knew all about it and just turned the other way. She ignored his abuse. You know what she said when I came home from the hospital? She told me to go to my room and stop acting like a whiny bitch. And Del, well, he just did the same thing that he had been doing and it only made me want to die all the more. I was drowning, Connor. Then I met you and thought, maybe the world wasn't all so bad, maybe I wasn't screwed. And now they're both dead and I have you and I am glad. But the baby? No, she didn't deserve to die. God no. Not in a million years. But the more I think about it the more I decide she was probably better off anyway. Can you imagine what she would have gone through growing up in a family like this? I would have had to raise her myself. But what about when I turned eighteen and moved out? I wouldn't have been able to. I would have known the baby wouldn't be safe so I would have stayed with them to make sure she was all right and continue living through this miserable hell. Del would have kept on having his way and I would have wound up pregnant and you know what would have happened next? We would have ended up with our own fucking reality show on MTV. We would become rich and exploited. That's what happens when a tragedy strikes. They don't make it better—they only make it worse. They showcase it with a million tiny video cameras and sell T-shirts of your favorite characters. If I wasn't too busy being distracted from raising my stepfather's baby I would have gotten so embarrassed I would've ended up trying to kill myself again, but knowing me I would have only failed. The paparazzi would have a field day. Can you imagine the headlines? So yeah, I guess it is a miracle that they're all dead. The whole fucking lot of them. It makes me feel like the most horrible person in the world to say that but it's the truth. God, what is wrong with me? I don't know. Sometimes I feel like I'm so far gone I'm passed insanity. I don't know why people are so focused on sex or why it's important enough to inflict violence on someone else. I don't know why people like to hit other people but I do know that I'm sick of thinking about it all. I want to go away and start a new life, one with you. I like you, Connor. I even love you. You're the only person I've ever met who doesn't make me feel pity for the world. Well, I still do, but it's a different kind of pity. When I'm with you I pity everyone else for not knowing the happiness you give to me when you're not even trying to do anything. When I'm with you I forget about everything else. I feel safe. I forget how much I despise breathing. And when we're separated, I hate being alive. It seems like a waste. But now nothing is holding us back, Connor. We're free to go where we want. So let's go. Let's be free."

She took a deep breath.

Connor didn't know what to say, so he just reached over and kissed her. He drew back and said, "We're gonna need some help."

"I know," she said, and this time she kissed him.

21

MADDOX KANE EXITED the Sting carrying a large briefcase. He stored it in the trunk of his Cadillac and took off, wondering again if perhaps this was a mistake.

The entire trip back to the trailer, Maddox found himself thinking about the events that were scheduled to commence the following day. He didn't like it at all, but knew this one job would be all he needed to buy Addy's freedom—if Sheryl was willing to make a deal, of course. Somehow he thought she would agree. Junkies did not have a sense of dignity. All they cared about was their next fix. The amount of money Maddox planned on offering would take care of their next three thousand fixes.

King had made an interesting point. Who knew what this drug's future held? Maddox pondered possible scenarios as he drove down the Dan Ryan. He had witnessed Jericho's cruel infliction on its host. King had claimed there were already numerous customers on demand and the numbers were only rising. Was the DEA investigating this yet? They were on top of everything it seemed. What about the news then? Were they reporting it? He made a mental note to ask Benny if he had seen anything on TV about it when he returned to the trailer.

The nightmarish image of test subject number eighteen shaking like that in his chair played over and over again in his head. The ominous purple mist violating his lungs, it made him feel queasy, destroyed all appetite—even for butter rum Lifesavers, as unheard of as that sounded.

He visualized mall consumers spraying breath fresheners in their mouths, only to become the victims of a cruel trap. Maddox could see it now: millions of eager consumers standing in lines located in a million similar shopping malls all across the globe, all of them squirting on their new perfume or mint candy spray. He could, very vividly, watch from his Cadillac as they all realized one by one how much of a mistake they had made, that their purchases were tainted with a deadly plague, all of them falling to the ground like a pack of crazed dominoes or running wildly through the streets and leaping through plate-glass windows. People would attack one another. They would kill for the next hit, or perhaps it would just be a simple case of phantom self-defense. Who really knew for certain the type of hallucinations this intoxication would bring upon the abuser?

Of course, this was all very long-term. It would take time, oh yes, years to come, but he feared this to be the truth if this drug continued feeding on the souls of desperate Americans. God knew where else it was being distributed. Someone needed to step up while it was still early and prevent these disastrous events from taking place. Maddox wondered if he was the one meant to stop it all. After all, he was in the possession of an entire briefcase full of this destructive product. But what could he do with it? Take it on down to the police station and say, "Yeah, that Vincent King guy is paying me to sell this. Please go arrest him."

Yeah, and if he said "pretty please with sugar on top" the lot lizard holding herself hostage in Benny's trailer would just pack up and leave, because life was simple and everything could be solved by polite conversation.

To hell with the future. He wanted to be with his daughter. He wanted her to be happy. And if that meant dealing a briefcase loaded with America's possible downfall to a notoriously violent pimp for this objective to become a reality, then so be it. He didn't care anymore.

But if his predictions did come true, and this Jericho did cast some kind of chaotic shadow across Earth's atmosphere and spin into complete and utter anarchy, well . . . he would just have to cross that bridge when he came to it.

* * *

It was a little after sundown when Maddox entered the trailer, discovering his brother curled up into a ball on the sofa, sucking his thumb with his eyes glued to the television.

He could very clearly hear that hooker animal sex cry from the bedroom. Maddox went to the fridge and grabbed a beer. Screw it, he thought, and came back in the living room and sat down on the recliner. He popped off the lid and took a deep, long swig, figuring since he was already breaking one vow, it wouldn't hurt to break another. The alcohol tasted so good flowing down his throat that it came to a bit of a shock to him when seconds later he reached the bottom.

He belched and glanced pitifully at his ostensibly scarred sibling. "What happened to you?"

"Don't wanna talk about it."

"You all right?"

"I dunno." He removed his thumb. "I think I have crabs now."

"You *think?*"

Benny stood up and faced his older brother. He began to reach down his long johns before Maddox held up his hands. "Whoa, whoa, what the hell are you doing?"

"Showing you?" Benny said, confused. "I'm not sure whether I have them or not and there's no way I'm going to see a doctor about this."

"Well, um, do you itch?"

"God yes."

"More than usual?"

"Oh yeah. Way more."

"Then you have crabs. So there's no need to show me."

"I was afraid of that," Benny said miserably, lowering his head.

Maddox looked over at the TV. Either that one beer had already gotten him drunk, or he was actually witnessing Steven Seagull kickboxing a guy dressed up in a Spider-Man costume. Either way, another brew was sure to solve the problem. He retrieved it from the fridge and sat back down.

Benny was still on the couch. Now he had the waist of his long johns stretched to their limits while he peeked at his groin region. "That's not all," he said.

"What?"

"It's all black and blue, like it's broken or something. You sure you don't want to see?"

Maddox flinched away, careful not to spill his drink. "No, that's quite okay."

"And I keep pissing blood."

"You should see a doctor." Maddox reached the bottom of beer number two.

"I was afraid of that," Benny repeated.

The screams from the bedroom rose and then abruptly fell quiet once again. Moments later the trailer was occupied by Jazzy's eerie snores. "We need to help your roommate," Maddox said. "I don't think he's going to survive much longer."

Benny shook his head, still looking down at his crotch. "She's taken him, Mads. It's no use. Floyd's on her side now. The dark, creepy side."

"What are you talking about?"

"Earlier she left the room to go to the bathroom, so I sneaked in to smuggle him out. But he wouldn't come with me. He says he loves her now. How can anyone possibly love that thing? I think she broke my dick."

TOXICITY

"Really?" A third beer was looking awfully promising.

"Yeah, I told you, if you would quit being a baby and just take a look you would know what I'm talking about."

"No, you idiot, I mean about Floyd."

"Yeah," Benny said, "I think he was a virgin."

"Oh."

Maddox downed a few more beers. He could feel the buzz coming. After a while he asked Benny if he had a gun.

Benny shot his head up from his crotch with excitement. "You're gonna *kill her?*"

"No, it's for a job."

"A job of *killing her?*" Benny asked, eyes pleading.

"No!" Maddox said, although he would be lying if he said the idea hadn't crossed his mind more than once. "I found this job today, and it requires the handling of a firearm. So, do you have one or not?"

"Well, that depends." Benny smiled.

"Oh?" He dreaded where this was going.

"This a job for a certain Mr. King?"

"It could be."

"Can I come?"

Maddox sighed. Of course, he didn't really want his younger brother tagging along with him tomorrow, but he also knew a piece would come in handy just in case anything fishy went down, and he didn't have anyone else to turn to.

"If you do exactly as I say," he said.

Benny slapped his thigh and grinned. "Then of course I got a gun."

149

22

JOHNNY WAS FORCED into the back of a limo and the driver sped away in a hurry.

Isolating himself in the corner of the backseat and tugging frantically at the overhead hand grip, Johnny did the best he could not to go tumbling all over the place. He spotted his girlfriend edging toward him with a look of comfort on her face, telling him to calm down, everything would be okay.

She was lying, of course. Nothing felt like it would ever be okay again. But when had it ever?

"What the hell is going on?" he shouted. "What're you doing? What is this? Answer me!"

She placed a motherly hand on his shoulder and he shook it off violently. "Don't you touch me until you tell me what's going on."

"Relax, Johnny. I'm your girl, remember? It's my job to take care of you. So, that's what I'm doing. I'm taking care of you."

"You're going to kill me?" He felt his heart freeze and he forgot how to breathe for a moment. He didn't want to die so soon, not like this.

She offered a very obvious smile. "No, silly, I'm going to get you clean."

"Clean from *what?*"

She patted his shoulder again and this time he couldn't find the strength to defend himself. "Don't play stupid, Johnny. I don't have time for your games. There's a really big sale coming up at the mall and I'm going to need you to be in top shape."

The drive seemed to take forever. He wasn't sure where they were going. What exactly had she meant by 'getting him clean'? He half expected the limo to pull up alongside a river full of Baptists eager to dunk his head in the water. Or maybe she really was going to kill him. How could he have been so foolish? He should have never trusted this traitor. Hell, she was probably working for the fucking flies.

Why did these insects want him out of the way? Moreover, what did they want at all? The greater good? That was what their leader had claimed—before Johnny drank It. How was he supposed to help save the world? It was all just so confusing, and now he wished he had listened a little longer before swallowing the Fly. Maybe then he'd remember what peace and quiet truly meant. This constant buzzing was going to be the death of him.

Assuming, of course, his girlfriend didn't kill him first.

Johnny gulped as the limo came to a slow stop. He could practically smell the blade hiding behind his girlfriend's back—but then he stopped to consider what a blade actually smelled like, and couldn't come up with an answer. As the driver got out and opened their door he could feel his flesh tightening against bone. This was it. The executioner was waiting on the roof of the automobile with his giant ax, waiting for that split second Johnny stepped outside so he could behead him once and for all.

His girlfriend grabbed his hand and pulled. "C'mon, Johnny, let's go."

But he resisted. This would not be a voluntary suicide— if it was going to happen it would be forced and as tragic as tragic could be. There may not have been a lot he knew, but what he did know was there was no way he was going to go out without a fight.

"No, I wanna go home," he whined.

"Oh, don't be a baby. Now let's *go!*"

And this time she tugged a little too hard, and he came

spilling out on the icy cement that was the sidewalk of downtown Chicago. Rolling over on his back, he shielded his face and winced at the blinding sun stained into the sky. The anticipation of a ready executioner quickly drained as he realized there was no one standing on top of the limo wielding an ax.

There was, however, a small bird perched at the edge of the car's roof, cocking its head at him in a rather queer amusement.

So much for putting up a fight.

Johnny got to his feet and brushed the snow off his butt. Before he had time to actually look around and study his environment, his girlfriend was yanking his arm forward and dragging him toward a solitary wooden door in the center of a brick wall. There was no sign to identify what was inside this building, nor were there any noticeable windows. He had never seen a place quite like it. Perhaps this was where the executioner hid in waiting; crouched in the darkness that camouflaged his wickedness with his huge bloody ax.

Johnny tried to dive back into the limo but his girlfriend's freakish kung fu grip was too strong for him to overpower. Like a five-year-old on his first day of kindergarten, he was violently dragged through the murder door on his hands and knees, fingernails digging into the wet cement. The last thing he saw before being completely swallowed by the building's cold darkness was a sign hanging from across the street—it was too faint a glimpse to be positive, but he was pretty sure it was the portrait of a zombie butterfly.

He screamed as the heavy wooden door slammed shut behind them.

He was given time to stand up and compose himself. There was no retreating now—the door was closed, what else could he possibly do but move with the current? Johnny was led down a short set of stairs into a dim lobby. His girlfriend directed him to a line of chairs propped up against a wall and left to talk to a woman standing behind a counter.

There were three other people sitting down in this lobby: two men and a woman. The woman held a tiny compact mirror in her palm as she stared critically into the glass, sliding her tongue out and licking her lips. A man next to her, wearing a suit two sizes too big, bounced his knees up and down as he waited his turn, gnawing away at his dirty fingernails. The other man, this one in a trench coat, wore dark colors in a poor attempt to disguise the hideous scars burned into his flesh. He looked like he'd been to Hell and back on more than one occasion. His outfit gave him the appearance of a private investigator for the undead.

Johnny sighed and took a seat next to the Devil's private dick. The man glanced down at him and grunted approvingly. "What're you here for?"

Johnny shrugged. "I'm not even sure where it is that I am."

"We are everywhere. We are here and we are there and we are inside and we are out. I can feel it and so can you."

"Um."

"We all begin as an egg. We all begin as an egg." The man coughed. Purple spit flew from his mouth. "Then comes the maggots. Oh, hellish legless white spawns! We feed! We feed! We feed!" He coughed again, and this time the man reached inside his mouth, as if digging for something stuck in his teeth. He pulled out a dead fly and flicked it across the room. "Then the transformation—the motherfucking metamorphosis of a nation! Oooohhh baby, yes! And then? Oh yes, oh yes. And then? And then, and then, and then we are grown, we are adults, we are . . . we are . . . WE ARE INFINITE!"

"What the fuck are you talking about?"

The man burst out into hysterics and Johnny realized the man had no lips, no nose, no eyes. This sent him shooting off the chair and hurrying over to the front desk with his girlfriend. The lady, dressed in all white, was handing her a stack of paperwork.

She pulled out a rectangular nametag and said, "Addiction?"

His girlfriend said, "Excuse me?"

The nurse clicked her pen and huffed belittlingly. "What is the participant's addiction?"

"Oh, he does purple."

Now it was the nurse's turn to be confused. "What in the world is that?"

She shrugged. "I dunno. Purple. Jericho. Soul spray. Ya know, comes in like a black can, shoots out this purple mist shit?"

"Ah," said the nurse, as the words clicked in her brain. "I know what you're talking about. I'm still not used to it yet is all."

She moved the pen along the nametag and wrote: *HYPNOSPLICE*.

Johnny's girlfriend grimaced, as if the word was enough to make her vomit and insult her mother alone. "What the hell is a hypnosplice?"

"It's the shorter version of *splictic hypnotranical oxide*, the correct title for that ungodly drug you kids seem to be calling—for reasons that escape me—'Jericho'."

"Oh," she said. "Uh, I knew that."

"Uh huh. Just fill it out, will ya?" The nurse turned her attention over to Johnny, who had tried to make himself as invisible as possible. "Are you the junkie?"

Johnny squealed at the sound of her voice and leaned forward. "Are you going to make the flies disappear?"

The nurse nodded. "Yeah, you're the junkie."

She pulled out a tiny plastic cup and placed it on the counter in front of him. "We're gonna need a sample of your urine. Go down that hall and the first door on the left you'll come across a bathroom. Make it snappy."

Johnny fearfully obliged. He grabbed the cup and left his girlfriend to fill out the forms, skipping off down the hallway to whatever may.

TOXICITY

The bathroom was a small dingy thing. He locked the door behind him as he approached the mirror and turned the facet, splashing water in his face. He wasn't sure what this place was, but maybe they could help him, after all.

These goddamn flies . . .

Would they ever go away?

The buzz.

It was louder in this bathroom. Much louder than he had ever thought possible.

The piss cup fell from Johnny's hands and he doubled over into a coughing fit. Palms smashed into his skull as he tried to beat the noise from his conscience, but he just wasn't strong enough. He would never be strong enough.

He pounced over the toilet and discharged a stream of vomit into the bowl. It ricocheted back into his face, which only caused another spell of puke to spray from his exhausted mouth.

Hell, he didn't even have the strength to pull his head out of the toilet—how could he be expected to fight the flies in his own head?

His neck went limp. His head just dangled there in the toilet, hair soaking in the ruined water. He closed his eyes and prayed for an answer. Any reasoning for the madness that consumed him. For the evil that ate him alive day after day.

Why was this happening to him? What had he ever done to deserve such cruel treatment? Better yet, who was it that was in charge here anyway? God? Satan?

The . . . the *Fly?*

"Dig deep for the answers you seek."

Johnny mumbled a series of words that were barely intelligible even to himself: "Who are you?"

"I am the one who holds the key."

"To what?"

"Everything."

Johnny tried to laugh but he just couldn't find the energy. This mysterious voice couldn't have been any cheesier.

"**Dear Johnny, I'm afraid the only cheese here is *truth* cheese.**"

"That makes no sense."

"**Nothing will ever make sense without risk. Now take a risk and dive into the truth.**"

"How?" At this point he would try anything. He craved to understand the meaning of peace again.

The voice spoke one last word before it faded away: "**Swim.**"

And that's just what Johnny did.

It wasn't hard. He had seen the same thing happened once in that movie, *Trainspotting*.

Every muscle in his body loosened as he surrendered himself to gravity, allowing its magnet pull to drag him down into the toilet water with his own puke. Soon enough, his skull was squeezing through the hole like a wet tissue. The rest of his structure liquefied along with it, and before anyone could say *splictic hypnotranical oxide*, Johnny Desperation had vanished into the Chicago sewer system.

He had followed the buzz into its home.

The powerful current of recycled feces carried Johnny through the series of mind-numbing tunnels like a running back carries the football toward the end zone. Nothing could ever interrupt this mighty flow. Nothing at all.

Except, of course, the brick wall constructed in the center of the tunnel, blocking all water from continuing forward. One would assume the same consequence would be held for the human body as well, but it was not the case. Expecting at the most, death, and at the least, a bloody nose, Johnny braced himself for the approaching impact.

He smacked into the concrete at full speed. There was no pain. The wall was not solid. When his face smashed into the bricks there was no blood. As it turned out, it only had the appearance of bricks. Instead it was made of . . . marshmallows?

When he connected with the blockade, Johnny's pace only slowed down slightly. The spongy material of the wall absorbed him whole, and before he could give the circumstances a second thought, it was spitting him out on the other side. Feeling like Mother Nature's placenta, Johnny shot through a new dimension covered in the portal's sticky goo, splashing into the shallow shores of a deserted beach before he could truly comprehend the reality of leaving the bathroom.

An ashy wave threw him forward and he found himself rolling in the sand, stinging particles burning his eyes while whirling a cloud of dust. Choking on the sand, Johnny sat up and wiped his eyes. This, of course, only made it worse. He screamed out and blinked furiously until the burning subsided.

He looked around at the vast emptiness of this new world. The sky was electric and purple.

"I don't think I'm in Chicago anymore," Johnny said, and immediately felt like a moron.

Johnny searched as far as his eyes would allow, but he did not see any other sign of life. There were no buildings off in the background—there was no anything. The sand, the miserable old sand, it just stretched on and on, finally coming to a stop at the edge of the globe.

The water continued forth, sharing almost the same distance as the land. But, as Johnny studied it longer, he determined the water was not like any other water. It was not blue, and it was not in the least bit clear. The liquid was more ashy, like a darkened gray that had failed to fully die.

Like a cosmic astray.

Johnny recognized that he was truly alone in the world. No one was real anymore. He wasn't even sure if he was, either—but at least he was aware of this fact, unlike the rest of the masses.

A thousand sketches drawn into a notebook and only one character realized it was a drawing. It was whatever the artist told it to be. It did not have a mind of its own. It did not have freewill. The other sketches ignored this drawing, and continued to remain in place until finally fading away over the years.

Which of the subjects survived the longest?

"HELP!" Johnny screamed, hands cupped around his mouth. "IS ANYONE HERE? HELLO! PLEASE, IS THERE ANYONE AT ALL? HELP, *HELP* ME!"

It was useless. No one was here—Johnny probably wasn't even here. But where was he, then?

Did it matter?

Johnny raised his head at the sky. No, it didn't matter all. Die or live, people would continue as if nothing had happened. He was just another pawn in a big scheme of bullshit.

There was no sun in this new world, and yet there was still a projection from the sky brighter than any sun he'd ever laid eyes on. He squinted as he studied the purple textures above. Any sign of clouds were long erased. Leftover was a straight sheet of violet, taped against a plain board lacking any distinguishable features.

It may have been a basic and goosebump-inducing sky, but man, was it a bright one.

Johnny snapped away, at last breaking from its hypnotic spell. Quickly transgressing into a cold sweat, he began trudging down the sand in hopes of discovery. But after two days of walking, he realized in horror that he had failed to take even a single step from his original marker.

Wherever he was, he was stuck. Worst yet, it had been two days and the need to eat had yet to arise. Sleep did not feel necessary. The only thing that mattered was to keep on moving—and he couldn't even do that.

Johnny gave up and collapsed to his knees. Tears erupted down his face as he raised his fists toward the sky, daring to pursue the layers beyond the purple.

"What is this? I give up. I'll do anything you want. Please, just someone, any*thing*, any*where*, please, just talk to me. Say *something*."

And finally, a voice:

"This is your future, Johnny."

He recognized the voice. Of course he did. It had only

been following him around for his whole life—that is, when it wasn't buzzing like a little bitch. It had no face, only words projected within the nerves of his own brain.

"This is what your world is coming to. Total and utter nothingness. Soon enough the water will swallow the land, and hidden survivors will drown in its wake. This is the sea of Armageddon, Johnny. The final ocean to ever flow over this planet. No one will survive this war. Every soldier, on either side, will perish. There are too many of them out there. We may be stronger, but we are outnumbered. We need the advantage, Johnny. We need your help."

"What do I do? Just tell me what to do and I'll do it. Get me out of this fucking place and I'll do whatever you want, I swear."

"Join our legions—take a step forward into the light. Fight for us and you will never suffer at the bottom of this tyrannical sea, strangling in its abusive seaweed. The demons of tomorrow will be the close encounters of yesterday. What you humans speak of paradise—Heaven—we can offer you the real version. Follow my commands, without question, and you will be taken care of as long as the stars burn in the universe."

"Why me? Why am I so special?"

"You are one of the few who have the ability to open their eyes wide enough to understand. The mist in the bottle is your key to surviving this war. Under no circumstances must you lose your token. Otherwise, all will be lost."

Johnny gulped. Shit had just got *real*.

"What do I have to do?"

"Further instructions will be delivered when the time is right. There is no backing out of this, Johnny. Your devotion has been saved and locked. You are one of us now."

"Who *are* you?"

There was a pause. **"I am the Fly that buzzes last."**

Johnny had more questions to ask, but before another word could leave his mouth the beach crumbled beneath him, opening up a pit of darkness. A waterfall of sand kept him company on a fall that lasted more than his mind could ever comprehend. After he lost the will to be scared, he closed his eyes and accepted the indefinite fate that waited for him at the bottom.

If there was a bottom.

And when Johnny opened his eyes again, he was no longer falling, but instead back at the methadone clinic, in a fetal position beside the toilet.

He felt the sharp bottom of a high heel stabbing into his fragile spine. His girlfriend was kicking him awake, looking awfully pissed off. "What do you think you're doing? Get up."

Johnny grabbed the toilet and propped himself to his feet. He wiped a coat of sweat off his forehead. "What happened?"

"How the hell should I know? Come in and you're on the floor like a damn crackhead. C'mon, we're getting outta this place."

She grabbed his arm and led him out of the bathroom, away from the hallway, through the lobby.

"I thought they wanted my pee!" Johnny squealed, not particularly fond of being rushed like this.

His girlfriend grunted and said, perhaps a little too loudly, "Yeah, well, turns out they won't touch you unless you're eighteen or you have 'parental consent'. Like your folks are really gonna bother with something like that. Oh well. Sorry kiddo, but looks like you'll have to die at seventeen because of a fucking law. God forbid someone try to help someone else. Bunch of fucking cowards."

Johnny shrugged. "Well, that's okay."

Considering what he knew now, he would have rather

died than be taken off his medicine, anyway. Hell, he *was* clean. It was everyone else who was so dirty.

His girlfriend slammed the front door of the clinic hard enough to scare the wind. "No, it is *not* okay!" she cried, throwing Johnny into the limo like he was nothing. "This sale is going to be a once in a lifetime opportunity!"

DAY THREE:

PUPA

23

I**T WAS ONLY** 7:00 A.M. when Addison woke up, wrapped in a warm quilt, sinking into a cloud disguised as her boyfriend's mattress. She loved sleeping over at Connor's house. His bed was always so comfortable. There wasn't another one like it.

She was alone in the bed. It would have been better if Connor was there to hold her like he had last night until she fell asleep. She had liked that a lot. But now he was gone. Off to the bathroom maybe, who knew. She stayed there until she felt strong enough to start the day and crawled off of her wonderful cloud of quilts and pillows.

Addison yawned, stretching her sore limbs, and went to the bathroom for a quick pee. She had to bite her tongue to suppress a scream, forgetting how much urinating burned right now. She washed up, pretending the pain didn't exist. Maybe one day it wouldn't, although she doubted it.

She made her way out into the kitchen, nostrils following the meaty scent of bacon.

And sure enough, there was Connor, hovering over the stove frying a pan full of bacon strips. He glanced over his shoulders and smiled at her. "Morning, baby."

"Morning."

"Go ahead and grab a seat. You want some coffee? Orange juice? Milk?"

She sat down at the kitchen table. "Since when do you cook?"

"Girl, I'm the best cook in the Midwest."

"You've never cooked for me, before."

"Well I am now, so shut up before I throw it all in the trash." He poured a cup of coffee and brought it to her.

He returned to the stove. Addison looked at the large plate of pancakes and bacon on the table before her and dropped her jaw. "Jesus, Connor, I don't think we can eat all of that. Where's your dad?"

"Already went to bed," Connor said, finishing up the last set of food. "But, um, we have a guest joining us."

"What?"

She couldn't think of a single person. Except for his bandmates, of course. But if they suddenly showed up, she was leaving. Those kids were nothing but freaks. She didn't understand how Connor could hang out with them so much.

Connor opened a cabinet and brought out a jar of peanut butter. He put it down on the table with the rest of the breakfast and everything clicked. Then there was a knock at the kitchen door.

Addison gaped at Connor. "You didn't . . . "

He looked at her and shrugged. "I had to."

He opened the door and let in an old friend, one they hadn't spoken to in quite a while. She walked in the kitchen with the same spiky pink cotton candy hair, the obnoxious piercings, and a tight tank top.

"'Sup, bitches!" Candy Blossom said, and saw the plate of bacon on the table. Her green eye shadow broadened. "Aw shit, you guys are too cool."

And without another word, she was sitting down across from Addison, digging in. She took a knife and spread a glob of fresh peanut butter on a pancake, folding it around a pile of bacon and taking a large bite.

Addison adjusted her position in the chair and winced. Her appetite was lost. She sat there sipping her coffee and nibbling on a strip of crispy bacon.

"You gonna eat that?" Candy asked.

TOXICITY

Addison willingly handed over her share. "Knock yourself out."

Connor pulled up a seat between them and helped himself to a couple pancakes and a tall glass of milk. They sat there, eating in silence. Then Candy said, "So, what'd y'all wanna talk about?"

"How do you eat so much of that stuff and never get fat?" Addison asked. She couldn't help it. It was driving her crazy.

"Bulimia," Candy replied.

"Seriously?"

"Yup."

"Well, that's fucked up," Connor said, and shook his head. "No, that discussion can be saved for later. I called you for a different reason. We need some help and don't know who else to turn to."

"What happened? You guys kill someone or something?" She laughed.

Connor and Addison exchanged looks.

"Oh," Candy said. "Well, shit."

"Yeah." Connor sighed. "I know."

"Christ, what did you guys do?"

He told her.

It took a while, but he told her everything that had happened to them since Friday night. It was only Sunday morning now, but God, did it seem like so much more time had passed—a lifetime.

Most of this storytelling session Addison spent in the living room, watching episodes of *The Twilight Zone* on Netflix. She couldn't bear to listen to him talking about it very long. Eventually he finished and she joined them again in the kitchen with a fresh cup of coffee.

"So, what do you think?" Connor asked.

"You guys are racking up a body count and you want *my* advice?" Candy said, a little shocked. "What makes you think I'm some kind of expert?"

"Well, we don't know anyone else we can trust."

She seemed touched. "Really?"

He nodded.

"Okay," she said. "Then I advise you get a shit load of cash and get the hell out of Dodge as fast as you can. How's that sound?"

"Well, yeah, we already figured that," Connor said. "But the problem is, how? How do we do that?"

"Hell if I know. Go rob a bank or something. Invest in stocks. Mow a lot of lawns."

"It's November!"

Addison wasn't really sure why Connor had gotten Candy involved, but maybe there was something she wasn't seeing. After some bickering Addison interrupted them. "What about my father?" she asked. "I already have him trying to come up with some money. Maybe he will."

"Maybe so," Candy said. "When was the last time you talked to him?"

"He was the one who dropped me off yesterday before . . . you know."

"Well, do you know his number?"

Addison nodded, reaching in her pocket. "He gave me a place to call." She pulled out a crumpled-up sheet of paper with a number scribbled across it.

"Then call him and see what's up," Candy said.

"Now?"

"Why not?"

24

MADDOX WAS AWAKENED bright and early the next morning by a pair of eager hands shaking him. He opened his heavy eyes to spot his brother leaning above him, more excited than a kid on Christmas morning. He was dressed in a black and white suit.

He bounced up and down. "Ready to go?"

Evidently, someone had gotten into the coffee.

"What in the hell are you wearing?" Maddox attempted to sit up but sunk back down as exhaustion overwhelmed him. He felt like vomiting and going back to sleep, and then possibly vomiting some more.

"What do you mean?" Benny asked, apparently offended. "This is what they wore in *Reservoir Dogs!* Remember?"

"This isn't *Reservoir* fuckin' *Dogs*, Benny. Now go change out of your bank robber costume and get into something more casual before I change my mind about this whole thing."

"Fine!" Benny stomped his feet down to his bedroom. The same bedroom where the lot lizard had held up camp for the past day or so, shrieking like a dying coyote in heat. And if Benny was going in there, that meant . . .

Reluctantly, Maddox cranked his head over to the sofa where Jazzy was lying with Floyd resting between her legs. This happened to be one of the rare occasions in which Maddox had seen the beast in actual clothes, and he counted it as a blessing.

The lot lizard was scratching her long swamp green

fingernails along Floyd's shiny scalp. He purred like a cat with each motion of her claws. They were watching a show that seemed to portray the simple life of two ditzy blonde chicks.

"What are you two all dressed up for? Leaving already?" he asked hopefully, and yawned.

"We're coming with you," said Floyd, wearing gray sweatpants and a white university T-shirt that was three sizes too big for his body. Excluding freaky monkey noises, this had been one of the very few things he had said since his first encounter with Jazzy. She seemed to have calmed him down considerably.

"Excuse me?"

"You thoughts youse coulda gotten away from me dat easy, sugar?" Jazzy laughed, dressed in the same biker attire as before, including the leather whip holstered at her side, looking as menacing as ever.

"I don't know what you're talking about." Maddox gulped. It was suddenly very humid in the trailer and he wanted to leave as quickly as possible.

"Oh *puleaze!* I knows what youse two were plannin'. Hit the road Jackie-boy and thinks I'd never get my money, huh, my deserved paycheck, is that it? Well nice try, honey! That hyper little boy in there told me all abouts it this mornin' while you was asleepin' away. I knews somethin' wasn't right, and of course my suspicions were correct. After a little torturin', I founds out what I needed to know all right. Oh yeah!"

"Oh God, what did you do to him?"

She winked. "Oh a little of this, a little of that . . . "

"You sick twisted bitch," Maddox whispered, feeling pity for his poor stupid brother.

"As I understands it, I'll finally be gettin' paid today, yes?"

"Yes, sweet Jesus, yes! You'll leave afterwards, right?"

"O'course," Jazzy said. "Along with my lover." She squeezed her large chicken wing arms around the blushing

Floyd and slobbered along his head, leaving it all wet and squeaky.

Benny walked out wearing blue jeans and a gray flannel. He gestured to the outfit. "Better?"

"I do believe you look like a redneck, Benjamin," Floyd said.

Maddox cleared his throat. "Bring the gun."

"Way ahead of you, bro."

* * *

The Cadillac pulled into the Super 8 parking lot at 11:20 A.M. Maddox had to borrow forty bucks from Jazzy for gas, which had of course raised their tab from three to five thousand. He was seriously debating just killing her. He probably would have, too, if not for the fear of likely failure. Would bullets even pierce through the reptilian scales she considered skin?

Benny sat next to him in the passenger seat while Jazzy and Floyd relaxed in the back. She reeked profoundly of motor oil. The repugnant odor was finding a permanent home in his poor leather seats.

Rocking back and forth in the seat, Benny asked if he was ready.

"Do you even know what you're doing?" Maddox killed the ignition but left the key hanging there. There was, after all, a chance of a speedy getaway, and he didn't want to delay essential time digging in his pockets for the car keys.

Benny stopped rocking and scrunched his face as if in concentration. "Not a clue. What *am* I doing?"

Maddox sighed. "All right, pay attention, 'cause I'm only gonna say this once. You listening?"

"When am I not?"

"You're going to fuck this all up, aren't you?"

"Absolutely not."

Maddox didn't believe him for a second, but what other choice did he have? "Okay, fine, just pay attention. You're gonna sit right here in the car, okay? And I'm gonna go way over into room 23 with a briefcase. Now, this is where you come in, all right? If I don't return in *fifteen* minutes, I need you to get up outta the car and come running in, gun blazing. Gun blazing, Benny. You know what that means? It means you don't ask questions, you don't say a single word. You just start shooting . . . and whatever you do, you *do not shoot me.* Understand? Chances are, if I'm not out in fifteen then that means it's a double cross and they're planning on killing me. Do *not* let them kill me, Benny. If you do I swear I'm going to kick your ass so bad . . . "

"How you gonna kick my ass if you're dead?" Benny grinned.

"I'll come back from the grave as a ghost and haunt the shit out of you."

"What kind of ghost? Bruce Willis or Casper?"

"No, I'm not going to be friendly. I'll be a drink-all-your-beer kind of ghost. You want a ghost drinking all your beer? Huh?"

Benny stopped grinning. "No, no I do not."

"All right," Maddox said, "then don't get me killed."

"You two are so cute!" Jazzy cut in, leaning forward between them. Loud smacks echoed from her mouth as she chomped her rotted teeth down on a wad of bubblegum. The stench of motor oil blew forward like a rancid gust of wind.

Maddox ignored the beast and trained his attention on his younger brother. "Repeat my instructions."

"What?"

"Repeat my instructions."

"Oh, um, okay. Uh, you're going to room 32 . . . "

"No! 23!"

"Yeah yeah, whatever. You're going to room 23, and if you're not out in fifteen minutes I go in there guns blazing. Shoot first, ask questions later—but not you, 'cause your ghost will drink all my beer. Anything else, chief?"

"I don't know," Maddox said. There was still about

three minutes left to kill before show time. His vision traveled aimlessly until they came upon the black pistol shaking nervously in his brother's lap. "You know how to work that Beretta, right?"

"That *what?*"

"The Beretta. Your gun."

"Oh yeah, right, right, right . . . yeah, sure I know how to work it. I ain't no damn kid, ya know."

"What's the magazine's capacity?"

"Huh?" He seemed thoroughly puzzled. "I think I have an old *Rolling Stones* back here somewhere, if that'll do."

There was suddenly a loud obnoxious snort of laughter from the lot lizard in the backseat. A chunk of thick snot sprung forth and splattered against the dashboard, making her giggle. "Whoops."

Silently grateful the snot had missed his face, Maddox went on: "No, you idiot. How many bullets can it hold?"

"Oh! Uh, twelve, I think."

"Is it fully loaded?"

"Of course."

"You have no idea, do you?"

"Not really."

"I figured," Maddox said. "It doesn't matter. You shouldn't have to use all twelve—hopefully you won't need to use any. I have to go now. Just remember, fifteen minutes, room 23."

"And don't shoot you."

"Correct."

"Go ahead, Mads. I won't disappoint you."

Maddox doubted that, but felt there was no need to press the issue. He clicked the trunk-release button and stepped out of the Cadillac, but was interrupted when Jazzy's large pit bull head came poking out of the window, nearly giving him a heart attack.

"Can I have your car?" Her tone was surprisingly less threatening than usual. It was almost human.

"What?"

"When you dies, coulds I have your car? It's so cool."

"I'm not going to die."

Jazzy winked at him as he lifted the briefcase out of the trunk and slammed it shut. "Trusts me. I knows who this guy is you're about to see. Jules is my pimp."

Maddox stopped, caught off guard. "He's *your* pimp?"

"O'course he is." She pointed to the fishhook scar running across her face. "Who you thinks give me this beauty right here, huh?"

"Oh."

"Yeah, youse fucked."

"Thanks."

"Anytime, big boy," Jazzy said. "So, can I keeps your ride or not? I'll be takin' real good care of it and all."

"No way!" Benny shouted. "I already have dibs."

"It's true," Maddox said. "He did call dibs."

"Damn!" Jazzy returned to the backseat.

Maddox managed two feet before he was interrupted once again. This time it was Floyd.

"Hey, you."

"What?"

"You think you could maybe score me a couple of those little bottles of motel shampoo? I just love those things. Oh, and some bars of soap! You can never have enough soap."

"I'll . . . I'll do my best."

"Thanks," Floyd said. "I'm gonna go do the sex now." And with that, his head retreated back inside where Jazzy was waiting for him.

Maddox cringed and turned away. He climbed the slick motel stairs with the briefcase of drugs swinging in his hand. Tightening the Cubs cap against his scalp, he knocked on the door once, paused, added four more in rapid-fire, and finished with a duo. The infamous code knock of crime lords. Although, in Maddox's humble opinion, he felt it lacked originality. Sadly, he did not make up the gangster rules. Other gangsters did. Gangsters much more gangster than himself.

TOXICITY

The door to room 23 swung wide open and a pair of large hands dragged Maddox inside, the door shutting quickly afterward. No one outside the motel noticed. He didn't even have a chance to scream for help.

25

MADDOX WAS SLAMMED into the wall face-first. Large hands worked their way in between his legs and spread them, quickly patting him down for any weapons—like, say, the Beretta he had left in Benny's possession. *Ha!* Maddox spat silently, and then was roughly spun around to face the dimly lit motel room. The blinds were pulled closed, making the small television resting on a nightstand across from the bed the only source of light.

The fat man standing beside him, the one who had pulled him inside, was wearing a short golf hat and a tight leather jacket. "He's clean!" he announced, and stepped away, hands folded behind his back like a true professional. It was a bit amazing the guy was able to wrap those short stubby arms around such a wide body.

The bathroom door creaked open and a ghostly sheet of light escaped into the main room. Out stepped a short scrawny little black guy, no more than five-five. Maybe a hundred and ten pounds. He wore a white suit, along with a white fedora and a set of white dress shoes. Hell, he was even holding a white cane.

"I take it you're here on account of Vinnie." His voice was high and squeaky, reminding Maddox of the times his brother used to inhale air from balloons.

The pimp approached him and stuck out his free hand—the other wrapped firmly around the crystal ball of the cane's head. "Jules."

Maddox shook it and introduced himself.

"That's a fine name."

"Thanks," Maddox said.

"You know, that name, it sounds familiar. I know you?" Jules tilted his shades a notch down his nose, exposing his eyes.

"I don't think so . . . "

Jules snapped his fingers and pointed at him. "Yeah, I know you! You're that crazy cracka who got busted the day of his first game, right? I remember hearing about you! That shit was *hilarious*."

Great. "You a baseball fan, huh?"

"Oh, you best believe it. Ain't nothin' better than the good ol' black and white, baby."

His grin brightened as he revealed his fandom for the Sox, and it took all Maddox had to stop himself from punching the guy's lights out.

Shit.

"You were gonna be a Cubbie, ain't that right?"

"Yeah, that's right."

"Well, if you ask me," the pimp said, "getting pinched was the best thing that could've happened to ya. Put you in line, got you thinking straight, didn't it? Jesus, boy, why the hell you wanna go around playing for that silly little team in the first place?"

Maddox breathed in, breathed out. It was obvious where this would lead to if someone didn't end it soon. "Do you mind if we got down to business?"

"Got somewhere else you gotta be, do ya?"

"Yeah, kind of," Maddox said, stressing over Benny's sense of time. The adrenaline of his dream as a criminal finally coming true might override the boy's patience.

Instead of the bullet Maddox had been expecting, however, Jules repaid him with another smile. "Well shit, why didn't you say so?"

He plopped down on the mattress, letting the springs bounce him up and down, and spotted the briefcase locked in Maddox's kung fu grip. "That what I think it is?"

"Depends on if you have what I need," Maddox said. *Vague, yet to the point. Very smooth. After ten long years you still got it, baby.*

"Yeah, I got your money. You got what Vinnie speaks so highly of?"

Maddox lifted the briefcase and set it down on the bed. "Sure do."

Still lighting the room with his teeth, the pimp said, "Well, a'ight, let's get down to business then, shall we?" He bent down and dragged a black duffle bag out from under the bed. Struggling to carry it, he heaved it up next to him and unzipped the top.

Maddox peered inside and his rhythm of breathing skipped a beat or two as the bag's contents overwhelmed him. Sure enough, inside was a shitload of money. Who knew how much? It was full, nearly overflowing of cash. The bag was going to be damn heavy.

"Now," Jules motioned to the briefcase, "your turn."

Maddox noticed the bodyguard tensing as he unlatched the briefcase and opened it, as if there was a gun waiting for him. It hit him then that a gun very well could have been hiding in there, since he had never looked inside. King had just given it to him and that had been that. Now here he was.

Nope, no gun. More like four rows of twelve small black bottles; each fastened against the cushion of the briefcase's interior by thin straps. Forty-eight potential destroyers of civilization.

The pimp whistled in awe. "Just as he promised.".

"Are we good?" Trapped in such a dark enclosed space, it was impossible to judge the passing of time. For all he knew, this transaction could have been going on for hours now. Days, even.

"Shoot, boy, you sure are in a rush." Jules looked up at him. "Where you gotta go anyway, huh?"

"Just would like to get this over with, if that's all right with you."

TOXICITY

Jules leaned forward. "You know who I am?"

"You're Jules."

"That's right. I'm Jules. You know what Jules does, Maddox Kane?"

"No—what?"

"He keeps bitches in line, that's what he does."

"Oh," Maddox said. "That's nice."

"Now," Jules continued, "don't get me wrong. It takes years—I mean *years*—to fully master pimping a ho. You wouldn't believe how much practice it takes to tell when a bitch is holding something back. It's not as easy as it seems, ya know? You don't just have to learn the art of facial expressions, no, but you gotta study every single movement of the body. I'm even talkin' about the fuckin' hips. The way their toes wiggle. Everything, you feel me?"

Maddox nodded, although he was not feeling the pimp at all. He had no idea what this guy was planning and he didn't like it. He also had to consider the fact that if Jules didn't really intend on a double-cross, then Jules himself would surely suspect one when Benny came barging in shooting up the place.

"So," Jules said, "I can't help but look at you with the same attitude I would approach one of my girls with. And man, I have to say, you're showing quite a few signs of a bitch in need of a good beatin'. It ain't that hot in here, boy. The AC is maxed and yet here you are, sweatin' like some kind of goddamn pig. You're bouncing up on the soles of your feet like you're just *begging* to get the hell outta here. It's clear as all can be that you're hiding something from me. Don't try to deny it."

"I just want to finish this."

Jules laughed. "*Finish this?* Boy, if that ain't code I don't know what is." He turned to the bodyguard. "Roach, you clearly missed the bug up this fool's ass. Give me the fucking Glock."

The pimp stood up off the bed. There was no mistaking the determination of murder in his stance.

Maddox threw his hands up in the air. "I'm not wired! Jesus Christ, I just got out of the joint. You said you knew that yourself. This is just a favor for King, nothing else. I am *not* working for the cops. Trust me, okay?"

The bodyguard, Roach, was in the midst of pulling out a pistol from his waist when Jules stopped him. He paused and awaited more directions.

"Vinnie did put in a good word for you, and your tone's implying you're telling the truth . . . or that you're a really good liar, one of the two. Which is it, huh? You a fuckin' rat?"

"No," Maddox said calmly, "and if you accuse me of being one again, I'm going to drive that cane down your throat."

The two men stared at each other coldly. Maddox thought he had it under control again. Just a simple death threat was all that was needed most of the time in a situation like this. You made these gangster assholes know you meant business, otherwise they walked all over you.

Jules cracked first. That smile returned and he clapped Maddox on the shoulder. "You're all right, boy." He sat back down on the bed. "What do you say we finish this up? Maybe a drink afterwards?" Jules pushed the duffle bag of cash to him. "It's all there, but I'll understand if you wanted to count it. I know I would."

"I trust you." King hadn't exactly informed Maddox how much he was picking up—just that his pay for deliverance would be quite charitable.

"Good man." Jules cracked a smile. "You mind if I test out the product real quick?"

"Knock yourself out."

Maddox thought of the hostage from the day before. How he had twitched in his chair, utterly helpless.

The bony fingers of the pimp piano-walked across the bedspread, stopping at the opened briefcase. They climbed upon its clean interior and ventured toward one of the bottles. He pulled away the Velcro strapping and caressed the black metallic capsule.

"Cold," he whispered. He took the bottle in one hand and softly tapped the side of it with the other. "So very cold."

"Yeah, uh, it's supposed to be."

Jules raised his brow. "Oh yeah?"

Maddox nodded, hoping it wasn't obvious how full of shit he was.

"What, am I supposed to keep it refrigerated or some shit?"

"That would probably be best."

"Funny," Jules said. "Vinnie never mentioned any refrigerating bullshit at the meeting. You sure?"

"Uh . . . " Stalling, he searched for a lie strong enough to get his ass out of there. And then, just like that, it came to him. "Yeah," he said.

"Oh-kay," Jules said. He studied the bottle some more. "So I just spray it in my mouth, right?"

"I think so."

He sniggered. "Would be pretty fucked up to find out you swapped these with some pepper spray or something, huh?"

"Sure would."

"Hmm." Jules raised it closer to his face and shrugged. "Well, here goes nothin'."

He moved his index finger to the top of the bottle and opened his mouth. He pressed down on the trigger and . . .

And nothing.

He pressed again.

And still nothing.

He shook it and then tried once more.

Nothing.

Fuck.

Jules looked up, puzzled. "Is there something I'm doing wrong? Why isn't it working?"

"Um."

The pimp investigated the drug a little while longer and sighed. "Boy, how long have you had this briefcase in your possession?"

"Since yesterday evening. Why?"

"And where, exactly, did you store it between then and now? And please, please do not tell me you were stupid enough to keep it in your trunk."

"Um."

"Because if you did, and I'm thinking you did," the pimp said, "that would mean the briefcase stayed out all night in the cold. Now, that would have probably been all right if it was maybe July or somethin', but no, it's November. The beginning of fuckin' winter, man. And obviously, this was some liquid type of shit we were dealing with." He stared at Maddox, shaking his head disapprovingly. "You know what happens to liquid when you leave it out in the cold, boy?"

Maddox couldn't move. Couldn't talk. Couldn't do shit. He just stood there, frozen.

"Roach!" Jules called out.

"Yes, boss?" the bodyguard asked.

"Tell this lost soul what happens."

"It freezes, boss."

"Correct! You know what that means, Maddox Kane?"

Maddox could only stare at him. Where the hell was Benny?

The bottle of Jericho smashed into Maddox's forehead.

His first thought was: *He wasn't kidding. That really is cold.*

The second one was: *Oooowwww!*

"It means it's fucking worthless," Jules said, and swung his cane at Maddox's knees, knocking him down to the floor. He felt a large bump already forming on his head as Jules brought the cane down upon it.

The pimp did all of this while staying seated.

Maddox couldn't help but question his own status as a tough guy. Perhaps prison had weakened him.

The sudden blood rushing down from his skull didn't

seem to help matters either. Jules hit him again and again with the cane and told him had he screwed with the wrong pimp.

Shit, I knew this was going to happen.

* * *

Benny was fantasizing turning around and emptying the entire clip into that evil bitch's dirty ugly face.

He gripped the pistol's handle tighter and tried his best to relax, but with them kicking his seat every other second and howling into his ear like a couple of dying animals, he didn't think relaxation was much of a possibility.

If he shot her in that ridiculous glass eye, however, he thought things might be different.

Benny smiled childishly, and probably would have done it if there wasn't a chance of spilling hooker blood all over his brother's leather seats. Best to wait until he caught her outside. Maybe when they took her back to the truck stop. She'd step out, with those supernaturally strong legs of hers, and *BLAM!* she'd die right there in the snow.

POP! goes the lot lizard.

Why doesn't anyone stop this? It wasn't as if the motel's parking lot was totally empty. Plenty of people had strolled by since Maddox's departure. Although, the guy inside this motel was supposedly a dangerous pimp— maybe it was the neighborhood's norm to pass a car with two people screwing in the backseat.

Maybe it wouldn't be a bad idea to check out if there were any apartments available to rent out here. Passing by automobiles full of fornication could totally turn into a hobby of his, he reckoned. Something to do on a Saturday night. Hell, maybe if he was smooth enough he'd get in on some of the action as well. It then crossed his mind that, like now, Jazzy—or something equally horrible—could very well be one of the occupants of these idealistic shagmobiles.

The dream died instantly.

Jazzy kicked the seat once again and sent Benny springing forward against the dashboard, nearly pulling the trigger against his own thigh. He wondered why he was holding the gun so close to his crotch.

That's it, I can't take this anymore. I'm gonna shoot her. I swear I'm gonna shoot her. I don't care what it does to the . . .

Benny's vision fell upon the time on the car radio. 11:51 A.M.

Crap, did he leave at 11:30 or a quarter 'til?

He briefly debated asking either Jazzy or Floyd if they remembered, but felt it would probably be in his best interest to not disturb them. They were doing a pretty phenomenal job of disturbing him enough as it was.

What was he supposed to do—wait another four minutes, or just go for it?

Another four minutes with the hooker and his roommate would be akin to an eternity in Hell. Also, they'd been going at it for a while now, and it could end any second.

Benny feared being this close to them when the time . . . came.

He shivered, said screw it, and leaped out of the Cadillac. Holding the Beretta against his side, Benny headed for the motel across the parking lot. He placed one foot on the icy steps and nearly slipped on his ass. And if it wasn't for the handrail, he would have.

Pulling himself back up, Benny wondered how many of those shagmobile gawkers had witnessed his embarrassing slip. *Thank God the gun didn't go off,* he thought, and cautiously made his way to room 32, ready to blow away the first sonofabitch he came across.

Guns blazing, baby.

* * *

TOXICITY

Fuckin' canes, thought Maddox Kane.

The pimp bashed the cane against Maddox's ribs, still seated. He was laughing. This was fun for him.

Maddox raised his hands up and blocked the incoming bash, shouting, "Wait! Stop!"

And to his utter disbelief, the pimp stopped.

"What?" Jules said, irritated.

"Stop hitting me!"

"Why?"

"Because it hurts?"

"Oh . . . well, why didn't you say so?" Jules asked, and brought the cane down once more across Maddox's cheekbone. He then twirled it around his hand and rested it on his lap. Maddox didn't really think he was done being smacked just yet—perhaps just some breather room for the next bloodbath.

After a moment of painful silence, Maddox felt it was finally safe enough to move again. He slowly sat up, panting heavily and leaking a fair amount of blood. Most of his jean jacket and undershirt were now a brownish color. His Cubs cap had fallen off his head ages ago and now lay on the carpet beside him. The bill was stained crimson.

He wiped the blood out of his eyes with the sleeve of his jacket and looked up at the pimp weakly, who was staring directly back down at him. He wore a very cruel expression that Maddox just did not particularly care for.

He gulped. It was a struggle not to swallow too much blood.

"You're one stupid motherfucker, you know that, Maddox Kane?"

When Maddox didn't reply, the pimp went on: "Boy, man, sometimes you people crack me up. I mean, of all the things you could have done, you leave it out in the snow. A fortune of drugs . . . ruined! What were you thinkin'? Huh?"

Maddox coughed and told the truth. "That fuckin'

hooker would have stolen it if I took it inside with me. She already took Floyd. She's evil, pure evil."

The pimp eyed Maddox queerly, finally letting out an understandable sigh. "Well, we've all been there."

Jules cracked a small laugh, merrily tapping his fingers along the side of the cane.

"You know," Jules said, "I bet you would be a pretty all right guy to hang out with."

Maddox felt a tiny gleam of hope.

"It's a real shame I'm gonna have to kill you."

Oh, well, that's more like it.

"Roach," Jules said, still not breaking eye contact with Maddox.

"Yes, boss?"

"Shotgun me."

"One shotgun coming right up, boss."

Roach bent down near the closet and retrieved a sawed-off shotgun, handed it to Jules, and backed away.

Maddox watched the weapon in Jules's grip with horror. Where the hell was Benny? He was going to die and there was nothing he could do about it.

"Opened or closed?" the pimp asked.

"What?"

"Do you want your coffin opened or closed during your funeral? Jesus, boy, and I thought you called yourself a gangster."

"Why don't you just reconsider this whole funeral idea in the first place?" Maddox suggested.

"And what would that do to my ego? You can't let one motherfucka slide, 'cause then you're gonna be lettin' all kinds of motherfuckas slidin', and that's just bad business right there."

"I suppose so." Maddox hung his head low and thought, regretfully, that the pimp actually made a solid point.

"Now," Jules said, "I'm only gonna ask you this one last time, and if you don't give me no answer, you ain't gonna get no choice. I'm gonna decide for you, ya dig?"

TOXICITY

He laid the sawed-off shotgun across his lap, next to the cane, the barrel aimed dead at his head.

"So, what's it gonna be, Maddox Kane? Opened or—"

A sudden report of gunfire erupted from above. Everyone in the room snapped their heads toward the ceiling. Somewhere upstairs, a woman screamed.

Maddox smiled through bloodied gums.

Benny, you magnificent bastard.

* * *

Benny kicked in the door and pulled the trigger without even looking. The TV ahead of him exploded and the room was filled with a piercing shriek. Covering his ears, Benny looked over to the bed and spotted a woman dressed like a dominatrix screaming her lungs out, a branding iron falling to the ground. A naked man was tied to the bed beside her, ass sticking up in the air, all red and . . . branded. But of *what?* Jesus Christ, it looked like a tiny duck smoking a cigar.

"Where the hell is Mads?" Benny asked. She continued screaming. Then it dawned on him. "Crap," he said, "this is the wrong room, isn't it?"

"*What?*"

"Nothing . . . my bad, my bad." Benny backed away. "Um, carry on."

He gave her a remorseful shrug and creeped out of the room, rushing down the stairs where he hoped there was still time to save his brother's life. He gulped, fearing a life where all his beer would be consumed by a ghost. The thought sent shivers down his spine. No way was he gonna let that happen.

Then he heard the gunshots and nearly jumped out of his own skin.

* * *

Staring at the ceiling, the pimp said, "Now, what the hell do you suppose is going on up there?"

Maddox snatched the sawed-off shotgun from the pimp's hands.

"Hey, what the hell—"

Roach reached down for the Glock. Maddox unloaded one of the two shotgun shells into his gut. The bodyguard flew back against the wall, sliding down on the TV stand and crushing it into a sparkly explosion.

Just like riding a bike, Maddox was thinking, and turned the shotgun on the pimp. He resisted his urge to pull the trigger.

Jules laughed. "I'm impressed, I tell ya, and I ain't one to be easily impressed."

"Shut up." Maddox rose to his feet with the shotgun. He wiped another glob of blood from his face and tried to stable his balance.

"Aw, is somebody cranky? Well, that ain't—"

The other shotgun shell exploded into the pimp's left ribcage. Jules flung across the bed, skull bouncing off the headboard. He curled into a small ball, his hands pressed firmly against the missing half of his side, screaming.

"OH MY GOD! YOU SHOT ME! WHY WOULD YOU SHOOT ME?"

Maddox dropped the empty sawed-off and cracked his neck. He spat out a chunk of blood and glared down at the defenseless pimp. A rage built inside him, making him want to hurt Jules just as badly as he'd hurt him. Worse, in fact. Much worse.

He couldn't allow a *Sox fan* to get off with a simple gunshot wound to the ribs. Maddox spotted the cane laying there on the floor, sticking halfway from under the bed, and picked it up.

He flipped the cane around so he had a clean grip on the bottom. He cracked the glass topper against the bedpost, leaving behind a few dozen shards facing outward.

He approached the side of the bed, staring at Jules as he squirmed on the crimson comforter. Holding the end of the cane, he raised his arms over his head.

"Hey," Jules said, "that's my cane," just before Maddox slammed all of his force down upon the pimp's face. The glass shards leftover from the crystal ball punctured through his right cheek and half of his eye socket. A mini volcano of blood and eye jelly erupted, splashing Maddox with the grotesque fallout.

Benny kicked open the door and barged through, waving the Beretta wildly.

He stopped, gasping at the scene. "Whoa."

Still feeling the brutal effects of killing two people, Maddox turned around, panting profoundly, vision hazy and sweet tooth stronger than ever. The things he would do for a goddamn cookie right now.

Maddox cocked his head to his brother. "I'll deal with you later. Cops are on their way—almost here, by the sound of it. Grab the briefcase and let's go."

Benny nodded and latched the case of Jericho closed. Maddox tossed the strap over his shoulder and, grunting, lifted the duffle bag of cash off the bed. Wiping the room clean of his prints crossed his mind, but he figured there was enough blood soaked into the carpet alone to connect him to the scene of the crime. Plus, there was simply no time.

He left the cane sticking in the pimp's skull, then stepped back out into the cold and slammed the door shut.

The cool wind on his face was heaven compared to the humidity of the motel room. As they rushed toward the end of the balcony it occurred to Maddox that the number of the motel room had, in fact, been the same two digits as the ones tattooed across his back: **23.**

He wondered if there was some kind of significance there.

They reached the top of the stairs and Benny went down first. Maddox followed closely behind him, struggling to carry the duffle bag.

Benny's foot landed on a patch of ice on one of the steps midway down, sending him tumbling down the stairs. As he landed on the hard cold cement his arm smacked the ground, forcing his hand to close around the trigger of the Beretta.

Maddox staggered back, somehow staying on his feet, his hand gripping the shot shoulder. He looked down at the bottom of the steps at his brother, watched him trying to regain his own balance while juggling a pistol in one hand and a briefcase in the other.

"You shot me," he whispered, too soft for anyone to hear.

Benny finally got to his feet and studied Maddox fearfully. "Did I shoot you?"

"You shot me."

"I did?"

"You shot me."

"Oh," Benny said. "My bad."

"Your *bad?* You shot me!" Maddox stumbled down the stairs.

"It was an accident!"

"I am going to kill you."

"Oh yeah?" Benny said, as they moved briskly across the parking lot. "Well, you kill me, then *I'm* gonna come back as a ghost and drink all of *your* beer! HA! I'll be the sexiest ghost there ever was!"

Maddox ignored him. He had to. Otherwise he really would kill him. His arm felt like it was on fire as he slid into the driver's seat and punched the trunk release button, ordering the idiot to put the duffle bag and briefcase inside.

"Well, ain't you a mess," Jazzy said from the backseat.

Maddox started up the car. "Bitch, it is not the time."

She fell silent.

Benny jumped in the passenger seat as sirens in the nearby distance droned closer and closer to the motel. "Holy crap, man, let's go, let's go."

Maddox skidded across the parking lot, spinning out onto the street and speeding away from the motel. "Give me a towel. Anything to wipe this shit off me."

TOXICITY

Floyd leaned forward and handed him a stack of baby wipes. "Always come prepared, am I right?"

Maddox took the wipes without answering and began to clean his face as they fled from the crime scene.

"So," Floyd said, "you remember my shampoo?"

26

IT WAS GETTING to the point where Johnny was high even without taking the purple. It was as if he had taken so much, that the drug's chemicals were soaked into his brain—had completely fried his mind to always perceive a hallucinogenic reality.

When he looked up at the sky, he saw red instead of blue. When it rained, it felt hot. When someone shook his hand, it was as if Johnny's hand was dissolving into the other person's. And God help whoever that other person may be. That person was *not* his friend. That person was his enemy. That person was some kind of camouflaged demon spy trying to uncover the secrets buried deep down in Johnny's soul—something these *monsters* didn't have. They were everywhere.

He became more paranoid at school. The kids he once considered friends—always *laughing*, always *fighting*. It was barbaric. He watched them interact with each other from faraway, drooling purple saliva, coughing up his lungs, hiding his hard-on. It never went down. He took care of it and an hour later his pants were tightening around his groin again. It was mystifying. How could someone be so disgusted with humanity and yet be so horny all the time?

It was that purple shit. It had to be. What else? *Teenage hormones?* No, these urges were too strong. Sometimes he caught himself thinking like some sort of psycho rapist and had to pinch himself until the thoughts diminished. Sure, he liked to think differently, but he knew

TOXICITY

the truth. He was just another one of the animals out there in the schoolyard, walking numbly back and forth among the masses of replicas with their hard silly dicks in their hands, wondering when something interesting would happen.

The students here weren't any different from other kids. The only difference was they wore suits and skirts. Some of them were demons and some of them were humans on their way to becoming demons. They were all waiting in line for that fang to sink into their neck, for that vacuum to suck up their soul, for that darkness to blind them.

Including Johnny.

He knew where he was, and what he was surrounded by. The purple had opened up his eyes. He hated it. He preferred to still be in the dark. But this, this *awareness*, it was all too much for him. It kept him up at night. He saw their eyes and their lack of faces and the deep coal pits replacing their withering hearts and it made him want to kill himself—to kill everyone, to kill the whole goddamn planet.

And then he met the Fly.

While that first hit of purple had been the gunshot to start the race, the Fly would be his guide in completing it. The Fly would lead him to the finish line. When he had been first introduced to It the morning before, Johnny had simply shrugged It off as some sort of asinine hallucination and swallowed It with his glass of water. But by the end of that day, Johnny had made a complete turnaround. It hadn't just been some illusion. The Fly convinced him otherwise. Now Johnny bowed to the Fly. He *worshiped* It.

Because now he knew what the Fly was.

The Fly was his Savior.

* * *

It was the day after meeting the Fly when everything started spiraling out of control.

It was a Sunday. He had spent the whole morning in the bathroom staring down stupidly at the toilet. It was beautiful, what he saw.

There was no water in the bowl—all gone and replaced with billions of flies, buzzing and buzzing and buzzing. There were just so many, it overwhelmed him, like a black colony of everything right in the world. Inside the toilet was heaven and outside the toilet was the shit.

Sitting on the seat by Itself was *the* Fly. *The Savior.*

"Soon, soon the time will come."

"For the end?"

"And the beginning."

Johnny had no idea what the Fly was talking about, yet at the same time he understood It perfectly. Not only what It was saying now, but he understood the whole world. He understood everything and was just as confused as before. The answers, he knew, were much clearer inside that toilet. All he had to do was dive in, headfirst, and swim with the flies. He wanted to drown in the knowledge of the universe.

"After it's over and after it starts, you will finally be one of us. All your hard work will be rewarded. You will join us down here in our bliss and never hurt again. You will be a god, Johnny. A real god. You will be fucked by many and worshipped by all. You will be at the top, you will be everything you've ever dreamed. Soon, Johnny, soon! But there is still much to do. Our soldiers are still caged, our animals are still imprisoned. You must attack first, before it's too late. Now leave us! Go! Free the beasts! Free the heathens! Free them all, dear Johnny! Go!"

And with that, a phantom finger pushed down on the flusher and the mass of holy flies swirled away into the sewer system. The Fly cannonballed after them.

27

THE CADILLAC CRUISED smoothly for a solid ten minutes before anyone else said something. Of course, it had to be the lot lizard.

"I am fucking starving."

"Too bad," Maddox said, having finally accepted his face wasn't going to get any cleaner.

"I'm kind of hungry, as well," Floyd said.

"Me, too," Benny said.

Maddox sighed. Every ounce of him ached. "Eat at the trailer."

"Oh come on, Mads," Benny said. "You know there ain't shit there to eat."

"What do you expect me to do, then?" These people were unbelievable.

"Right there!" Jazzy pointed ahead at a McDonald's. "I wants a Big Mac!"

Maddox looked at the fast food restaurant in disbelief. "You can't be serious."

"I haven't eaten all day!" Benny rubbed his stomach for extra effect.

"No," Maddox said. "This is ridiculous. You are ridiculous. There's blood everywhere! And I'm shot!"

"Oh, quits yo baby hollerin'," Jazzy said. "Just go on to the drive-thru reals quick. C'mon!"

Maddox shook his head stubbornly. "No," he said. "Absolutely not."

The three passengers sighed and settled back in their seats. He couldn't believe what he was hearing. They had just barely escaped from a motel full of pimps, pistols, and pigs—the three Ps, respectfully—and they wanted to go eat? He was practically bleeding to death and all they cared about was a Big Mac.

"You know," Benny said, "I saw a commercial the other day that was advertising these new sugar cookies McDonald's has. They're crammed with like these giant M&Ms? Only a buck for three of 'em, too . . . "

Maddox maneuvered the Cadillac into a hasty U-turn, thinking that sweet tooth of his would be the death of him one day.

"Yay!" Jazzy clapped.

"Fuck you," Maddox said bitterly, turning into the McDonald's parking lot.

He only had to take one look at the drive-thru to determine there was no way he was going to wait that long in line. When bleeding through multiple places on the body, it was seldom possible to have patience in fast food drive-thrus.

He swerved into the nearest empty space he could find and turned the car off.

Maddox sat there for a moment, head leaned back, eyes closed, just enjoying the silence.

"Well?" Jazzy said, ruining the peaceful moment he had going. "I wants a Big Mac!"

"Wait, who's going in?" Floyd asked. "Oh God, please don't make me go. I hate standing up there, waiting in line, giving orders for more than just myself. It makes me feel like such a fat cow. And all the people behind me, you just know they're thinking the same thing about me. *Fat cow, fat cow.* No way! Too much pressure, man, way too much pressure."

"I will," Maddox said. He didn't open his eyes, though, or make any hint of getting out of the car at all, for that matter.

"What?" Benny said. "Are you crazy? You're fuckin' shot, man. You can't go in there. They'll call the cops!"

"I'm going." Maddox leaned forward and pressed the

trunk release button. He winced. Every movement seemed to drive another jolt of pain through his shoulder, which would then explode into an agonizing spasm located at the center of his nervous system.

"Big Macs for everyone then?" he asked.

They all nodded.

"Fries?"

"Um, I don't know," Floyd said. "Is anyone else going to have some if I get some? I will if you guys will. Otherwise I'll feel all fat and stuff."

"Jesus Christ, Floyd, you're skinnier than I am," Benny said.

"Don't you dare hurt my emotionals, Benjamin!"

"No one wants fries," Benny said. "Just go on and get the Big Macs and let's go, huh?"

"Yeah," Maddox said. "And then I kill you."

"Deal."

"Catcha later, lover-butt," said Jazzy. The lot lizard leaped forward and planted a small sloppy kiss across Maddox's cheek, leaving behind a faint rancid outline of swampy green lipstick. "Thanks for murdering my boss."

"Anytime." He headed to the back of the car and lifted up the ajar trunk. He quickly unzipped the duffle bag and took out a hundred-dollar bill. He figured one hundred out of what could be millions would hardly be accounted for. Hell, if he wanted to, he could probably even take a couple thousand. It wasn't the time to commit unnecessary risks. He would even inform King of this one minor bill and tell him to take it out of his own pay.

Maddox stuffed the bill in his pants pocket. He took off his bloodied jean jacket and tossed it in the trunk before closing it. It was too much of an eyesore to be wearing out in public. He walked into the McDonald's and headed straight down the hall toward the bathroom. The men's was locked.

"*Ocupado!*" said a man who clearly did not speak Spanish.

Shit, Maddox thought, and looked around. He made

sure no one was watching and slipped in the women's bathroom, quickly locking the door behind him. He rushed to the sink and turned the faucet on, splashing cold water in his face. He pulled up his sleeve and grimaced at the hole in his upper arm, blood slowly gushing out.

He took some paper towels, wet them, and cleaned up any noticeable blood. It took a while but he felt he had done a pretty decent job. Except for his arm. It was still oozing a little. He spotted a sanitary pad dispenser located next to the sink and he grinned.

Maddox ripped the dispenser's opening apart, a waterfall of pads collapsing to the floor. He picked one up and peeled away the bottom. *I can't believe I'm actually doing this.* He flattened the pad against his gunshot wound. It stuck to his flesh just as good as a Band-Aid, maybe even better. It actually wasn't so bad at all.

He rolled his sleeve back down, covering up the pad. Its shape was still visible through his shirt, but he doubted anyone would come to that sort of conclusion. Maddox inspected himself one last time in the mirror and frowned. His face was swollen, nose purple, lip busted.

His Cubs cap was missing, too. Must have still been at the motel, abandoned at the scene. This pissed him off more than anything else.

Maddox walked out of the bathroom and stood in line. Everyone stared at him when he came out, gasping at his injuries. No doubt they were ridiculing the pad concealed under his sleeve. Bastards. He briefly debated retreating back to the trailer. To hell with the lot lizard's complaints. He would drop them all off at the trailer, deliver King his money and collect his reward. And then find the nearest gas station and reload on sweets, where he would then race back to the trailer so he could pay off the bitch to finally leave them alone once and for all. It sounded like one hell of a fantastic idea.

But then he saw the cookie bin resting on the counter up there by the register. Rows and rows of fresh sugar cookies, each one caked with giant, seductive M&Ms. Benny hadn't been lying. They looked absolutely delicious. It was exactly the type of medicine he needed to treat his ravenous sweet tooth.

The sign pinned to the front of the bin read: **3 for $1**

Maddox decided to wait in line after all.

A young punk sporting a green Mohawk stared at Maddox. "Whoa, man, the fuck happen to you?"

Maddox looked at the kid miserably. "Got screwed by an inside-out Oreo."

"Oh . . . well, we've all been there . . . " He turned back to the front of the line, possibly disturbed for life.

Maddox waited as the only cashier in the place slowly took everyone's order. Twice she made a customer repeat themselves. He didn't understand what was so hard about "double cheeseburger", but whatever, it wasn't his problem. He just wanted a damn cookie.

Someone tapped him on the shoulder. He turned around expecting to be interrogated by another nosy punk, but instead discovered his brother.

"Benny? What the hell? Go back to the car."

"I will in a minute."

"What is it?"

"Well, Maddox, I was sitting in the car a few minutes ago, and I got to thinking about something. I thought long and hard, too, believe me."

"About what?" *Oh God, what now?*

"Now, trust me, I really thought about this and—"

"What the hell are you talking about? Spit it out."

"And I think I've made the right decision—"

"Benny! What do you *want?*"

He sighed. "I want . . . fries."

Maddox could have sworn a blood vessel was on the verge of popping. His fists clenched. His teeth gritted. "Benny. Go. To. The. Fucking. Car. Right. Fucking. *NOW.*"

Benny took a defensive step back. He looked hurt.

"Okay, okay, fine," he said. "Off I go. 'Bye, Mads. I'm

going. If you need me, I'll be in the car. I'll be in the car if you need me. The car is where I'll be. See ya later. Catch ya on the flip side. Going to the car now. Remember my fries! Thank you! 'Bye!"

He ran out the doors.

Maddox wanted to clock him. He really did, so very badly, right in his stupid face. But that would come later, he decided; teach him to shoot his big bro in the shoulder. Some actions just couldn't pass without consequence.

It was his turn in line so he approached the counter. The cashier gave him one glance and flinched, fearing the worst. After a moment or two of soothing, she finally took his order.

Maddox gathered the food in his arms and gladly left the building. He walked out to the space where he had parked the Cadillac—only now, instead of a car, there was only Benny, sitting there on the icy pavement stuck in some sort of melancholic state.

Maddox knew what had happened right away, but still, he had to ask anyway. "Benny . . . where's my car?"

"Well, do you see it?" Benny asked, carefully dodging eye contact.

"No, Benny, I sure don't."

"Yeah, me neither . . . "

Maddox whipped his fountain drink of Pepsi across the parking lot and it splattered like a carbonated grenade. "What the hell, Benny? Why didn't you just stay in the goddamn car like I told you to?"

"I'm sorry, Mads," Benny said. "How'd they steal it anyways? It's not like you left the keys in the ignition or anything . . . Oh, you did? Shit. Why'd you do that?"

"Excuse me for not thinking clearly," Maddox said, "but it's kind of hard to concentrate with a *bullet in my fucking shoulder!*"

"Oh come on, there's no need to bring up the past like that."

"The past? *The past?* It wasn't even a fucking hour ago! Do you realize how much money was in there?"

"No—how much?"

"Millions!"

"Well, I just don't know what to say," Benny said. "They stole from us. I can't believe it. Floyd was like a brother to me. A brother that wasn't so overly violent. But that bitch, that *succubus,* completely turned him against me. I wasn't even in there for a minute, too . . . " He spotted the McDonald's bag in Maddox's hands. "But hey, let's look on the bright side. More food for us, right? Speaking of, can I have my sandwich please? I'm still pretty hungry. I would have liked a pop or something with it too, but, you know, someone kind of lost their temper and now we don't have any. It's okay, though. I forgive you. Nobody's perfect."

The vessel popped.

"You want your sandwich, Benny?" Maddox asked, derailing off into total hysteria. "Your little fuckin' *Big Mac?* Here, take your stupid goddamn sandwich!"

He reached into the bag, pulled out a cardboard sandwich box, and threw it at his brother. It exploded against his forehead, thin sheets of lettuce being carried away by the wind like green dandelion seeds.

"TAKE THEM ALL!" Maddox threw the whole bag at him.

Benny just sat there and took it, licking Big Mac sauce off his face. It wasn't enough. Maddox wanted to beat his face in—beat him until his knuckles were raw. He almost did, too, but at the last second managed to stop himself.

Somehow, Maddox bit his lower lip and held back the anger. "I'm sorry," he said. "I shouldn't have done that. It's just that you really screwed me, Benny. What am I supposed to tell King? That my car, with his money in the trunk, was jacked by a hooker in a fast food parking lot? He'll kill me!"

Benny stood up and hugged him. "I accept your apology," he said.

Maddox kicked a hamburger bun across the parking lot and stared up at the sun. It felt like it was staring back down, mocking him. "We're like two miles from the trailer. Let's get walking."

"All right," Benny said. He bent down and searched for scattered food in the snow. "Umm . . . Mads? Where're my fries?"

"Oh, I'm sorry, you must have forgotten to tell me," Maddox said, walking away.

Benny followed. "Man, that was a real asshole move on your part."

"Benny?"

"Yeah?"

"Shut up."

28

SUNDAY AFTERNOON.
Johnny's girlfriend came over and found him in his room, scribbling messages on his wall with a permanent marker.

"Johnny, what the hell are you doing?"

He stopped and looked over his shoulder. "What do you mean?"

"Why are you writing all that crap on your wall?"

"What crap?" Johnny turned back around. He studied the wall and its markings. There was one consistent phrase written over and over:

OBEY THE FLY OR ELSE ALL WILL DIE

He held the marker up and shrugged, tossing it on his dresser. He looked back at his girlfriend. "I didn't write that."

"You did too! I just saw you."

"You're crazy," Johnny said.

"*I'm* crazy? I'm not the one with a million candles in my bathroom. I couldn't even sit on the toilet. And *I'm* crazy? It's like a damn praying station in there."

"It is what it is," Johnny said. "Now what do you want?"

Her jaw dropped in disbelief. "What do I *want?* You haven't called or visited in almost a week! What on earth have you been doing?"

"Preparing." Johnny sat down on the bed. He began picking at the numerous sores occupying his body.

"Preparing for what?"

"War," Johnny said. "The apocalypse. The uprising. The stars. The beginning. The end. The alpha and the omega. The buzz."

She rushed over to him. "Oh my God, how much purple have you taken?"

"All! I've taken it all. I've swallowed the sky and chewed on the long grass. I have drunk the clouds! I am fucking *aware*, baby!" His legs were trembling. He rocked back and forth as if he'd just downed a thermos of coffee and snorted a mountain of cocaine.

His girlfriend sat down next to him with her face in her hands. "You're completely lost, aren't you?"

"No," he said. "I'm found."

"What's my name then? Can you even tell me that? You don't even know my name, do you?"

"Of course I know your name."

"Then what is it?"

"*Beelzebub*."

"Dear Jesus."

"Yeah, he'll be there all right." Johnny smiled. "And you'll be begging for his mercy."

"Johnny, what are you talking about?"

"Just you wait, bitch."

"Excuse me?"

"Your time will come," Johnny said. "The Fly will rise and Its people will follow. It will bring Michael and he will slice your miserable fucking throat. Don't think I don't see through your pathetic charade. *I SEE ALL!*"

"I'm leaving," his girlfriend said.

"You won't go far."

"Far enough from you." She stood up.

Johnny reached over and grabbed her arm. "Baby, it isn't me you gotta be afraid of."

She looked down at him and snorted in disgust. "Oh my God, do you have an erection?"

"It wouldn't surprise me."

"Let me go."

"Let's screw."

"You just called me the Devil."

"All women are," he said. "Let's fuck."

"You're insane."

"I know. Now get on the goddamn bed. Maybe I'll save you yet."

"Go play with your fly."

"Don't joke about the Fly," Johnny said. "Take off your clothes."

"Why don't you go fuck your fly instead?"

"You dirty blasphemous bitch! I'll kill you!"

She swung her free arm around and dug her fingernails into Johnny's face. He released his grip and fell back, blood streaming down his cheek. He howled.

His girlfriend spun on her heels and fled the bedroom, leaving Johnny on the bed in his own shame. He screamed threats but didn't get up to carry them out.

She would get hers. They would all get theirs. And he would be king of all. The Fly would make sure of that. It had promised him.

Johnny reached into his pocket and pulled out a bottle of his medicine. He inhaled a sea of purple euphoria and sighed in content. This was all he needed. Screw everyone else.

Then there was a knock at the door.

"Come in."

He heard the door opening but whoever it was didn't say anything. He opened his eyes and sat up, spotting his girlfriend standing there in the doorway, looking at him. Teary makeup stained her cheeks. He knew what she was there for and accepted her apology. Johnny even felt a little bit of pity for the poor girl. She had no idea what was coming down the road. She had no idea just how utterly doomed she was.

Johnny stood up, walked over and grabbed her hand. "It's okay," he said, and led her back to his bed. He laid her down on the mattress, reached down and kissed her. His lips touched her nose. It was so cold. He kissed her again and again. She tasted so good, he wanted to have more. He wanted to have all of her. The Fly would forgive him.

He licked her all over, groped his hands along her magnificent body. "I love you," Johnny told his girlfriend, even though he didn't know her name. She turned over and stuck her ass up in the air from him. Johnny pulled down his zipper and entered her; she whimpered in ecstasy.

After the deed was done, they lay in bed together, spooning like the poetic lovers he imagined them to be.

Then the door opened and someone came in.

"I forgot my purse. Don't you dare try to do anything or I'll—what the fuck?"

Johnny looked up over his girlfriend's sleeping naked body and saw his girlfriend standing there at his dresser, picking up a purse.

"What?" he asked.

Lip quivering, she pointed at him. "What did . . . don't tell me . . . oh my God . . . no way . . . "

"*What?*"

He looked back down at the figure in bed with him and his eyes widened. His girlfriend had been switched with something much hairier.

The family dog, Zooey Deschanel, turned around and ran her long, wet tongue across Johnny's face.

"Oh, fuck," Johnny said, gagging.

"Yarp!" Zooey Deschanel barked. Some kind of canine pillow talk.

He vomited right there in bed.

"Holy shit," his girlfriend said, backing away. "That is beyond disgusting." She brought out her cell phone and snapped a picture of the scene. "I can't wait to post this on Facebook!"

She escaped before Johnny could catch her.

Zooey Deschanel stayed in bed and licked up his puke. It was purple.

29

OUT OF BREATH, Maddox stumbled through the front door and headed straight for the kitchen. He took off his T-shirt and tossed it to the floor.

"Towels," Maddox said, opening the freezer, "lots of towels."

He pulled out a bag of frozen peas as Benny came running in with a handful of beach towels.

"Um, Mads?"

"What?"

"Is that a pad on your arm?"

Maddox ignored him and sat down at the table, drenched in sweat. He unpeeled the pad and discarded it in the trash can next to him. He pressed the bag of peas against his wound and winced. Blood poured down his arm. He made a mental note never to get shot again.

"Yeah, that's a pad all right," Benny said, checking the garbage. "I don't even want to know. Okay, maybe I do. Yeah, I'm gonna need details here."

"Shut up, Benny."

"Okay."

Maddox got up and went over to the counter. Scavenging through a drawer, he came up with a large knife. Benny stood beside him watching with sincere interest. To him, this was really exciting. Just like in a movie! Maddox wanted to take that movie and shove it right down his brother's throat.

He held the knife in his right hand, trying to work up the courage to do what needed to be done. "You got any whiskey?" he asked, eyes glued to the sinister glimmer of the blade.

"What?" Benny said. "Oh, yeah, sure, sure, of course I do. Jameson all right with you?"

"Just get it. Quick."

Benny jumped up and grabbed a half empty bottle of liquor from the top of the refrigerator. He handed it over and watched as his brother took a long gulp of it.

"Now what?" Benny asked.

Maddox grabbed one of the beach towels and stuffed it in his mouth. The last thing he could afford right now was a concerned neighbor of the trailer trash colony butting in and calling the cops all over some lousy girly screams.

Benny looked the other way as Maddox slid the tip of the blade into the jagged hole occupying his shoulder. He gasped and bit down on the towel as he dug through it. Blood oozed out, dripping down his arm and splashing against the porcelain sink.

The knife halted in action as it made contact with the bullet hiding in his flesh. Fearing that if he hesitated any longer he would never finish the job, Maddox wiggled the blade under the bullet for more leverage. His teeth sank through the fabric of the towel as he pried it out of his shoulder. His head was swimming, vision blurring. The bullet flung up in the air and landed back in the sink, clinging down the drain and into the sewers for the rats to find.

He spat the towel out of his mouth and let out a short croak: *"Whiskey!"*

Benny turned around just in time to witness a volcano of black blood erupting from Maddox's shoulder. "Whoa."

Maddox blindly reached for the Jameson on the counter and chugged half of the bottle down, then slashed some against his wound. He gestured to the knife, which had clattered into the sink, and said, "Hot—make it hot. Hold it over the stove. Hurry."

"What? No way! This is my good knife."

TOXICITY

"BENNY THIS IS NOT THE FUCKING TIME!"
The phone rang.

"Don't you dare answer that," Maddox said.

"What if it's an emergency?" Benny asked, and picked up the phone. "Hello? Oh, yeah, sure, here he is." He handed it to Maddox. "It's for you."

Thinking it was his daughter, Maddox grabbed the phone and pushed it against his ear. "Yeah?" he said, breathing heavy.

"Hello, Maddox, this is Lionel Turner, your parole officer."

"Oh, shit."

"I'm just making my daily required call. I called earlier, but nobody answered. Please make sure you don't miss my phone calls in the future."

"WHAT THE FUCK DO YOU WANT?"

"There's no need to be so hostile. Just make sure you report to work tomorrow. Eight o'clock sharp at the Booth Bacon packing factory. Be there or be . . . *in jail.*"

Maddox hung the phone up and tossed it on the counter. "Benny, are you going to heat that knife or what?"

"Yeah, yeah, I'm doing it, don't get your panties in a bunch." Benny flicked on the stove and ran the blade carefully through the blue flame until it glistened into a charcoaled black. "Why am I doing this again?"

Maddox soaked his flesh with more of the whiskey, pouring the last quarter of the bottle down his throat. It was a blissful burn. He grabbed the knife and exhaled. He pressed the burnt end of the blade against the bullet hole, which had widened considerably during his bullet scavenger hunt. A crazed yell escaped his lungs as he cauterized the wound, leaving behind a messy, raggedy scab.

Maddox dropped the knife and backed away, collapsing down at the kitchen table. He leaned his head back, eyes closed, panting, trying his best not to think. Thinking about not thinking—an agonizing paradox.

"Benny."

"Yes, Mads?" Benny was still at the counter, gaping at all the blood staining his sink.

"You got any gauze or anything?"

Maddox licked his lips, wishing he hadn't wasted those cookies. His shoulder still hurt like a sonofabitch, but he knew it would recover with time. Given the circumstances, he thought he did a pretty good job. Maddox had absorbed a lot of valuable knowledge in prison.

He glanced over at the phone on the counter. It'd been nearly twenty-four hours since he'd last spoken to his daughter. He suddenly felt a strong urge to call her. But she would probably only ask about money. How was he supposed to break it to her that he was practically a dead man? That he wouldn't be able to free her like he had promised, after all? This realization hurt a thousand times more than the hole in his shoulder. He couldn't let it happen. He didn't know how, but he would find a way out of this jam. He would *not* disappoint his daughter again.

Benny entered the kitchen carrying a roll of gauze. He caught Maddox staring at the phone. "Expecting a call?"

"Not really," Maddox said, taking the gauze and wrapping it around his arm. He felt like a mummy.

"You know," Benny said, sitting down across from his brother, "I forgot to tell you, but earlier this morning some chick called asking about you. It was like really early, though, and you were still sleeping, so I didn't think you would've wanted me to wake you up . . . "

Maddox's head shot up. "What? What did she say?"

"She asked to speak to you. I said you were sleeping and you needed to rest because you had a big important job later, so I wasn't allowed to disturb you until it was show time."

"I never once said that, Benny."

"But it was implied."

"How the hell was it implied?"

"I dunno—it just was. Anyhow, I tried telling her you'd call back but she had already hung up. Who do you suppose that was, huh? You *do* have a girl waiting for you, don't you, you sly dog you? Shit, man, why didn't you say something in the first place? I would have never had to rent that fuckin' bitch succubus if I'd known that. Just think, you'd still have your car!"

"That was my daughter, you idiot," Maddox said.

"Oh, right."

"What's today? Sunday?"

"I think so." Benny nodded. "I'm pretty sure my Starbucks suspension ends this week. Or maybe it was last week. Who knows. Why?"

Sunday meant no school, which meant that Addison would most likely be home. He thought it'd be a nice surprise to drop over unexpectedly. He didn't think he'd have the heart to break the bad news, but at least they'd be able to spend one last moment together. Maybe they could go out for coffee again. That had been nice last time. He did have about eighty bucks left from his change at McDonald's.

It might also be his last chance to murder the hell out of that bastard Del.

The little things in life, that's what kept you going.

30

CONNOR SWUNG THE Ford Fiesta into the parking lot and pulled to a stop next to a dumpster. It was filled to the brim with moldy furniture. It was always like that. Even after garbage day, not two days later and someone was dragging out an old broken chair or a loveseat some dog pissed on.

"Why'd you park way over here?" Addison was asking.

Killing the engine, Connor said, "For all we know, your parents were discovered and the police already have an APB out on you."

"A what?"

"All points bulletin." He gave her a pitiful look. "Have you never seen an episode of *COPS?*"

Addison craned her neck to the windshield and peered toward the apartment building. "No one is here."

"Exactly. Makes me suspicious. Ten bucks says there's a Green Beret or something hiding over there in that bush, waiting for you to walk past so he can inject you with a sleeping tranquilizer."

Addison snorted. "You definitely need to stop watching so much TV."

"Yeah, well, you need to, um, shut up," Connor countered.

They got out of the car and approached the building, pausing at the door. Addison tilted her head up, spying on the third-story window of her living room. The room appeared completely dark, as if some great devil had taken over as tenant. She cleared her throat, gaping at this distressing darkness, this cave that seemed to welcome her with cold hands, and she suddenly had an urge to flee back to the car.

And she would have, too, if Connor hadn't sneaked his arm around her. "You all right?"

She shook her head. "I can't go up there."

"Well, why don't you just wait out here then? I'll go in," he said. "Tell me what you need."

"You sure?"

"Of course." He kissed her on the side of the head, strands of hair sticking to his lips. "I wouldn't want to go up there, either."

But he went up there, anyway. He left Addy waiting outside, leaning against the residential mailbox with a light gust of snow whirling in the air. She noticed someone had scribbled on the metal, in sloppy block letters:

*JEROME **WAS** HERE! NO LONGER LIVES THE WHITE MAN!*

And below that, in a different colored marker, was:

BELLA FANGS EDWARD (AND SO DO I! OMG!)

God, she hated this neighborhood. For the seven or so years they'd live here, she couldn't remember it being nice at all. Nothing but crack dealers, junior KKKs, and *Twilight* fanatics. Despicable.

She stood there in the cold with her arms crossed, shivering, wishing he would hurry up. They didn't really need to come here, but he had insisted. He told her she couldn't live the rest of her life with just the clothes on her back. An Asswarts T-shirt could only get you so far.

"I'll buy more," she said.

But he said they were going to need to save all the money they could get their hands on. Anything they could salvage for free, they must. It was going to be a long, bumpy road ahead, and they needed all the breaks they could manage. According to Connor, it was a tad bit difficult to get away with murder.

How could that be considered murder? They were just

kids, for Christ's sake. In the wrong place and the wrong time. They weren't murderers.

"Yeah," Connor had chuckled on the drive over, "try telling a judge that."

Now here they were, a body count of two. Both monsters. Both deserved what they got. She thought about it and decided it was a pity the deed hadn't been committed sooner.

So where would they go? She had never even left the state before, travelled only through magazines. She remembered seeing photos of this beach somewhere in California. It'd looked beautiful. She had never seen the ocean in person before, but judging from the pictures, nothing else compared. She wanted to be on that beach, wherever it was. She wanted to kick her shoes off and feel the hot sand pounding into the soles of her feet as she ran toward the sea. She wanted to dive into the water and float with the fish, and then she would finally know what freedom was.

She could practically smell the salt from here.

Standing outside the apartment building, thinking about California, Addison smiled.

It was then she heard the footsteps gaining in on her, heavy in the snow, and a voice: "Addy? That you?"

Addison snapped out of her reverie just in time to spot a man in a black T-shirt and blue jeans walking her way. It took her a minute to recognize him without the Cubs cap and jean jacket. Either way, it was still her father.

Leave it up to her luck to have a convict as a dad. An ignorant heroin addict as a mother. An abusive molester as a stepfather. A dead baby doomed from the womb as a little sister.

Hell, this guy may have been her only living relative in the world. And she barely knew him.

"What're you doing out here, Addy? Aren't you cold?"

"What about you?" she asked. "At least I have a hoodie."

TOXICITY

He looked down at his own appearance and shrugged. "The walk kept my blood running."

"You *walked* here? Where's your car?"

Maddox studied his frosted-over boots. "Stolen. It's a long story."

There was a bulge under his shirtsleeve. It revealed a tiny snip of what could only be a large bandage. A dark brownish splotch was staining through.

"What happened to your arm? Are you hurt?"

"Nah, I'm fine. Just got shot."

"What? Who shot you?"

"My brother," Maddox said. "Like I said, it's a long story."

"I see." At least he wasn't the only living relative left. Or, on second thought: "What'd you do to him?"

"Do to who?"

"Your brother."

"Nothing," Maddox said. "Where's Del? I need to speak to him."

Addison tried to clear her throat but only ended up choking on her own air. "Why? Do you have the money?"

He shook his head. "I just have to talk to him."

"About *what?*"

"Never you mind."

Then she had an idea. "Are you going to kill him?"

"What if I am?"

"I don't think that will be necessary."

"Why not?"

Addison struggled with what to say next. She thought about telling him the situation, spilling the beans and showing him the corpses upstairs in the apartment. But what if he freaked out and called the police? How would he look at her knowing what had been done?

"Just . . . don't," she said.

She broke down in tears. Maddox stepped forward and she allowed him to hug her. It was surprisingly comforting.

"Killing him is just going to make things worse," she

said. "You'll go to jail. I'll be sent to a home. I can't do this. I just can't do this. Please. Just, just get the money, okay? I don't want anyone else dead. I can't handle this anymore. I just want out. I want to be free."

Maddox gently patted her on the back. "I will, sweetheart," he said. "I promise you I am going to make everything okay. I'm on my way now to this man who might be able to help us. It'll be all right, Addison."

She returned the hug, squeezing him for dear life. For a moment, it felt like he had never gone to prison, that he had always been there for her.

"I should probably be leaving now," Maddox was saying, drawing away. "I'm sure he's expecting me."

She nodded. "Thank you."

"I'll be back, sweetheart. I love you."

31

PEOPLE WERE GETTING smarter with their cars. There were just way too many goddamn alarms on these things. Maddox tried almost the entirety of the Wal-Mart parking lot before giving up. He started walking down the street and, to his amazement, spotted a cab passing by. He hailed it down and gave the cabbie his desired location and off they went.

He stepped inside the Sting knowing there was a good chance he'd never leave it again.

Sorry, Addy, he thought, as the desk clerk led him downstairs to King's lair.

The boss himself was already sitting at his desk waiting for him. It only took a second to see that Maddox's hands were empty. No Jericho, no money, no anything. Just a soul for the killing.

Vincent King sighed. "You screwed up, didn't you?"

Maddox nodded. "Kind of."

* * *

Benny heard a rumbling and ventured out on his porch just in time to see the giant yellow Hummer pulling to a stop in front of his trailer.

And to his astonishment, his older brother was stepping out of the passenger seat, alive.

Zombie? Benny wondered hopefully, but decided against it.

"Mads?" He watched as his brother and a muscular

man walked toward him. He didn't know this guy, whoever he was. He wore a white tank-top, tinted sunglasses, a black fedora, and gray dress pants.

"Who's this?" Benny asked. They pushed past him through the door and headed straight for the kitchen. "Well, all right," he said, following them inside. They were already at the fridge, drinking all his beer. People were always drinking his beer. And they weren't even ghosts!

Unless . . .

"Mads, tell me the truth." Benny sat down at the table. "Are you a zombie?"

"Benny, shut up."

"Okay."

Maddox grabbed two more beers and joined him at the table. The man remained standing by the fridge, ready to tear both their heads off at a moment's notice. Benny now understood how his brother had felt when he introduced him to that deceiving bitch of a lot lizard.

"So . . . what's going on?" he asked, breaking the irritating silence. He hated not being filled in on a situation. It made him feel like a child.

Maddox took another swig of booze. "Well, he gave me twenty-four hours to come up with the money . . . or else."

"Whoa," Benny said, "that was nice of him."

"It's a million dollars, Benny."

"Oh."

"Twenty-four hours, that's all we have. If I don't have the money by then, I die." He gestured over to the fridge. "You see that guy there? His name is Winston. He's King's personal bodyguard. He's going to be babysitting us until this time tomorrow. If we're still a mil short, he's the one that gets to kill us. Isn't that right, Winston?"

Winston nodded.

"I think he might be a mute," Maddox said. "Guy hasn't said a single word the whole drive over here. I don't know what's with him."

"He scares me," Benny said.

"Me too."

"How are you gonna come up with the money?"

"Well, I figured we'd go out and rob ourselves a couple of banks."

"*We?*"

"Yeah, Benny, 'we'." Maddox finished off his beer. "Don't you remember that little talk you gave me before? This is a 'we' situation, correct? Then *we* are going to go rob some banks. And we're not going to stop until we have a million dollars, understand?"

"Dude, it's Sunday," Benny said.

"So?"

"So, the banks are closed."

"Oh," Maddox said. "Well, shit."

And just like that, their plan was ruined.

They were stumped. Doomed. Well, at least Maddox was. Benny didn't see any reason why Mr. King would kill him, as well. He was innocent. He just wanted fries, for Christ's sake!

Then Benny had an idea. And it was actually a good one.

"What about one of those currency exchange places?" he asked. "Maybe not as much money as a bank, but I'm sure it's still a lot, right?"

Maddox raised his eyebrow. "Whatever you're doing differently," he said, "Keep doing it."

32

JOHNNY SAT IN his chair, staring at the computer screen in disbelief.

He had to hand it to her—the bitch was fast. He guessed that came with the territory of being the Lord of Darkness.

On the screen of his monitor, there was a photo of himself, in bed. Zooey Deschanel was next to him.

There was a blurred spot at his crotch where his dick was hanging out from his zipper.

A talented observer would have spotted the dark wet stain between them on the bed sheet.

His name had been tagged in the pic. A notification was sent to him via Facebook. There was already a mountain of comments below it. None of them were pretty. All of them had claimed to be his friend at one time or another, yet he didn't really know any of them, did he? Hell, he didn't even recognize their names. Their avatars were distorted. He couldn't make out anything.

Who were these people, these betrayers, these demons?

And why were they buying into this devil's blasphemy?

He moved his cursor to the comment box and typed:

FAKE! PHOTOSHOPPED! NO ONE BELIEVE THIS BITCH'S LIES! NICE TRY YOU STUPID EVIL WHORE! YOUR TIME IS NEAR!

Content, he clicked on COMMENT and watched as his protest became public.

Not sure what to do next, he ventured over to his own

profile. He was a bit taken back at first to discover his wall was the same message written over and over. All of them by the same person. The same Messiah.

The profile's name was The_Fly.

His wall read:

OBEY THE FLY OR ALL WILL DIE
OBEY THE FLY OR ALL WILL DIE
OBEY THE FLY OR ALL WILL DIE

Johnny clicked on "Like" and a thumbs up icon appeared above The_Fly's post. That was a good message. More people should have taken it to heart.

He clicked back to his girlfriend's profile one last time to check out the photo. Someone else had already commented after him. It said:

JOHNNY U R PATHETIC

And the comment after that:

UR NUTHIN BUT AN ANIMAL Y DON'T U GO BACK 2 TEH ZOO WERE U BELONG!?!!!?????

He was pathetic? These monsters, these wasters of life, they had no idea what life was. They didn't know what was going to happen. They weren't the ones chosen by the Messiah. These useless drained souls, they had no idea just how pathetic they actually were.

He typed into the comment box:

YOU ARE ALL FUCKED

Not even a minute passed before someone else replied:

NO I THINK U R MISTAKING US 4 UR DOG!!! LMFAO!!!

Johnny screamed and drove his fist through the computer screen. A burst of sparks shot out, his knuckles starting to bleed.

He looked at his hand and trembled at the thin streams of toxic purple mixed within his blood. He stuck his tongue out and licked it.

The taste was incredible.

Johnny paused and glanced at his reflection in the broken monitor. He frowned, wondering if maybe those "people" were right. Maybe he really was just some animal. But then again, wasn't everyone else?

He didn't want to be like everyone else, though. He was different. He was the Chosen One.

He was Johnny Desperation, leader of the Fly's holy army.

Zooey Deschanel whimpered in the background and Johnny slumped his head down. What had he done? It was horrible. He felt like the biggest piece of shit in the world. God, he was disgusting.

Where was the Fly when he needed It the most?

"Where are you?" Johnny shouted. "Show yourself!"

He ran into the bathroom and put his head down into the toilet. "Show yourself dammit!" he screamed. "I need you."

But the Fly never appeared. He didn't know where It was, but apparently It wasn't constantly looking over his shoulder like he had once believed. Maybe, hopefully, It was merely off preparing for war—instead of the alternative.

Instead of not existing.

"What in the hell?" said a voice from the bathroom door.

Frightened, Johnny jumped back, staring at a large melting swamp monster. He believed it used to be his older brother, James.

"What do you want?" Johnny backed up against the tub. This was *his* private bathroom, so what was this foul creature doing rotting in it?

"Why the hell are there so many candles in here?" James asked. "Is this some kind of, um, ritual jerkoff ceremony?"

His black, empty eyes spotted Johnny's hand, the one he had punched the computer screen with.

"Don't tell me you're using blood as lube now, too."

Blushing, Johnny hid his hand behind his back. "*Why are you here, demon?*"

James offered a gargled, hideous chuckle. "You're

tripping balls, aren't you? That's too cute," he said. "Nah, I just wanted to say I saw that pic on Facebook. Man, that was my dog too, you fucking animal. You should be ashamed of yourself. I'm telling Mom."

And with that, the swamp monster slithered away.

Animal?

Animal?

ANIMAL?

Johnny screamed, his voice reverberating against his own skull, and he leaped to his feet. He opened the medicine cabinet and grabbed an emergency bottle of Jericho he kept stored there. A minute later the can was empty. It dropped to the floor, bouncing one, two, three times against cracked linoleum.

Everyone thought he was an animal. Even he was starting to believe it. Animal, huh? Then what was he doing here, in this house of evil? He belonged with his own kind— with the other animals. These "people" could just go to hell.

And they would, once this was all over with.

They would burn.

Then he heard a voice. It was one in his head, but it wasn't his own. It was his Savior.

"Release the army. Free them all."

* * *

Caught in a wild sprint, Johnny approached the Loathsome Public Zoo at a frantic pace. He knew it was closed for the winter so he didn't waste any time and started climbing the stone wall. Nothing was going to get in his way.

Feet crushing soft snow, he was starting to wish he had bothered to put on a pair of shoes before leaving. But then again, what animal actually wore shoes?

And for that matter, what animal wore any type of clothing at all?

Besides humans.

Which he no longer was, and would never be again.

Johnny let out a growl and ripped the clothes off his body. Looking down, he blushed. It *was* extremely cold out here.

Thank God no one's here, he thought, and bolted like a bullet for the first building in sight.

He kicked in the door and barged inside, foot swelling from the impact. He knew where he was. This was the answer to the age-old question "Where do the zoo animals go during the winter?"—they kept them locked up at an interior habitat. A couple zookeepers would visit every day and feed them, but still, it must have been hell never being able to go outside.

Never being free.

"I have arrived!" Johnny yelled, and was answered by his own echo.

He ran through the building unlocking all the cages. It was crazy, how they all just piled out like that, as if they'd been waiting for his arrival this whole time. Awaiting their savior. They all knew where to go. Johnny watched them head out the door.

The purple had him accelerating like a madman. Building to building, he bounced from lock to lock, tearing them all open with his bare, bloody hands. One cage to the other, until every last one was opened.

He was going to free the whole damn zoo.

Such were the commands of the almighty Fly.

Obey or die, obey or die, obey or die . . .

And afterwards he would break down the gate separating the animals from the humans. He wondered if anyone would be able to tell a difference.

Who would be more civilized?

Gloating, he thought about how proud the Fly must have been of him, and moved on to the next building. This one was full of goats. Lots of 'em.

One by one, Johnny Desperation saved them all.

33

MADDOX TOLD WINSTON to pull into the Walgreens coming up.

"What're we doing here?" Benny asked from the backseat.

Maddox pulled out a twenty and handed it to him. He told him to go pick up two ski masks. "And a pack of cupcakes," he added.

"What? Why?"

"Because I'm hungry."

"No, I mean the masks."

"Are you really that stupid?"

There was a pause.

"Oh-kay," Benny said. "I'll be right back then."

After Benny left, Maddox tried to strike up conversation with the bodyguard but the man refused to respond. Instead, Winston reached over and flipped on the radio.

Several minutes later, Benny returned, and once again the Hummer took off, heading to a currency exchange building called Loathsome Cash.

After finishing his cupcake, Maddox told his brother to give him one of the masks. Benny handed it over and Maddox gave it a double take. He held it up with his thumb and index finger, curiously.

"Benny, why is this mask pink?"

"What does it matter? What, are you homophobic or something?"

Maddox cleared his throat. "Well, Benny, it is generally considered common criminal knowledge that you wear a black ski mask. Who the hell wears a *pink* one?"

"They were on sale."

"Jesus Christ. Just give me your gun."

"What gun?"

"Your Beretta."

"Oh," Benny said. "I don't have that, anymore."

"What are you talking about?"

"It was in your car."

"Goddammit, Benny."

"I'm sorry!"

Maddox looked over at Winston. "You wouldn't happen to have any weapons on you?"

Winston did what he always seemed to do and nodded. Then he hit the trunk release button and refused to do anything else.

What a stubborn little mute, Maddox was thinking, stepping out of the Hummer. His brother followed him to the back and they lifted up the trunk, revealing an arsenal of weapons.

"God bless America," Benny said. "Is that a rocket launcher?"

"That," Maddox said, "that sure is a rocket launcher."

"Can we use it?"

"Don't be an idiot."

"Okay."

Maddox scooped up two Uzis and handed one to his brother. Both guns were already loaded. This guy Winston, whoever he was, was prepared for a major battle. A battle with *who* was unknown.

"You ready?" Maddox asked.

"Hells to the motherfuckin' yeah!" Benny said.

"Ugh. Okay. Let's go." Maddox pulled the pink ski mask down his face.

They marched across the street and entered Loathsome Cash. There were maybe two or three customers inside, and neither one of them seemed to notice Maddox and Benny's presence.

Maddox pushed them out of the way and stepped in front of the line. Pointing the Uzi ahead at the cashier, he said, "I want all the money you people have. Now."

And she laughed, looking at their masks, saying, "Are you guys serious?"

* * *

The Kane brothers fled from Loathsome Cash like two bats out of hell, a stream of bullets brushing inches from their flesh. Both now unarmed, they maneuvered recklessly around traffic like a bad game of *Frogger*, making their way across the street and leaping into the Hummer.

Wheezing, sweat pouring down his temple, Maddox whipped the pink ski mask off his face and threw it out the window. He glanced at the driver's seat only to realize Winston was asleep.

The getaway driver was taking a nap.

"GO!" Maddox shouted, snapping him awake. *"DRIVE! NOW!"*

Winston gave him a dirty look and took off. Police sirens droned on in the distance, gaining more and more territory with each passing second.

Maddox turned to the backseat and slapped his brother across the cheek.

"Ow!" Benny rubbed his cheek. "What was that for?"

"What do you think? How the hell could you screw that up?"

"Oh, come off it! That wasn't my fault and you know it. That dude came out of nowhere. Did *you* see him?"

"Benny, he was in a wheelchair."

"Yeah, well, he rolled fast, okay?"

"I can't believe you let him take your gun." Maddox buried his face in his hands.

"He took yours, too!"

"Yeah, he did, you're right," Maddox said. "He took it because he was pointing *your* gun in *my* face, you moron."

Benny pounded his hand on the leather seat. "I am *not* a moron!"

"Are too."

"Am not!"

"Are too."

"Am not!"

"Are—*WATCH OUT!*"

There was no time to react.

The goat sprung out from a bush on the side of the road and stopped in the middle of the pavement, frozen, eyes widening at the approaching vehicle. Maddox managed to catch a single glimpse of it before it smashed into the front end of the Hummer. The initial impact sent the animal in the air, flying at least a good ten feet, before landing on the road again and rolling to a gruesome stop.

Winston slammed down on the brakes and they came to a halt, everyone inside the Hummer staring dumbfounded at the sight before them.

Maddox's heart was skipping a thousand beats a second. He couldn't take his eyes off it. Of all the things . . .

It made sense. In a strange, screwed up way it made all the sense in the world.

Finally, Winston said, "Is that a fucking goat?"

"Did you just talk?" Benny said.

"No," Winston said.

"Oh."

Maddox stared at the animal bleeding out there on the road, shivering its last few dying breaths away. This goat, it was a sign. It was an omen. Something had to be done.

"A goat," Maddox whispered, amazed. "Cursed. I'm cursed. That's all there is to it."

"What are you talking about?" Benny asked.

"It's . . . a . . . *GOAT!*" Maddox shouted, and shot his elbow out into Winston's jaw, driving his face against the window. He didn't waste any time grabbing a hold of the bodyguard's fedora and smashing the man's face against the steering wheel with blunt force.

"For Christ's sake, Mads," Benny cried out, "what the hell are you doing?"

Maddox pounded Winston's bloody face into the wheel a few more times before reaching over and opening the driver's door. Sucking in a breath, he kicked him out of the car and sent him flying out onto the road with the goat. He closed the door and slammed his foot down on the pedal. There was a strong series of bumps underneath as he ran over Winston's legs and then the goat.

There was no backing down now.

* * *

"Hey, what's wrong with you? Why'd you go all psycho on Winston?"

Maddox finished off the very last beer in the fridge. "Because there's no way in all of blue hell we were gonna come up with a million dollars by tomorrow. So, it was either him or us. I took my pick. Also, you need more beer."

"Yeah, no thanks to you."

The trailer was filled with a sudden ringing.

Benny screamed. *"What's that?"*

"That's your phone, you moron."

"I am not a—"

"Why don't you just answer it, huh?"

Benny picked up the phone. "Hello?" he said, and waited. Then: "I'm sorry, who is this again? You work for King? Huh? Yeah, well, you can just tell him that we already took care of his pansy ass bodyguard and will do the same for any other piece of crap he throws our way, *capisce?* You'll get your money in hell!"

Benny punched the END button on the phone and tossed it in the sink.

"Who was that on the phone?" Maddox asked.

"I don't know. Some girl asking for you. I think she was one of King's henchmen."

Maddox rubbed his temple. "Or was it my daughter?"

"Highly possible."

"Why do you have to ruin everything?"

"Why do you have to drink all my beer?" he countered, and sat down at the couch, flipping on the television.

Maddox hurried to the kitchen and scavenged the phone out of the sink. The torn phonebook page was no longer of use; he already had the number memorized.

But it just rang and rang and rang until the line finally went dead.

After a while he gave up and surrendered to the living room with his brother, wishing he had more booze. "What're you watching?"

"*Good God, that's Odd,*" Benny said.

"The hell is that?"

"This show that interviews these people with weird-ass collections, I guess. I don't know—it's new."

"Sounds like a waste of time."

"Shh, it's starting!"

Maddox leaned back in the recliner and tried to relax.

Catchy annoying theme music spat out from the speakers and a banner ran across the TV in big bold letters, declaring the show's title. A man with slick hair combed straight back appeared onscreen, wearing a cheap suit and holding a microphone up to a pseudo-grin.

"Good evening, America," the man spoke. "I would like to welcome you to a brand-new program presented for your viewing pleasure. Allow me to proudly introduce you to *Good God, that's Odd!*, the newest family member of the acclaimed LOL Network. I am your host, Jimmy Beam. For our first episode of thirty golden minutes, we will be featuring three separate individuals who collect some truly *wacky stuff!* Whether it be creepy dolls, fungus, or social security numbers, we are *guaranteed* to entertain! So sit back, relax, and prepared to be amazed at the *wacky stuff* your fellow Americans are into. But first, a word from our sponsors!"

"Man, I hate commercials," Benny said.

"I wish there was more beer," Maddox said.

"I thought you quit drinking."

"Mind your own business," Maddox said, and drifted off into his own little world, which was cut short when the show returned from the commercials.

Rather than showing off the host's Hollywood gleam, the screen now showed the flabby face of a woman standing in front of one of the biggest houses Maddox had ever seen. When she spoke, the nicotine stains on her teeth were clearly visible.

"My name is Ruth Desperation," the woman announced, "and I am the sixty-million-dollar winner of the Illinois State Lottery." She waved her hand back behind her. "This is my home."

The camera shot past the woman and zoomed into the mansion, leaking through the closed door and finding its way inside the living room, showing off an interior just as ridiculous as the exterior.

Benny pointed his finger enthusiastically at the TV. "Holy crap, I know that place! I remember reading all about these people in the newspaper like, what, a year ago? I'm not even sure. Who the hell is named Desperation, anyway? Lucky sons of bitches."

Leaning forward in the recliner, Maddox told his brother to be quiet.

The host, Jimmy Beam, was narrating as the camera panned over each room in the mansion, showing off a giant 72-inch Sony, leather furniture, a basement dedicated only to video games, and a fountain of chocolate located in the center of the kitchen.

"Gaining popularity for hitting the jackpot with the simplest simpleton's set of digits—one, two, three, four, five, and six—Ruth Desperation did not waste any time at all in rewarding herself with the greatest of life's pleasures.

But what most people are not aware of is the extensive collection of dolls she acquired once coming into this seemingly bottomless barrel of good fortune. Until today. Now, please, let me proudly introduce you to the rest of the Desperation family that very few have had the pleasure to meet."

A sudden montage of doll faces emerged on the screen, flashing endlessly. With each image the woman, Ruth, declared their name. One had to wonder where she came up with all of these names, nonetheless how she kept track of them all.

Michelle. Jason. Amie. David. Bill. Ted. Russell. Phil. Cody. Stephen. Tyler. Jessie. Amanda. Christian. Jake. Nathan. Polly. Pollyanna. Anna. Howard. Anthony. Samantha. Chloe. Logan. Xander. Melinda. Dylan. Echo. Max. Lori. Todd. Etcetera.

No, really, one of the doll's names was "Etcetera".

The montage concluded in the back yard of the mansion, where at least five hundred of the dolls were propped up on chairs. They were all pointed toward a small plastic altar. Standing at this altar were three more dolls— one a groom, one a bride, and one a minister.

"That there getting married are my very own Adam and Eve," Ruth Desperation explained. "I know, it's kind of weird, but I'm a sucker for romance."

An audible interview commenced as the camera slowly rolled up and down the aisle. It made a very foolish scene look quite dramatic. Maddox had to give the cameraman props.

"Do you have any particular dreams pertaining to your dolls?" Jimmy Beam asked.

"Yeah, I guess it would be nice to populate an entire island. Like Arkansas or something."

"Do you happen to have a favorite out of all of them?"

"As hard as it is for a mother to favor her children," Ruth said, "I do have to admit that I am quite partial to my Aunt Jemima. She is just so *delicious*."

TOXICITY

The interview cut out and Jimmy returned to another solo voiceover: "Ruth then decided to abruptly end our conversation for another refill at her chocolate fountain, but fortunately I did manage to uncover a bit more information afterwards from various family members."

The next shots were of a camera appearing in front of the following individuals:

(Each asked the same question: *What do you think of Ruth Desperation?*)

A man with a gray beard and a pipe in his mouth, wearing a *World of Warcraft* blazer: "Well, I'm married to her." He then proceeded to relight his pipe and walk away without saying another word.

A twenty-something-year-old guy with rolls of fat hanging out from under his tank-top: "I think she loves them damn dolls more than she does her kids. Hell, she even gives them an allowance."

A blond-haired boy wearing swimming trunks plopped down on a lounge chair in the front yard: "My opinion? She's *[BEEP]*-ing crazy."

A girl in a bikini resting on a lounge chair next to the boy: "Who's Ruth?"

And, finally, a dog: "Yarp?"

34

RETURNING TO THE kitchen, feeling a mixture of confusion and disappointment, Addison sat down on the sofa next to Connor, basking in the warmth of his arm wrapping around her shoulders. Whenever she was in the dumps, she could nearly always count on his touch to comfort her back into a semi-sane state.

"No answer?" Connor asked.

"Someone answered all right," Addison said. "Dunno who it was, though. Some crazy guy. He told me I would get my money in hell. I don't think we are going to be hearing back from them."

"Okay. What should we do, then?"

"I don't know." Addison snuggled closer to him. "Just hold me for a while, 'kay?"

He squeezed her tighter. "Always."

"You mean it?"

He kissed her on the top of the head and they fell silent, drifting off into their own thoughts while their pupils kept themselves occupied with the *Harry Potter* movie on television.

Connor yawned. "What do you think of 'Quit, Bitch, Welcome to Quidditch' as a song name? It might have potential, huh?"

Addison erupted into giggles, rudely interrupting her state of sorrow. "You're such a nutnerd."

"Did you just call me a nutnerd?"

"Yeah, I sure did."

"That's just weird, Addy."

TOXICITY

The front door burst open and Candy Blossom stomped into the living room, tears drying on her cheeks, a bag of fast food crushed in her grasp. "Oh *hell* no! That bastard is gonna die!"

"Jesus, what's wrong?" Connor asked. "What's that in the bag? Did you bring food?"

"Who's going to die?" Addison said.

"My prick of an ex," Candy said, reaching in the bag and pulling out a large double bacon cheeseburger.

"Hey, where's mine?" Connor said.

"I need this to calm down." Candy paced back and forth in the living room, taking giant bites of the burger, carelessly flinging globs of mustard and ketchup all over the carpet.

"Are you talking about Johnny?" Addison asked. "What's wrong? What'd he do now?"

Candy snorted. "I take it you guys weren't watching TV. Because I was, and guess who I saw? Yeah, him and his whole fucking family. Including that skank of his. She was sitting right there next to him in a goddamn bikini, just flaunting off her two pathetic silicone injections."

"You're talking about boobs, right?" Connor asked, probably already picturing them in his head. Addison kicked his shin.

Ignoring his comment, Candy went on, finishing up her burger: "Where does he even get the nerve? It pisses me off so bad. It just, I don't know. He turned into such a fucking jerk."

"I'm sorry, Candy," Addison said. "It isn't fair."

"Yeah, we both agree, that kid became a major dickhead," Connor said. "Just forget about him. He wanted to drop us so badly, he was never really our friend in the first place, then."

Candy stood for a moment in the center of the living room, sucking a splotch of mayo off her finger. She seemed to be contemplating Connor's suggestion. Then she nodded and said, "Okay, sure, I'll forget about him all right. Right after we go and TP that fucker's house."

"Can't we do that some other time?" Addison asked.

Candy frowned. "Well, I suppose." She quietly retreated to a rocking chair.

Connor cleared his throat. "Addy doesn't think her dad is gonna help us anymore, so it looks like we're on our own. We don't know what else to do, though. Any ideas?"

Candy just sat there in her own gloom, all previous energy wiped out. Lips barely moving, she said if they were eighteen they could donate a lot of blood. They could donate semen, donate eggs, donate whatever else people paid to be donated. She suggested going door-to-door selling cookies and candies. If any of them were computer-smart they could start up their own pornographic website and charge outrageous prices for memberships. She even offered to star in some of the videos if it would help them out more. She said they could list her under the bacon fetish category.

And then again, they could always just steal the money. Hell, Candy worked at a gas station. Why not just rob the place? Or anywhere, for that matter? It didn't seem so hard. They could take out the gas station, a pawnshop, anything. They could even rob Johnny and his pisspoor family of all their lottery winnings. They could take away everything that had turned him into such a piece of shit.

Watching Candy spitball ideas, they saw that thin smile returning to her face, that smile they had become accustomed to over their years of friendship. It meant she had an idea, an idea that most likely wouldn't end well. It was her evil scientist look.

"That's it," she said.

"What?"

"You guys need money," Candy Blossom said, "and I need revenge. Why not take care of both at the same time?"

Connor snorted. "You want to rob Johnny?"

"Yeah—why not? Don't tell me that asshole doesn't deserve it."

"I agree, he *does*, but still . . ."

Candy slammed her palm against the armrest, angry tears searing her eyelashes. "But *nothing!* Who was it that was acting all big and bad last year, huh? I seem to remember hearing something about someone paying the consequences of someone's certain actions. Don't you?"

"Well, we lit a bag of my poo on fire at his front door," Connor said.

Addison spun her head to the side, disgusted. "I thought you said that was from a dog."

He shrugged. "You try finding a dog at three in the morning."

Candy said, "As nasty as that may be, we all know that will never be enough to satisfy our much-desired and justified vengeance. We *need* to do this. C'mon, what's the worst that could happen?"

There was a moment of silence as the three teenagers pondered the situation.

"Okay, say we did decide to do this," Connor said, "we're gonna need to come up with a plan. It can't be too complicated, because well, let's face it, we'd screw that up. We're gonna actually have to give this some thought."

"Actually, I figured we'd just show up there with a gun and tell him to hand over the cash or we'll blow a hole in his dirty, betraying face."

Her deadpan expression and frighteningly serious tone made it impossible to judge whether she would actually do this or not. They both thought she had it in her, though they really did not want to be the ones to push her to such limits.

"But we don't have a gun," Connor said. "What are we gonna do, bring along a butter knife?"

"Yeah, but how hard do you think it is for someone to get a gun? I mean, this is the twenty-first century, after all."

"But none of us are exactly connected with the whole

thug scene, now are we?" Connor said. "It's not like we can just walk into a 7-Eleven and come out with a cherry slurpee and a TEC-9. Besides, it still doesn't change the fact that we don't have the money to buy one in the first place."

"I know someone," Addison said.

* * *

It was starting to get late, so they called it a night.

"Tomorrow is going to be one of the most important days of our lives," Connor said. "We're going to need all the sleep we can manage."

Hopefully the last day of this life, Addison was thinking, *and the beginning of a new one*.

"Agreed," Candy said. "I am exhausted. Mind if I just crash here on the sofa tonight?"

"Knock yourself out," Connor said. "My dad might freak out in the morning when he comes home from work and finds you, though. Just a fair heads up."

"Thanks." She snatched the remote from the table and started flipping aimlessly through the channels.

Heading down the hallway, Connor took a detour into the bathroom, letting Addison go to the bedroom alone. She crawled into bed. The room was dark and cold, although the quilt she wrapped herself up in helped matters.

Head resting against the pillow, Addison wondered if she was really capable of following through with tomorrow. Could she actually hold up a gun and force someone to give them their money? It seemed like such a pathetic and desperate act—but then again, this was kind of a pathetic and desperate situation, now wasn't it?

When she thought about all the shit she had gone through the past couple days, she felt like she could take on the entire world. Not even just the last two days, either, but her entire life had been a constant battle. Tomorrow would only be the escape she'd been dreaming of since she was a little girl.

TOXICITY

She had fought Del. She had fought the monster in the woods. She had fought Loathsome. And when she woke up, she would fight whatever new obstacle stood in her way.

Tomorrow, she would win the life she deserved.

DAY FOUR:

IMAGO

35

HOVERING ABOVE THE toilet, looking at his own shameful reflection in the bowl, Johnny waited for the Fly's next order. He had been standing there for several hours now, and so far absolutely nothing had happened.

The zoo had been infiltrated. The prisoners had been set free. The city was a wreck with wild animals roaming the streets. So why wasn't the Fly out here praising him for his good work? Why wasn't he being rewarded for following his directions? Why was he looking at a goddamn toilet?

"Where are you?" he said out loud, his own voice startling him. He felt so tired, yet knew sleep would be impossible right now. Overgrown dirty fingernails dug into his palms. Eyelids clamped shut to block away frustrated tears.

"SHOW YOURSELF!" he screamed at the empty room.

But It did not show Itself.

He sighed. Maybe the time just wasn't right; maybe the Fly was busy and would appear as soon as It got the chance. It was, after all, almost Judgment Day. He could feel the anticipation in the air. All around him, the smell was much more complex than he was used to. His nostrils did not lie; they detected the End.

And, according to the Fly, the Beginning.

It was going to be oh-so wonderful. He couldn't wait. When the time came, he wanted to be resting on top of the biggest hill, spying down at the world as it burned, people so small they'd look like little pitiful ants, screaming and running away as fast as they could. And then, once the Fly's justice finally struck their cowardly souls, they would crumble to nothing but a pile of hellacious ashes.

Johnny grinned. Why couldn't it happen *now?* He was sick of waiting. What else could there possibly be left to fulfill? What other trials were there to complete?

He turned away from the toilet, intending on checking Facebook again, when he caught his reflection in the mirror. He froze, horrified at what he saw.

His skin was red, as if he had been swallowed whole by an infectious rash. His cheeks were scarred with deep gashes from long nights of digging his fingers into them, scratching away at unceasing irritations. His body was covered in them, all over—those bumps, those sores, like mini volcanoes erupting seas of pus and blood. It came to no surprise that the blood held a strange purple glow to it. Hell, by now his whole aura was probably purple. He bled what he breathed, breathed what he bled.

Standing in front of the mirror, gaping at a decaying version of himself, he thought, *Is this really me?*

There was one hell of a throbbing bastard pulsating on his left cheek. Just the sight of it alone was enough to make Johnny gag. He hadn't even felt it until he noticed it in the mirror, but now that he was aware of its existence, the itching was unbearable. Tremors of anxiety scalded the interior of his mind, cooking the exterior until it was nothing but a black charcoaled mess of ruined brains. Arm shaking, his fingers climbed up his chin, over his mouth, stopping at this swelling located in the center of his cheek.

All it took was one simple touch to send his senses into overdrive, a white burning light of pain searing his nerves to obliteration. Teeth sunk into his fleshly muscle of a tongue. Blood soaked into his gums. Johnny couldn't resist the incredibly powerful temptation that baited him.

He plunged his fingers into the sore, breaking through the surface, digging deep into his cheek. But even that didn't stop him, but rather increased the level of irritation. In a back and forth motion his disintegrating nails slashed through the gash like a set of vicious windshield wipers, burying themselves further into his skull, blood and pus dripping down his hand, flinging against the mirror. The smell was horrendous, like a removed tumor or popped boil, but it kept him alert. It kept him trained on his mission, and that was to satisfy this evil burden of an itch. At that moment, it was the only thing that seemed remotely important anymore. Everything else could wait.

He dug until there was nowhere else to dig. The tips of his fingernails scraped against something smooth and hard, almost like bone. Who was he kidding? It *was* bone. He had dug all the way through his flesh to the cheekbone. He had hit the bottom and yet it still wasn't good enough.

Fuck it, he thought, and began grinding his fingers against the bone, his nails tearing away as well as the skin. It was as if his face had turned into a blender and he was gladly offering his flesh up for the slaughtering. The pain was tremendous but he didn't care; the itching outweighed any other sensation one could ever feel.

And it was only growing stronger by each scratch.

Screaming through bubbles of blood, he felt his cheek giving away, a gruesome flab of skin freefalling to the sink, going *SPLAT!* against the already crimson porcelain. Now he could actually *see* the white space of bone visible where his cheek once dwelled. The smell was becoming too much to handle and he let loose a lumpy discharge of violet-colored vomit. The glob exploded in front of him onto the mirror, erasing his reflection.

He gasped, drawing his hand back, staring wildly at the mirror. Did it only take a puddle of puke to erase yourself from existence? He fled to his bedroom. Using the only hand he possessed that wasn't deformed, he reached in his drawer and pulled out a can of medicine. He raised it to his mouth and sprayed, not letting go of that nozzle for the whole world. He felt the purple spraying through the gash in his face, smearing against his cheekbone. A warm trickle of urine dripped to the carpet, leaking down his bare leg, and he thought, *When the hell did I get naked?*

Where am I?

Why am I?

And where are YOU?

"I am here."

Johnny spun around, the can of Jericho falling from his grasp and clattering to the bloodied hardwood floor. *"Where?"*

"HERE!"

Johnny's eyes rolled back against his skull. His legs turned to flimsy rubber and he collapsed, smacking his head on the floor.

When he opened his eyes again, he was not in his own body—or *any* body, for that matter. The Fly had led him into some type of wicked astral projection. His spirit floated among the clouds, or at least he thought they were clouds. More like a cloudy mist; not in a sky but rather a sea, he realized. A sea covered with an intricate fog.

Where had he been taken?

And then, just like that, he knew.

This was what would happen to the world. After everyone was dead and washed away on the shore of Hades, this would be the remains.

And unless he wanted to be left stranded out here in this vast emptiness, he had better sure as hell get himself back in gear and prepare for the last of his orders. There would be no more embarrassing scenes in front of mirrors. No more mistakes or he would quickly find himself erased for the rest of eternity.

He was just a pawn. He needed to shut his mouth and follow directions and that was all. Then after everything was done, after the war was over, he would receive his rewards.

The ocean's chromatic water seeped through his ears that weren't there, through every orifice that wasn't there, whispering apocalyptic secrets and lunatic enigmas, and he knew, he knew this was knowledge to hold close to his heart that wasn't there, either.

He realized that this entire sea, the whole damn thing, it was only one entity. One deity. The most powerful one of them all. And seconds before regaining consciousness, Johnny came to a confounding epiphany that what he was swimming in was *the Fly*.

But at the same time, the Fly was swimming inside Johnny.

Whatever the fuck that was supposed to mean.

36

"BENNY, WAKE UP."

Maddox lightly slapped his brother across the cheek, sending him into a delirious stirring fit on the couch. He opened his eyes mumbling, "What? What's going on? What do you want? What time is it?"

"You know that show we were watching earlier?" Maddox asked, towering over him. "You know, with the dolls?"

Benny yawned. "Yeah, what about it?"

"You told me you knew who they were, right?"

"What—the Desperations?" Benny said, sitting up and stretching. "I don't *know* them, like not personally or anything. They were just in the news a while back. Why?"

"That mansion they showed—the place where that woman won the lottery—is it nearby?"

Picking away eye snot, Benny said, "Yeah, man, it's up there at that Libertyville place. People like to drive by and take pictures of it. Me and a buddy went up there a couple months back just to see what the big deal was. It's not worth it. Just some house, a lot bigger than most, but still just some house."

"So you could take me there?"

"I . . . I guess." Benny nodded. "Hey, what's all this about?"

"We can't stay here much longer," Maddox said. "Someone is going to find Winston and he is going to call King, and when he does, all hell is gonna break loose. The first place they'll check is this trailer."

"What are you saying?"

"I'm saying we need to be gone by morning."

Maddox started walking away and Benny jolted to his feet, at last realizing the situation. "What, you mean *abandon* my trailer?"

"Yes, Benny, that is exactly what I mean."

"No way, man! I still haven't even paid this baby off yet."

"That's because you're being scammed."

"I think I would know if I was being scammed, Mads."

"Sure you would." Maddox gestured back to the couch. "Why don't you go back to sleep and we'll talk more about this in the morning? We'll need to get up early and leave as soon as possible. We should actually leave tonight but I just can't think of anywhere else to go right now."

"But where are we gonna go in the morning?"

"Well," Maddox said, "you're gonna take me to that mansion we were talking about, and I'm gonna get us some quick cash for our little trip coming up. Then we're gonna pick up my daughter and hightail it the hell out of Illinois before the shit further hits the fan."

* * *

It was the creaking that woke Maddox bright and early Monday morning. A creaking of a door lightly being pushed open, moving at a pace so slow it was conspiratorial. He heard the soft steps of heavy boots carefully entering the trailer behind him and he knew this was no wanted guest; a mysterious stranger short of the most valuable resource one needs the most when trespassing into another's home: an invitation.

Maddox kept his eyes shut. The blaring silence in the room gave away the intruder's presence. Maddox detected a strong stench of chewing tobacco from the guy's foul breath, well-practiced exhales of crude air warming the back of his neck.

He heard each step the man made, could feel how close

they were. Of course the intruder was aware of Maddox's presence on the chair, but the question was whether or not he believed he was sleeping.

There was a sharp clicking as a pistol's hammer was thumbed down. Obviously a hit man, and an amateur at that. Who in their right mind would wait until after entering the target's home before preparing their weapon? Besides, any true professional knew damn well cocking your pistol did nothing but make you sound like an idiot. Cocking hadn't been required since the days of the Old West. There was a sudden need to smack him. Seriously, this was like Gangster 101.

He felt the side of the barrel tap against his head, a voice saying, "I know you're awake."

Maddox moved his head away. "How?"

"Because no one sleeps while holding their breath," the intruder said. "Now where's the other one? Boss said there were two of you."

Maddox surrendered and opened his eyes. The intruder was dressed in a black-striped suit, the buttons of his jacket threatening to pop off of his straining gut. A shaggy beard covered his chin and most of his neck, ending at the cheap knockoff of a tie clipped on to his undershirt.

"That is a really small gun," Maddox said. He was surprised the thing even fit in his hand.

The hit man glanced at the pistol and shrugged. "So, who cares if it's small?"

"I just think somebody your size should be packing something a lot bigger, like a shotgun."

"Well I happen to be partial to this gun, thank you very much. It was my father's, and his father's before his. They . . . they were much smaller than myself."

"I can believe that," Maddox said. Then: "I take it you're from King."

The hit man chuckled. "Unless you've pissed off more than one millionaire drug kingpin. Where's your brother?"

"I don't know. Probably in the bathroom."

"He's hiding somewhere, isn't he?"

"I don't think where my brother is really matters."

The hit man raised his eyebrow, amused. "Oh?"

"Yeah," Maddox nodded, "considering that he's not in the room, but the Smith & Wesson currently under my blanket *is* in the room, I think there are other more important matters to discuss."

The hit man snorted. He studied the throw blanket across Maddox's lap, at the elevating bulge in the center of it. His face turned pale.

"Bullshit," he said.

"Is it?" Maddox smirked. "Well, it's either a gun or I'm very happy to see you. No offense, but I don't find you particular sexy. The beard, it just doesn't do it for me."

"You're bluffing."

"Am I? You care to bet your life on that?"

"Bullshit."

"Why don't you take a seat so we can find a way out of this without either of us leaving in a body bag?"

"Okay." The hit man slowly nodded, sidestepping the couch and sitting down. "But just for the record, I still call bullshit."

"Of course." Maddox smiled. "I'll just keep pointing this massive erection your way."

"They told me Maddox was the smarter Kane brother. I take it that's you."

"What else did they say about me? Did they talk about my huge dick? Some people say it's the size of a locked and loaded Smith & Wesson, you know."

"They told me, whatever I did, not to let you get hold of a gun."

He grinned. "Then it's a good thing I'm just jerking off over here, huh?"

The hit man sighed. He settled back on the couch.

Maddox cracked his neck. "Tell me, what's your name?"

"Elvis," the hit man said.

"Come off it."

"Come off what? That's my name."

"Your *real* name?"

"According to my birth certificate. What's wrong with Elvis?"

"Nothin'. Just a little odd, is all."

"And Maddox ain't?"

"Good point."

They sat there, staring at each other, trying to predict the next move—who would draw first, who would live, who would die—all that gunslinger-standoff bullshit.

Then the toilet flushed. Elvis took his eyes off the chair, looked down the hall. Maddox blew a hole through his blanket, through the thick unwelcoming air, and through the abdomen of the hit man, sending him into a spasm on the couch. His arm jerked to the side and squeezed the trigger, sending a bullet just a hair's inch from Maddox's own cheek.

Maddox released two more shots, making sure he'd stay dead.

The bathroom door burst open; rapid footsteps trampled down the short hall and turned into the living room. Benny stopped in his tracks, gaping wide at the corpse on his couch.

"Who the fuck is this?" he yelled, a sheet of toilet paper stuck to the bottom of his foot, pants barely even buckled.

"One of King's assassins," Maddox said.

"And he's dead, right?"

"Well, he ain't alive."

"Jesus, what are we gonna do?" Benny said.

"Whatever you don't want to lose forever, put in a bag. We're leaving in ten minutes."

"Where are we going?"

"We need to pick up my daughter before they get to her."

Benny snorted. "You really think they'd hurt her?"

He was answered by a stone-cold stare. Maddox

retrieved the phone and dialed Addison's number, but over at the apartment it only rang and rang until it went to voicemail. Hand trembling, he let the phone drop to the floor.

Could they have gotten to her *already?*

The idea alone left a thick lump clogged in his throat, making it almost impossible to breathe, let alone think.

He couldn't imagine what he'd do if they touched even a hair on his daughter's head—and it scared him. Scared him even more than no one answering the phone.

In retrospect, Winston undoubtedly had a cell phone on him. Everyone he'd encountered since his release seemed to have one. Except for him, of course, but he had it marked as a top priority purchase once they were far away from Chicago and had a few expendable dead presidents.

"We gotta go. Now."

The Hummer skidded away, leaving behind a gust of snow.

Daddy's coming, sweetheart, Daddy's coming . . .

* * *

"Why can't I come in?" Benny asked. "What if there's a bunch of gangsters up there and you need my back? Then you'll be screwed, bro. Admit it: you need me."

"You go up there and you're just gonna end up shooting me again," Maddox said, reloading the lovely Smith & Wesson he had snatched from the back of the Hummer.

"Oh c'mon, Mads, you know I'm not going to do that again."

"Do I?"

"Well, you should." Benny lowered his head.

"Tell you what. You can be my lookout. You see anything fishy going on, honk three times. That way I'll know if I'm being ambushed. Sound like a plan?"

"You don't have to talk to me like I'm a kid, you know. I'm twenty-nine years old, for Christ's sake."

Maddox sighed. He had tried. "Okay, I'll stop treating you like a kid when you stop *shooting me*. How's that sound?"

"Man, whatever."

Snapping the now full clip into the gun, Maddox stepped out of the driver's seat, boots crushing icy snow. Rays from the sun pierced his pupils and temporarily blinded him until he managed to adjust his vision to the bright sky.

Jogging across the snow, pistol stuck in the back of his jeans, Maddox pushed his way inside the apartment building and up to the third floor. He headed straight for the door with the large wooden C nailed above the peephole. After a few knocks and no answer he grew frustrated and tried the knob, only to find it unlocked.

Beads of sweat dripping down his scalp, Maddox stepped inside and entered the living room. A blanket covering a large object on the floor. It was soaked with some kind of brownish liquid; there was no mistaking what was under it.

He pulled out his pistol as he bent down and uncovered the blanket, revealing the pale face of his ex-wife. Her eyes were still open—open, but not alive. She looked like a ghost.

"Jesus."

Shivering, he threw the blanket back on top of her and stood up. It took him a moment to regain his composure. He couldn't take another step forward. Who knew what else waited for him in this place?

Fuck.

Maddox stepped over a floor covered in trash, careful not to leave any fingerprints, and continued down the hall. Each room came up empty—until he entered the last door at the end.

He started gagging. The smell alone was horrible, but the sight . . . that was something else altogether. Crazy bastards hadn't even bothered to pick up the bowling ball.

TOXICITY

They'd just left it there, creating a gruesome crater in the man's face for eternity. He stepped away, unable to take his eyes off the gory corpse.

Where was his daughter? He searched the apartment one last time, shouting her name over and over, but it was no use. She was gone. So were her clothes. Someone had packed her stuff and taken her someplace—but where?

Like it wasn't obvious.

Who else? King had taken her. Of course he had.

His goons had come, killed Sheryl and her dickless husband, and snatched Addy. She was most likely being held hostage at the Sting with King himself, waiting to trade for the payment Maddox owed.

Undoubtedly, the place was heavily protected by a battalion of armed guards, so breaking her out wasn't an option. Realistically, there was only one way he could solve this dilemma and that was to come up with the money.

And when dealing with a tyrant like Vincent King, there was always little time for action. He had to move fast. He could not fail his daughter once again. No, this time he needed to be a hero. Her life depended on it.

His life depended on it.

Maddox stuffed the Smith & Wesson in the back of his jeans, turned around, and calmly walked down the three flights of stairs. Panic was not his friend; he could not accept it. He climbed into the Hummer and started the ignition, just sitting there with his hands on the wheel, his brother staring at him.

"Well?" Benny said.

Maddox closed his eyes and sighed. "Where is this mansion?"

37

ADDISON KANE FOUND herself in bed, body entwined with the man she loved the most, legs thrown over legs, arms wrapped around backs, faces pressed close together.

Almost as if he felt her gaze, Connor's own eyes opened, meeting hers. He did not have to push his head far before their lips connected, a soft smacking sound as they welcomed each other from their dreams.

"You ready for today?" he asked.

"Be there for me?"

"Always."

They got up and made breakfast. Connor grabbed the morning paper from the front porch and browsed through it with a cup of coffee. Candy, finally awake, stumbled into the kitchen, searching for her next bacon fix.

Addison nodded at the paper on the table. "Anything interesting?"

When Connor didn't reply, she waved her hand in front of his face. "Hey, are you all right?"

His expression was one of pure horror. He tapped his finger on the newspaper. Addison leaned forward, discovering an article about a bunch of escaped zoo animals. Focusing, her eyes read the portion Connor's finger directed to.

The part where it described a vicious cougar named Michelle digging up the corpse of a man out of the snow behind the local Walgreens. According to the article, a medical examiner declared the body already dead before the cougar encounter.

Addison found herself feeling very, very sick.

Candy slammed the refrigerator door shut and joined them at the table. "Uh, are you guys upset over this disastrous lack of bacon, too, or did I miss something?"

* * *

The Ford Fiesta cautiously turned into the trailer park, almost colliding with a large yellow Hummer gunning out onto the main road.

"Whoa!" Connor slammed down on the brakes.

In the backseat, Candy said, "Dude, that thing has no business driving in a place like this."

Connor slowly drifted down the street, parking in front of a familiar trailer. It was painted green, and every step leading up the porch was missing.

"I'll be back in a couple minutes," Addison said, opening the door, but Connor stopped her.

"Wait, we don't have any money, so what exactly are you going to do?" he asked, raising his eyebrow. "I think I better come in."

"Then he definitely won't help us," Addison said. "Dave's got a major jealously problem with you. Just let me handle this, okay?"

"I dunno . . . "

Addison leaned over and kissed him. "I'll be right back," she said, and slid out of the car. She could hear Candy cheering from the backseat and flipped her off without looking. Climbing up onto the porch, Addison rang the doorbell and waited until it opened, revealing a young man in a tank top and basketball shorts. His right arm was also replaced with a giant chainsaw, the tip of the dulled down blade pressing against the carpet.

The guy did not hold back his surprise to see her and Addison did not hold back her surprise at the chainsaw arm.

"Addison!"

"Dave?"

"What . . . what are you doing here?"

She hesitated. "Can I come in?"

Looking over his shoulder, he said, "Um, sure, but my grandpa is sleeping so we gotta be quiet."

Addison followed him down the hallway and into his bedroom, watching him struggle to drag the chainsaw along. He sat down on his bed and she found a small chair across the room. She couldn't not take her eyes off the machinery attached to his arm—but they were even, since he couldn't take his eyes off her boobs.

"So, what's up?" Dave asked.

"I could ask the same question."

He paused, first confused then amused. "What—the arm? You didn't know?"

Addison nodded. "I heard about it, but why is there a *chainsaw?* That couldn't possibly work. Doesn't it . . . you know, hurt?"

Dave smiled. "I was short an arm, figured I might as well go all out. I just never thought about how heavy a chainsaw actually is. But, on the flip side, it does make me look cool."

"Uh huh."

"So, what is it you wanted? How's loverboy doing?"

"Connor is fine," Addison said. "And I need your help with something."

"What's wrong?"

"I need a gun."

He leaned back on the bed, waving his free arm. "Whoa, what makes you think I can help with something like that?"

"Because you sell guns."

"I do not. That's illegal!"

"You sell pot all the time," Addison said. "I know you sell guns, too. C'mon now."

Dave settled back down. "I suppose you want a discount as well, huh?"

"Actually, I was wondering if you'd just lend me it for a couple hours. I'll return it, I swear."

"You're insane," Dave said. "What the hell do you need a gun for, anyway?"

"It's, uh, complicated."

"You're not going to tell me, are you?"

"Nope."

"And you just expect me to hand you over a gun?"

"Yup."

He shook his head. "You must think I'm stupid."

"Yes."

"Hey!"

Addison smirked. "I'm just teasing you, relax. Will you help me or not? You know I wouldn't ask you unless this was really important . . . " *And I was really, really desperate*, she silently added.

"Yeah, yeah, you know damn well I'll help." Dave sighed, adjusting his chainsaw. "But, um, you're gonna have to do something for me first."

She paused, hesitant to ask. "What?"

And this time it was him who was smiling. "You know," he said.

"Oh, God," Addison muttered. "You can't be serious."

"If you need my help bad enough . . . "

"You realize this is the whole reason we broke up in the first place. It's just too . . . creepy."

"I am who I am," One-Arm Dave said. "Now take off your shoe."

"You're disgusting," Addison said. "If Connor found out about this he would kill you. Or puke, I'm not sure which. Maybe both."

"Yeah, but he isn't going to find out, now is he? So off with the shoe already."

She kicked off her right shoe and held her leg up, telling herself that whatever she did, not to vomit.

"Only one lick," Addison said. "And make it fast."

"Will do!" Dave shouted in joy, leaping to the ground

and nearing impaling himself with his rusted robot arm. He slowly crawled toward her in a seductive way that did not seem the least bit seductive.

She winced in disgust as he took advantage of her pinkie toe, the whole time One-Arm Dave chanting, "This little piggy went to the market, and this little piggy went into my mouth . . . "

38

JOHNNY PACED BACK and forth in the shed wondering how he had gotten there.

He had no memory of anything that proceeded his euphoric confrontation with the Fly. It had all been a blur, an intoxicated blackout that hadn't ended until he was midstride in the middle of the shed. Something had finally flipped the light switch back on. His feet stopped moving. His body jerked to a stop.

Everything in the world suddenly made absolute sense.

He had to kill them.

He had to kill them all.

Johnny frowned. The prospect of slaying his family did not sound promising at all, nor the least bit fun. But he had to face reality—those "people" were not his family anymore. For Fly's sake, they weren't even people.

They did not belong in this world any longer and it was Johnny's job to exterminate. Of course, there were others of these humanoid replications roaming the planet, but who honestly expected one boy to take care of them all? According to the Fly, Johnny was not the only soldier in this army of righteousness. There were thousands.

And according to the Fly, today would be one of the most important battles in history. Whoever won today would most likely win the whole war. Everyone was depending on Johnny's success. If he failed, so did the Fly.

If he failed, evil would win.

But why the shed? He scanned the walls, the shelves.

The place was full of those goddamn dolls his mother collected. These were the outcasts that came after there was no longer any room in the mansion. These were the rejects.

Why did they have to be so creepy?

Johnny spotted what his subconscious had been searching for all along. Three large kerosene tanks rested in the far corner. Beside the tanks were five miniature gas cans.

He took a step forward, intending on getting straight to work, when a strange noise caught his attention.

His head snapped to the left. What the hell was that?

There it was again!

Some kind of laugh.

He cringed. Where was it coming from?

It grew louder, sharper.

Johnny collapsed to his knees. Where had it come from? Why was it here? What was so damn *funny*?

The noise was a hundred times worse than any chalkboard imaginable. He could feel his brain expanding against his skull—any second the whole thing would explode. *Ka-boom.*

Thoughts pulsating, ambiguous fears migrating, Johnny finally locked eyes with the monster.

Or, *monsters*.

The dolls.

But even that wasn't right. Maybe they used to be dolls—just like how the things living in his house used to be his family. But no, these were not dolls anymore. These were something different. Something . . . *dark*.

"*YOU WILL NEVER WIN!*" one of the dolls shouted.

"*VICTORY WILL BE OURS!*" another one yelled.

"*PREPARE TO BE DEFEATED, FRAGILE BITCH OF DIPTERA!*"

Johnny shot to his feet. His fall would not be so easy, no siree. These plastic fucks would have to work a lot harder than that.

TOXICITY

"You want a piece of me?" Johnny screamed at the dolls. "*Huh?* Well, here I am! *Come and get me!*"

One by one they poured down on him, gnawing at his now-deformed face, making his body leak an ugly purple.

He pulled a couple off and whipped them against the wall. He managed to pick up a hammer on the workbench and began swinging away at himself, smashing the steel against the demons and against his own flesh.

Finally, black and blue from head to toe and drenched in his own sweat and blood, he dropped the hammer. Smiling through layers of exhaustion, Johnny retrieved a gas can.

❊ ❊ ❊

Gasoline had never smelled so glorious.

Johnny stood back, hands on hips, admiring his creation. God, it was perfection.

This, this here, this was what people called a masterpiece.

A magnum opus.

Soon, he would be taking his last breath as a mortal.

Soon, they would all be destroyed.

Everyone; everywhere. The world. The demons. The humans. The grass. The trees. The backstabbing lies posted on social media.

It would all be gone.

It began in the shed. He had soaked the dolls' crushed corpses, had formed a puddle so thick surrounding most of the cement floor it might as well had been labeled Death's Volatile Pond. And resting in the center of that pond was the first kerosene tank, cap unscrewed and ready to go.

A stream of gasoline led from the shed to the patio, sliding under the second kerosene tank. The kitchen door was propped open by a block of wood (itself also soaked in gasoline). Half of the kitchen floor was coated, splashed against the walls and slowly slithering toward other rooms branching from the food wing.

In the center of the kitchen stood the beloved Desperation chocolate fountain; always running, always yummy. At first glance, it would be hard to notice the third and final kerosene tank floating peacefully along its pool of deliciousness, cap off, its vile contents contaminating his mother's pride and joy.

The stove was turned on, switched to gas, all the way to HIGH. Below, in the closed and inconspicuous oven, rested the last can of gasoline, still full.

This was fucking brilliant. *He* was brilliant. It was all brilliant. And they were all stupid, oblivious dogs waiting to be put down.

Feeling a tightness in his sweatpants, Johnny examined the bulge at his crotch. The atmosphere had excited him something fierce and he suddenly found himself wishing he could have a chance to make amends with his girlfriend so they could screw one last time.

Fuck it. He slid his arm down his pants, grabbed his cock. The world would end soon anyway. Stroking his precious organ, Johnny could hear people yelling from inside the mansion.

Feeling a tingling in his nostril, as if a sneeze was on the rise, Johnny sniffled and continued to stroke faster, faster, faster . . .

It didn't even interrupt his pace when the Fly buzzed out of his nose, hovering above his face, tiny wings fluttering in a purple blur. In his head, the Fly spoke:

"The time has come, Johnny."

No kidding, Johnny thought amusingly, and began to spasm. His head thrust upward into the clouds, eyes piercing through what others could not see, mouth slightly agape—a moan that would chill Lucifer's spine.

"You have served Us well."

And then the whole world was a fireball.

39

NEARLY DOUBLING THE speed limit, the Hummer raced down Libertyville. "There!" Benny tapped his fingers against the window. "That's it! That's the one! I'm sure of it."

"How?" Maddox asked. "Every single one is identical."

"It just is, all right? Doesn't that one just look more . . . uh, *richer,* to you?"

"You gotta be kidding me," Maddox said, swerving around a parked Ford Fiesta, gunning forward a few hundred feet and then slamming on the brakes in front of the designated mansion.

"I kid you not," Benny said matter-of-factly. "This is the place. I'd bet my last beer on it."

"You don't have any beer."

"Don't change the subject."

Maddox sighed. "I can't believe I'm going to steal from a *family.* This is beyond low."

Benny slapped the dashboard. "Ah fuck 'em! They have enough dolls to earn an entire new fortune. They'll be fine. We, on the other hand, will not. Now let's go rob us a crazy woman!"

"Benny, I never thought I'd say this, but you do make a pretty good point."

Benny blushed. "Aww . . . "

"But you are staying in the car again."

"*What?*"

"I don't have time to argue with you. My daughter is in trouble. I can't risk you ruining things. Just stay here, keep the motor running, and if you spot any trouble, honk the horn. Think you can do that?"

Benny lowered his head. "Man, I am getting so sick of this stay-in-the-car shit."

"Good boy," Maddox said, hitting the trunk release button and springing out of the Hummer. He lifted the trunk. He pulled out a double-barreled shotgun, and holstered a Desert Eagle in the back of his jeans for good measure. There was also his brother's discarded ski mask. This was a very rich community and there would most likely be many security cameras scanning the area. It wouldn't hurt to be extra careful.

Maddox pulled the pink ski mask down over his face, closed the trunk, and headed straight for the mansion. He approached the porch, wondering if he was actually doing this. He wished there was another way. Of course, there probably was. If only he had extra time to think things out, to actually form a *plan*, then maybe, just maybe, he could save his daughter without having to commit such a heinous, stupid deed.

Biting back his lower lip and, gripping the double-barreled shotgun with all of his might, Maddox Kane kicked in the front door of Desperation Manor.

40

THIS WAS THE first time Addison had seen the mansion, and she had to say, she was impressed.

And a little scared.

The place was huge. Not to say that every other residence in the community wasn't the same size, but still, it was a bit different when it concerned a friend.

The Ford Fiesta pulled over, the engine peacefully dying, light flecks of snow falling against the windshield. She held on to the handgun nervously in the passenger seat.

Behind the wheel, Connor gripped his own handgun, looking at it suspiciously. "You ever gonna tell me how you managed to get two guns for free?"

Addison blushed. "He's very generous, Connor. Leave it alone."

"All right. Fine."

In the backseat, Candy Blossom snorted. "He didn't lick your feet, did he? I heard that dude was weird like that."

Addison looked down at her lap in shame. "He does have a chainsaw for an arm, though."

Connor nodded in approval. "Well, that's badass."

"Indeed," Candy said.

"So, how do you want to—"

His voice was cut off by the roar of a yellow beast. Out of nowhere it charged, brushing within mere inches of the Ford Fiesta's wing mirror, scaring the holy bejesus out of the occupants inside. All three of them screamed like a pack of nuns accidentally stumbling across "2 Girls 1 Cup."

"Jesus, that thing almost nailed us!" Candy yelled.

The three of them watched the Hummer as it parked in front of Desperation Manor.

"I wonder if they're here about Johnny," Candy said.

A man wearing a pink ski mask stepped from behind the trunk. He was holding a shotgun.

As if on cue, they all gasped in perfect unison.

"Holy shit! He has a gun!" Connor said.

Candy paused in mid-scream and sniggered. "Well, so do you."

"Good point."

"Guys, what the hell is going on here?" Addison said.

They watched in bewilderment as the masked man casually walked up to the porch and kicked in the front door. He stormed inside and out of view. An audible scream caused a flock of birds to flee from the roof.

"That nerf herder took our idea!" Candy shouted, punching the seat with all the strength a scrawny teenaged girl could manage. "I cannot believe this."

Feeling utterly defeated, Addison leaned back. "Well, what do we do now? Run, call the police, what? We can't allow this to continue, right?"

"I say we get the hell out of here before the guy with the big scary gun sees us."

"No," Connor said, eyes burning into the mansion. "We're not going anywhere. At least not yet."

"What are you gonna do?" Addison asked.

"Well, for one thing, I'm not gonna just sit here and let our only chance of freedom slip away from us without putting up *some* kind of fight. We need this money, Addy. You know this just as much as I do. Plus, who the hell does this guy think he is? *We're* Johnny's friends, not *him*. No one is allowed to rob him but us."

TOXICITY

Tears dripped down Addison's cheek. "Connor, *no*. He could kill us."

Connor locked eyes with Addison. He rubbed her shoulder. "Addy, don't be afraid. This is nothin', okay? Just a minor inconvenience is all. This stuff happens all the time. Well, okay, maybe not exactly like this, but you get what I mean. He's in there now, with his back facing the door. That means I have the element of surprise. I'll make him put his gun down, get the money, and run like hell back to the car. You can even be my getaway driver. Sounds good, right?"

Addison shook her head. "It isn't worth it."

He leaned forward and gave her another kiss, one that seemed to last forever.

When their lips broke apart, Connor said, "Keep my seat warm, baby. I love you."

"I love you, too."

He reached under the seat and pulled out a silk wizard cape, which he promptly clipped around his neck. After noticing the strange looks from both Candy and Addy, he shrugged. "It's my good luck cape."

Then he was outside, hurrying toward the mansion, gun in hand, wizard cape fluttering against the cold November wind.

"Your boyfriend is such a nerd," Candy said.

"He's my nerd," Addison whispered.

41

FOR A RICH FAMILY, the mansion sure was a mess.

Lifting his legs over piles of dirty clothes, crusty dishes and throngs of discarded dolls, Maddox hurried through the little foyer and burst into the living room. He found a man and a woman on the sofa.

The woman was either in her late forties or early fifties. Maddox recognized her from the TV show. This was the one who'd won the lottery—what was it, *Ruth?* Legs stretching out unfortunate sweatpants and wearing the fanciest flannel ever designed, the woman sat there on the sofa with a large bucket of Rocky Road, a silver spoon shoved deep down her throat.

The man was much younger—twenty-five, at the most. He had a fistful of Cheez-Its, cracker crumbs foaming out of his mouth and consuming his shabby attire whole. Maddox recognized this guy, as well. He was the one who'd gone on that jealous rant about the dolls.

Maddox pointed the shotgun at them, yelling for no one to move. They both screamed and jumped back against the sofa.

"Shut up!" Maddox aimed the shotgun at the woman. "You're Ruth Desperation, correct?"

"The one and only," she answered smugly. "The hell do you want?"

"I want you to listen close, because if you make me repeat myself I will not hesitate in shooting your son here. He *is* your son, right?"

"Yes."

TOXICITY

"Well, he'll be your dead son unless you do exactly as I say. Do you believe me?"

Ruth glanced over at the man sitting beside her. He was nearly in tears.

"Yes," she said, shaking her head disappointedly.

"Good," Maddox said. "Now, I'm assuming you have a suitcase or a briefcase, yes?"

"Of course. What kind of trash do you take me for?"

"Excellent. What I want you to do, Ruth, is to go get that bag. Then you are to fill it up with cash, understand? I'm talking about that lottery cash. You don't look like the type to keep your money in a bank so I trust you have it stashed here in some kind of safe. Get to it—*now*. You have five minutes before I start blowing off body parts."

This was Maddox circa 1990s talking here.

But the lady wasn't moving, just staring at him. He kicked a glass bowl off the coffee table. *"NOW!"*

She fled the living room, wobbling like a horrified penguin. He hoped she wouldn't be stupid enough to call the police. At this point, he really didn't have anything to lose, and he *would* end up shooting someone.

He heard something crunch behind him and quickly spun around. Some kid with red hair had walked in the front door. He was holding a little snubnose, and he wore a cape.

Maddox whipped the shotgun around at him and said, "Who the hell are you and why are you wearing a wizard cape?"

The kid pointed his gun back at him. "I could ask you the same question! And that is none of your business!"

Back at the sofa: "Hey, ain't you Johnny's old friend? The little gay Harry Potter rocker, right?"

In the unison, the two gunmen redirected their aim at the dickhead on the leather sofa: "Shut up!"

Maddox and the kid were quick to return their aim back at each other. "You're here about the lottery money, aren't you?" Maddox asked.

"You, too, huh?"

"Why did you pick today?"

Scratching his head, he said, "Good day as any, isn't it?"

"You should probably leave now," Maddox said, nodding the shotgun at the front door. "There is nothing for you here."

"Um, yeah, there's like a shit ton of cash for me here."

Maddox cracked his neck, hoping he looked as intimidating as one could look while wearing a pink ski mask. "Do you honesty want to try your luck with me, kid? If you don't leave, you will die. Do you understand?"

The kid attempted to crack his neck as well, but came up empty. He shrugged it off and scrunched his neck. "Hey, bro, in case you don't see it, I have a gun, too. And I am not afraid to bust a cap in yo ass, mo'fucka."

Maddox couldn't help it. He burst out laughing. "What was *that*?"

The kid frowned, clearly regretting his wording.

"Kid, get the hell out of here. You're too much."

"I'm too much? At least I'm not wearing a freakin' pink mask."

"But you do have on a wizard cape."

"It's my lucky wizard cape, thank you very much!"

There was a loud thud off to the side. Ruth Desperation was standing there, fuming, a duffle bag at her feet.

"Well, here it is!"

"All of it?" Maddox asked.

She snorted. "If you think I'm handing over every cent to my name you must be out of your damn mind. There's about one fourth of the lot in there, along with a couple of dolls that'll get you a pretty penny on the market. One of them is Obama. You're welcome. Now, get the hell out of my house before I call the police."

Maddox gritted his teeth. There was just not enough time to bicker over this. Hopefully King would accept his money in installments. "Lady, you're lucky."

"And you're lucky I don't kick your ass," Ruth said. "Now shoo!"

Someone tapped his shoulder. He glanced back at the kid. "What?"

"So, um, you wanna split this down the middle, or . . . ?"

"Heavens to Betsy! Connor Hickory Murphy, is that you?" Ruth said.

Nearly dropping the snubnose to the floor, the kid, Connor, gasped and looked over Maddox's shoulder. "Uh, hello, Mrs. Desperation."

"What in tarnation are you doing here?"

The kid cleared his throat. "Well, ma'am, I'm afraid I'm here to rob you."

"You little shit."

"I know, I know." Connor suddenly tensed, eyes bulging.

Maddox smirked, seeing the wild black hair behind the Irish kid. "Took you long enough."

"I . . . I was interrupted," Benny said.

"Do I even want to know?"

"Uh, no, probably not. What's going on here?"

"I'm taking what's mine, that's what's going on here," Connor said.

Maddox had to give it to him—the kid had balls. Especially with two guns aimed at him.

Benny laughed. "Who the hell are you? And where did you get that cape? It's awesome."

"Let's just split the money, okay?" Connor said. Maddox saw the look in his eyes and he hated it. Now was not the time to feel pity.

"Don't you give me those puppy dog eyes!" he yelled. "I mean it!"

"*What?*"

Benny pointed forward with the expression one manages seconds before the finale of a car crash. "Mads, watch out!"

The shotgun was ripped from his grasp and he was left

with the frontend sticking right in his face. Judging from the look on the sofa hostage, he couldn't believe his luck, either.

"How did you move so fast?" Maddox asked. He sincerely wanted to know.

"I . . . I have no idea."

"That's my boy!" Ruth said.

"Thanks, Ma."

"Now kill them all!"

"Uh, what?" he said, glancing at his mother.

Maddox pulled the Desert Eagle from the back of his jeans, returning the shotgun's mean stare. He winked. "Too bad I'm faster."

"Whoa," he mumbled.

"You are a disgrace of a son." Ruth sighed.

Everything had gone to shit—total, complete shit.

Four guns—four targets. Benny's pistol at Connor, Connor's snubnose at Benny, Maddox's Desert Eagle at the sofa hostage, and the sofa hostage's double-barreled shotgun at Maddox.

Connor sniffled. "Uh, guys, does anyone else smell gas?"

And that was when all hell broke loose.

42

ADDISON WATCHED AS the man of her dreams dashed through the cold with a pistol and wizard cape. California, she thought, that would be perfect. That was where she wanted them to go. No more coldness, no more sorrow; only good things from then on. Life would be as perfect as life could be.

"Man, the amount of chick flick tension in this car is enough to make me puke," Candy Blossom said from the backseat.

They sat in silence for a while, trying to keep their minds off the present.

Then Candy jolted up, pointing at the mansion. "Hey, look! Somebody else got out!"

Addison watched as a wild-haired man approached the trunk of the Hummer. He lifted it, looking around, and slammed it shut. When he stepped closer to view she was able to spot a large pistol in his grip.

"Oh shit," she said.

The man headed straight for the mansion, but was cutoff halfway by a dog tackling him into the snowy front yard. She watched as his gun flew a few feet away. The dog refused to get off of him.

"Isn't that Zooey Deschanel?" Candy asked, baffled.

"Yeah, I think so." Addison nodded.

The man tried his best to struggle out of Zooey Deschanel's attack, but the attempt was futile. The dog slapped his face riotously with her tongue, knocking his head against the ground. They watched from inside the car, dazed and amused.

However, by the time one of them realized now would be a great time to do something, it was too late: the man had finally succeeded in wrestling away from the dog and was bending over to retrieve his pistol. Zooey Deschanel, insulted, jogged away with a frown.

They watched with their hearts on pause as the man walked through the front door. Addison gulped, fearing the worst.

"Well, I certainly didn't see that coming," Candy said.

"I gotta help him," Addison said. "I gotta do something."

"Like *what?*"

Addison hesitated. "I dunno. *Something.*"

She looked down at the handgun in her open palm. It felt cold against her skin. The gleam of the short barrel temporarily blinded her. Her love was in danger. The time to act was now.

Addison opened the passenger door and stepped outside.

"Where are you going?" Candy asked from the backseat, but did not receive an answer.

Addison was halfway to the mansion when her foot connected with a huge patch of ice, sending her legs up in the air and throwing her violently across the pavement. She screamed as her back landed on the road, skull smashing against concrete. The hand holding the gun came down hard, causing her to make a fist, index finger squeezing down on the tough trigger. A loud bang filled the street, and the next thing she knew Desperation Manor was up in flames.

43

HIS INITIAL THOUGHT was he'd died and gone straight to Hell.

Then Maddox realized he was still inside the mansion, only now he was on his back and the walls were melting.

Unable to find the strength to rise, he lay there with his head spinning back and forth, embracing the scorched scenery. Somehow, the entire mansion was ablaze. Sparks rained from the ceiling. Fire consumed available free space. Smoke contaminated once breathable air. His pink ski mask had burnt away to nothing, leaving behind a set of very tan cheeks.

What the fuck happened?

In the movies, actions scenes were always slowed down and easy to comprehend. You were able to see each move before it happened.

Why couldn't real life be so predictable?

The sofa hostage rose from the flames, most of his body charcoaled, pointing the double-barreled shotgun at Maddox. He screamed as he leaped forward, but was soon gunned down by Benny, who'd managed to climb to his feet at the last second.

He raised a victory fist in the air, smiling. "That's right, baby, I just saved your life," Benny said. "You totally owe me a beer."

And then a chunk of Benny's skull sprung from the center of his forehead and he collapsed to the floor. Standing a few feet away, the kid, Connor, stumbled forward with a face blackened from ashes. Maddox raised the Desert Eagle and plugged a bullet in the kid's gut, upped his aim, and shot the gun off again, a misty cloud of crimson spraying from the side of his neck.

He had barely fallen to the ground before Maddox heard a new scream—this one from a woman. He focused his vision across the room and spotted Ruth Desperation charging toward him, covered from head to toe with what looked like . . . *chocolate?* No, that couldn't have been right. Either way, he emptied his clip into her.

Maddox dropped the gun and backed up, slowly finding his way to his feet. He was shaking, his mind on the verge of a total breakdown. Sirens were closing in. His brother was dead. Everyone was dead.

Maddox scanned the room, searching for the duffel bag but could not for the life of him find it. He burnt his hand on an overturned coffee table and decided escape was either now or never. Maddox looked at his brother one last time, then ran out of the mansion and leaped into the Hummer, speeding away from the inferno.

44

CANDY WATCHED IT all from the backseat of Connor's Ford Fiesta, unable to blink. She watched the fiery cloud exhaling from the top of the mansion. She could see Addison on the ground, unconscious, but that didn't seem to fully register yet. Her attention was too busy gazing over the beautiful flares bleeding into the morning sky.

It was like the Fourth of July.

What finally broke her dreamy state was the sudden roar of gunfire. She jumped back, blinking for the first time in ages. Holy hell, was that loud.

What had just happened?

Addison fell, gun went off, and the mansion . . . what, *exploded?* Were the walls constructed of nothing but TNT?

Struggling to breathe, Candy tried opening the door, but her sweaty hand kept slipping off the handle. She could see Addison climbing to her feet and she wanted to go over and help her.

But then she saw something.

Stumbling from the side of the mansion, a tall figure led by Zooey Deschanel. The closer the person got, the clearer he became.

He was naked. Either he'd stripped, or his clothes had melted into his flesh, he was nude nonetheless. He moved like a zombie. From head to toe, burnt to a crisp. Layers of red, layers of black, charcoaled to death and back again, blood spilling onto the snow as he walked.

Candy watched in horror as the zombie strode toward

her. He opened the driver's door, allowed the dog to climb into the passenger's seat, and sat down behind the wheel. No one said anything for a minute; Candy once again unable to blink, air drowning her lungs.

She flinched as he turned the key in the ignition.

"Johnny?" Candy Blossom said.

The zombie turned around and offered a crusty smile, revealing a set of teeth that glistened compared to the utter blackness of his face. The glow sent her crawling back against the backseat. She dived for the door but it was too late: locked.

She turned back, expecting the worst.

"Hello, darling," he said, and stomped on the gas.

45

ADDISON SNAPPED AWAKE, head pounding like a disco ball. She was on her back staring into the sky, which had now turned a mischievous black. A cloud of smoke. But from what?

She sat up.

Desperation Manor was burning to the ground.

"Connor," she whispered.

She heard the Ford Fiesta starting up behind her. By the time she looked over her shoulder the car was halfway down the road, swerving between lanes recklessly.

A man barged out of the front door and broke for the Hummer. Addison had to give him a double take before realizing who it was.

"D-Dad?"

She watched him climb behind the wheel and start the engine. As he was pulling away their eyes managed to lock onto each other, both of their expressions twisted into oblivion.

Then he shook his head and made a screwed-up face. He kept on going.

Addison sat on the pavement for a moment until her ears finally accepted the approaching howl of sirens.

Connor, she thought, shooting to her feet. She ran toward the mansion, leaving her handgun back in the road, and charged headfirst into the inferno.

She started coughing. Everywhere she looked there were flames. The mansion didn't have much longer before it all collapsed on top of them.

Addison moved further into the living room and

spotted a pile of bodies. A small cry escaped her strangled lungs and she rushed forward. It was difficult to recognize them, but there were three men and a woman. She thought the woman was probably Johnny's mother, but who knew for sure? And why did she smell chocolate?

A light cough from one of the corpses startled Addison back to her feet.

"Addy? That you?"

"*Connor?*" Addison crouched down, taking her boyfriend's hand. Out of the rest of the corpses, he was the least burnt up. "Oh my God, are you shot?"

He nodded. "A little bit."

"Oh, shit."

"Took the words right out of my mouth," Connor said, risking a thin grin. One hand wrapped around hers, his other hand pressed tightly against his neck, where a river of blood appeared to be streaming out.

Addison lost it. "Oh God, oh God, oh God . . . "

"Come on," Connor said. "Please stop crying."

She sniffled, making an honest attempt to stabilize herself. "The police are on their way," she told him. "We have to get out of here."

"*THIS IS THE LIBERTYVILLE POLICE. COME OUT AND SURRENDER WITH YOUR HANDS UP.*"

Addison cried out at the blow horn from outside. "Shit!" she yelled.

"*IN CASE YOU ARE NOT AWARE, THE HOUSEHOLD YOU ARE IN IS ON FIRE. I REPEAT, IT IS ON FIRE. SURRENDER NOW.*"

"Shit! Shit! Shit!"

Connor giggled. "Such a dirty mouth you have."

"It isn't funny! We're screwed! And you're shot! Shit!"

Connor grunted, managing to sit up. "Shh, it's all right. I have the money."

"*What?*"

He nodded next to him at a duffel bag. "I fell on it when

that guy shot me. He couldn't find it because it was under me. We got the money, baby."

"But the cops!"

He winked. "Let me take care of them."

"What do you mean?" Addison asked, not liking the sound of this at all.

"I'm dying."

"Shut up. You shut up right now."

"Addy, it's true."

"No it's not. Stop talking like that."

"I was shot twice, Addy. Come on. Look at me. Don't let my death be a waste."

"*Connor!*" Addison couldn't believe what she was hearing. She wrapped her arms around him, careful not to squeeze too tight. "*No!*"

"Dammit, Addy, just listen to me. You still have a chance to get out of this. They don't even know who's here. You can escape. There's a window over there. I don't think we have long before that's on fire, too. We gotta hurry. I'll distract them."

"No . . . "

Connor sighed and looked her in the eyes. "Please. Do this for me, okay? Take this money and go. Leave this goddamn town, leave this whole fucking state. It's bad luck. Go to California. I want you to meet me in the ocean. I want you to breathe it all in, because that salty air you'll smell, that's me. I want you to live happily ever after, all right? Just like in the fairy tales. Touch your heart and you'll feel me there. You won't ever be alone again, okay? Be free, Addy. Please. Your time is now."

He kissed her one last time.

"I love you, Addy."

"I love you, too . . . "

Retrieving the handgun, Connor stumbled to his feet and headed out the front door. His words echoed in her head:

Don't let my death be a waste.

Sobbing, Addison picked up the duffel bag and ran for the window, dodging the spots completely swallowed by fire. She had barely managed to step one foot out onto the snow before she heard the first gunshot. It startled her and it took everything she had in her not to scream. It was followed by another set of blasts. She knew what had happened and it damn near killed her right then and there.

Addison took off through the back yard with the duffel bag of cash slung over her shoulder, climbing over the fence and fleeing into the snowy forest beyond.

She did not look back.

46

MADDOX DROVE WELL over the designated speed limit. His hand was swollen and throbbing. He had burned it pretty badly. The pink cotton mask melted into his flesh felt like someone had tossed a cup of acid into his face. He had killed two people. He was broke. His brother was dead. His daughter was doomed.

All in all, he was having one hell of a day.

Maddox cranked up "Master of Puppets" on the radio as he raced into the city. The music vibrated him in his seat. He turned the volume louder. The light was red but he didn't give a shit. He kept going. *Fuck it,* he thought, and then a semi-truck smashed into the side of him.

One second he was driving and the next there was a terrible loud bang and the Hummer was rolling across the road, smashing random automobiles. Maddox couldn't see—just a quick blur that ended when the Hummer crashed through the large picture window of a Macy's.

The Hummer finally came to a stop halfway inside the clothing store, flipped upside down. Maddox was sprawled out against the windshield, blood gushing from his nose.

He climbed out through the shattered passenger window. His back cracked with a jolt of thunder. Random shoppers cowered in the corner of the store, staring at the wrecked scene with a mixture of terror and fascination.

Maddox gave them all a once-over, brushed a few sheets of glass off his chest, and shrugged. "My bad," he said, and walked around the Hummer and onto the sidewalk outside to inspect the damage.

He whistled and a glob of blood shot from his mouth. The semi-truck had managed to stop a few feet after colliding with the Hummer. The driver was walking around, dazed but seemingly uninjured. Maddox noted with some amusement that on the side of the trailer, in big red letters, it said: HOSTESS. To his utter delight, he saw a pile of Twinkies spilled out behind the truck. It was like waking up on Christmas morning.

The street was littered with weapons. The trunk had opened in mid-crash, vomiting out Winston's private arsenal.

People were screaming and taking pictures with their cell phones. Maddox leaned against the wall and closed his eyes. He rubbed his temple, attempting to fight off a sudden wave of vertigo. When he opened his eyes again he thought he was hallucinating.

A 1974 Cadillac Eldorado was slowly creeping down the road. With the BLUE23 license plate and everything.

Maddox blinked again. It was real. He recognized the driver's bald head, too. Then she saw him as well, her jaw dropping. Numb as ice, Maddox pointed at her, silently ordering her to pull over. It was all he could do.

The lot lizard slammed her foot down on the pedal. And just as fast as the Cadillac appeared within vision, it was gone. Maddox could hear the evil bitch laughing even from where he stood.

He hurried out into the road and nearly tripped over a solid steel object. When he looked down to see what it was, he couldn't help but smile. There was no time to go over the pros and cons of what he was thinking about doing, so he just said screw it and picked the weapon up.

He rested half the rocket launcher on his shoulder and peered through the sight. Once the aim was matched with the back of the absconding Cadillac, Maddox squeezed the trigger. A recoil of flames exploded from behind him as a heavy missile instantaneously shot out through the rocket launcher's wide tube.

TOXICITY

He followed the projectile's journey with wonder. It whizzed through the air, coming within mere inches of bumping into multiple objects, until it finally connected with the bumper of his stolen car. He watched as a ball of fire blasted the back up in the air, sending it into a wild flip, the Cadillac skidding half a block with a series of metallic sparks shooting all over the place.

"Whoa," Maddox muttered, and dropped the rocket launcher to his feet. He bent down, scooped up a handful of Twinkies from the immobile Hostess truck, then turned around and ran like hell, knowing anything in the Cadillac that was once living was now dead. Sadly, if there had been any of the money they'd stolen from him left, it was now burned to a humble pile of worthless ashes, too.

As he ran, he visualized his fist sinking into Vincent King's fat face. He thought about beating him until there was nothing to beat. He'd find a can of that fucking Jericho and empty the whole canister down his throat. He would find his daughter and take her far away from here and they would finally be free to live life as it was meant to be lived.

As long as he didn't screw it up, of course.

* * *

It didn't take long for someone to spot a man covered from head to toe in blood running down a Chicago sidewalk.

The cop cruised alongside Maddox, matching his pace. He rolled down the passenger window. "Hey, you! Horror movie victim! Hey, I'm talking to you!"

Maddox glanced over his shoulder but refused to slow down. "Yeah?"

"Care to explain what the hell happened to you?"

"I fell."

"Is that so?"

"Basically."

"You gotta name?"

"Probably!"

"Well?"

"Well what?"

"You want to tell me your name?"

"Maddox Kane!" he shouted. "I was born April 7, 1977, opening day of Wrigley Field. We lost against the New York Mets, five to three."

"Kane?" the officer asked, checking his computer. "Says here you have a warrant out for your arrest."

"Tell me something I don't know! Besides, they're just Twinkies."

"*What?*"

"Nothing."

"Says here you're wanted for grand theft auto, that you stole a minivan . . . outside the prison where you'd just been released. Says they have the whole crime caught on tape. A certain Lionel Turner filed the report himself. Says here he's very angry with you. Hey, man, watch it—we're running out of road here."

Maddox stopped with the police cruiser. He bent over, panting. "What about the other stuff?"

"What other stuff?"

"Uh, never mind."

"Nice answer."

"You going to arrest me?"

"Well, I *am* a cop. You gonna resist?"

Maddox straightened his back, thinking it over. He thought about Addison, he innocent little daughter. She was still at King's. There was no way he was going to outrun this cop. He was at a loss. He could either try his odds at fighting the police, or talk them into working with him. Sure, he'd be going back to prison for a very long time, but at least there was a chance he could still save his little girl.

"Depends," he said.

The cop stared at him curiously. "Depends on what?"

"Sox or Cubs?"

47

IN THE BASEMENT chambers of Desperation Manor, the father and husband of the family, Roland, was having the time of his life. He was lost in the depths of his game vault, any noise from the rest of the mansion undetectable through the metal walls that surrounded him. Hell, he even had his own personal butler whose sole purpose was to light his pipe on command.

He was on the verge of beginning perhaps the biggest *World of Warcraft* raid of his online career when there was a sudden knocking at his vault door. It was very consistent and very annoying.

"Shall I answer that, sir?" the pipe butler asked.

Roland shook his head, figuring it was either his wife or one of his stupid children. "Hell no," he said. "But, since now that you're up, you *can* spot me a light, my good chum."

Little did Roland Desperation know, at the door was neither his wife *nor* one of his stupid children. It was, in fact, a team of firefighters ready to inform him that the rest of his mansion had burned completely to the ground—and to the best of their knowledge, he was the last surviving member of the family.

But he wouldn't find any of that out until after he'd finished his raid and went upstairs for dinner.

48

WHAT THE HELL *was she doing?*
Addison Kane stepped out of the bus station and sat down on a bench, the sun beating down upon her lonesome face. Her fingers traced the edges of the one-way ticket to San Francisco. She was still shocked they hadn't carded her. It was the first lucky break she'd gotten in God knew how long. The bus wouldn't arrive for another hour or so, so she lay down on the bench, staring up at the clouds.

What the hell was she doing?

She tried not to think about Connor but that was like telling somebody not to breathe. It wasn't fair. It wasn't fair at all.

She wondered how far he'd gotten out the door before the police took him down. Did he die instantly, or did he lie there under the sun, bleeding out?

Was he even dead?

Maybe he was on his way to the hospital, handcuffed to a stretcher.

What would the newspapers say in the morning? Would they call him a murderer? Would he go down in history as one of the bad guys?

Fuck what the newspapers would say. They didn't matter. Nobody's opinion mattered. Addison knew the truth. So did Connor. Everybody else could go straight to hell.

She shook her head, trying to think about anything other than a blanket being thrown over his corpse. Instead she thought about the way he'd held her on his porch swing, before everything went bad, the way they'd fallen asleep together.

On the bench, Addison's eyes wandered with the clouds as she waited for the bus to carry her away to the ocean.

49

JOHNNY SPUN 'ROUND and 'round on the merry-go-round as the world ended.

He could think of no other place to go. There were so many memories here—it was his true home, his forgotten home, his only home.

He had left his soul mate along with the mysterious cotton candy-haired girl back at the car, wherever he had parked it. He wasn't sure who the girl was, but she had acted like they knew each other. Perhaps they had been friends in a previous life. Whoever she was, he had given her full responsibility of the goddess, Zooey Deschanel. Hopefully she was in good hands. He didn't think he had hurt the girl. He hoped he hadn't. But he couldn't remember. His head was pounding too much to concentrate—pounding and buzzing.

Although he supposed it really didn't matter, considering the planet's existence only had a few minutes left 'til its expiration date hit.

Johnny grinned, proud of himself.

Spinning at an impossible supersonic speed, Johnny tilted his gaze up to the sky, or what used to be the sky. There was no more blue. There were no more clouds. There was no more *sun*. At first it had all been purple, but now it was black. It was the darkness of an infinite number of flies raining down from Heaven. They had come to deliver him to paradise. The Fly had kept Its promise.

The Fly always kept Its Word.

Obey or die,

TOXICITY

a million drowning sinners cry,
obey or die,
obey
or
die.
Die.
Johnny raised his fists to the fallen sky and screamed,
"TAKE ME!"
And they did.
They poured down upon nature like holy termites,
erasing anything they came in contact with. The army
swallowed all and soon Johnny could not see to see.
And when he and the horde embraced on that fateful
merry-go-round, it was not fear that he experienced, but
content.
Johnny Desperation welcomed them with open arms.
And when he died, all he heard was a Fly buzz.

AUTHOR'S NOTE

The life of a book is a peculiar thing. When does it begin living, officially? When the idea is conceived, when its writer first puts pen to paper, when its final chapter is concluded, or when it's finally published and available for readers? Officially, *Toxicity*—my debut novel—was first published by Post Mortem Press in spring 2014 a few months shy of my twenty-first birthday. So, if we're going by that measurement, that makes this 2024 reprint its ten-year-anniversary edition. But if we're going by when I started the original draft, when I first put pen to paper, we're looking at somewhere around eighteen years.

I was twelve, almost thirteen, when I started writing *Toxicity*. This would have been sometime in early 2006. It's also possible I may have been thirteen, almost fourteen, which would put us in early 2007. My memory here, for some reason, likes to flipflop. Either way, at this point in time the book didn't have a name yet, although it'd eventually go through many different titles—*Jericho* and *Black Cadillacs* being the top two contenders—before finally settling on *Toxicity*. Most of my books I have no recollection of the actual writing process. I certainly never remember *starting* them. But that's not true with *Toxicity*. I still have a very distinct memory of the first day I began working on it.

My older brothers had already moved out by then, so it was just me and my parents. We were experiencing the early days of a bleak situation that would last until I was sixteen. The situation is hard to explain, exactly, since it was never completely explained to *me*. I tried my best to analyze these years of my life in a novella titled *Indiana Death Song* (found in my collection *Abnormal Statistics*), so I recommend giving that a gander if you want to learn more details about my teenage years.

But, basically, this is what happened: one morning we woke up and the electricity in our house was out, which wasn't an uncommon thing for us. Usually it might be out for a day before the bill was paid and the city turned it back on. Except, this time, the power stayed off, and we soon started staying the night at various hotels around the area—starting with comped reservations at a casino hotel, thanks to my mom's dangerous gambling addiction (which, I imagine, was also the cause of us unexpectedly becoming unhoused).

Soon, due to transportation inconveniences, my parents withdrew me from school. I would never graduate the seventh grade (later, at the age of sixteen, I would enroll in an adult education program and earn a high school diploma shortly before my eighteenth birthday). In those first couple weeks of The Situation, whenever the casino hotel comps dried out, my dad would drop my mom and me off at the house before heading to work, then pick us up again after his shift and we'd find another cheap hotel to stay the night. The house remained powerless. My mom and I would sit either in the living room or out on the porch and wait out the day.

I remember going through the many, many stacks of library-sale paperbacks in our kitchen and plucking things out at random. One of them ended up being my introduction to crime fiction literature: Richard Price's *Clockers*. I must have read that entire novel in one afternoon. I was absolutely hooked on this thing and couldn't get enough of it. This would have been around the same time that, one bored afternoon while waiting for my dad to finish work, I opened a blank notebook and started writing a new story. Writing was not something new to me by then. I'd been doing it since the age of six or seven. But this would have been the first time I tried to write crime fiction. I wish I still had the writing saved, but I'm afraid it's lost to time at this point. But I do remember the scene, which I'll explain now (spoilers for *Toxicity*, if you haven't already read it):

A highly dysfunctional family, not-so-cleverly modeled off my own family, has recently won millions from the lotto. They are rich and famous and have the biggest house imaginable. The story I wrote back then opened with this family, the Desperations, sitting around their fancy living room watching reality television while eating junk food. Suddenly, the doorbell rings. One of the characters—my brother—gets up and answers it. He is immediately pulverized by a shotgun from someone who I'd later name Maddox Kane. What follows next is similar to what happens in the final version of the novel. A series of characters have all decided right now is the perfect time to rob this terrible family of their fortune, leading to a bit of a Mexican standoff where it's doubtful anybody's going to make it out alive.

I wrote this entire scene in one sitting, in a house without power, using only the light spilling in from the picture window in our living room. Something about the story immediately mesmerized me unlike anything else I'd ever attempted to write, and it's only now, however many years later, writing this author's note, that I realize why that may have been. Although I'd written stories before this, *Toxicity* would have been the first time I'd ever tried incorporating elements from my own life into fiction. It felt huge. Total game-changer shit. Also consider the fact that the Desperations were modeled off my own family, and they'd just won the lottery—meanwhile, while writing this book, we were literally in the process of becoming unhoused. In a way, this book was less crime fiction and more fantasy. And, even in my own fantasy world where we might win the lottery, I felt that we would still need to be punished somehow. Hence, the intruder with the shotgun, and all of the additional mayhem that soon unfolded.

Soon after starting *Toxicity*, the county would install giant locks on our front door, and we'd never step foot in the house again. Any belongings we hadn't already taken out would be lost forever—which accounted for pretty much everything that my parents hadn't already pawned (such as video game systems and DVD players). For the next several years, we would live in a series of cheap hotels. I would lose all contact with friends. I would become a hotel shut-in. The only thing keeping me company? Reading and writing. Writing what, specifically? Short stories, yes, but also this crime novel that I'd started back at the house. I rewrote the book over and over. Eventually I found a website called StoriesVille, which is now defunct, but back when it existed the site was wonderful for new writers trying to improve their craft. How it worked was simple: you uploaded stories, and other people in the community read and critiqued them. You were also able to upload serialized stories, which is what I did for *Toxicity* and a wide range of other writings. People read those early chapters and gave me their thoughts and expressed excitement to continue reading future installments and it was the coolest possible thing for someone my age to experience. Here I was, in this fucking hotel, so lonely and depressed that I genuinely considered suicide on a daily basis, suddenly gifted with the one thing every writer yearns for: an active audience. It inspired me to continue working on the book, yes, but it also motivated me to get better.

At this point, I have no idea how many times I've rewritten *Toxicity*. In either 2012 or 2013, it was accepted for publication by a micro press called Rainstorm, but shortly after signing with them I requested for a cancellation of the contract. Something about them felt off. I wasn't a fan of how they'd treated some of their other authors, and I wanted to jump ship as quickly as possible. Once that was sorted out, I signed with another press, Post Mortem Press, and they released the book in 2014. This would also prove to be a mistake. If I ever received any royalty statements from them, it would have been for no more than $50. This publisher, to the best of my knowledge, is no longer around, and that is probably for the best.

I forget when, exactly, *Toxicity* fell out of print. Time is weird. I haven't thought about this novel in several years, but readers have asked me time and again when it might return. There are a few other early books of mine that will never see a return to print—such as the short story collections *True Stories Told By a Liar* (2012) and *They Might Be Demons* (2013)—because there is no salvaging them. The writing quality is simply reprehensible. I feared the same might be true for *Toxicity*. Fortunately, upon revisiting it nearly ten years after its initial publication, I found myself relieved for the most part. While the writing is nowhere near as strong as my current output, it was not . . . *embarrassing*. I made a few tweaks here and there, but nothing too significant. It is still very much the same book I released a decade ago. It's not a great book, but it's also not terrible. Was I perhaps *too* inspired by the filmography of Quentin Tarantino as a teenager? No comment.

A few thank-yous are in order here: The entire web community of StoriesVille, Paul Michael Anderson for initially editing the manuscript all those years ago, Betty Rocksteady for the perfect cover art on this second edition, and Lori Booth for everything she does and continues to do. And a big thank you to *you*, dear reader, for giving me a reason to bring this book back in the first place. I hope you have fun with it.

Max Booth III
—February 5, 2024

ABOUT THE AUTHOR

Max Booth III is a novelist, screenwriter, editor, podcaster, and publisher. He is the author of *Abnormal Statistics, Maggots Screaming!, Touch the Night*, and many other titles too spooky to name here. His film, *We Need to Do Something*, was released by IFC Midnight in 2021. With his wife, Lori, he co-runs Ghoulish Books, a small press and indie bookstore based in San Antonio, Texas. Learn more about him at TalesFromTheBooth.com.

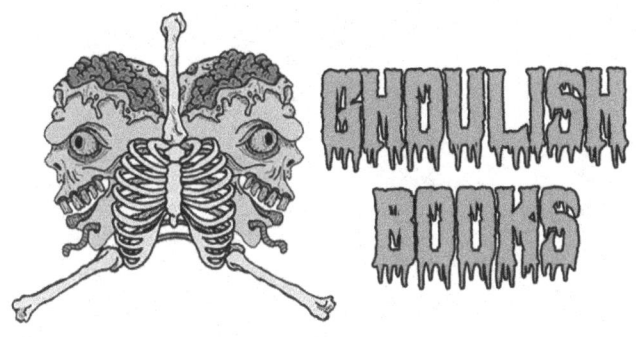

Patreon:
www.patreon.com/ghoulishbooks

Website:
www.Ghoulish.rip

Facebook:
www.facebook.com/GhoulishBooks

Twitter:
@GhoulishBooks

Instagram:
@GhoulishBookstore

Linktree:
linktr.ee/ghoulishbooks